"Guess I'll

Clay said abruptly.

Ann saw a spark of something breathtaking in his eyes. Desire. Fiery and strong, it radiated from his gaze. Her heart thudded in a foreign rhythm. She wanted him to go back to bed… she wanted him to take her in his arms and love her. Confusion swirled in her.

He stood, and the emotion she'd seen in his eyes was gone, making her wonder if she'd only imagined it.

"You sure you're all right?" he asked.

"I'm fine."

"Good night, Ann…. I hope the rest of your night is filled with pleasant dreams."

"Thanks." She turned and fled. She had a feeling her dreams would still be disturbing, although in a very different way.

CARLA CASSIDY

Carla Cassidy is an award-winning author who has written over fifty books for Silhouette Books. In 1995 she won the Best Silhouette Romance award from *Romantic Times* for *Anything for Danny*. In 1998 she also won a Career Achievement Award for Best Innovative Series from *Romantic Times*.

Carla believes the only thing better than curling up with a good book to read is sitting down at the computer with a good story to write. She's looking forward to writing many more books and bringing hours of pleasure to readers.

Carla Cassidy
Behind Closed Doors

FOR HER EYES ONLY

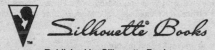
Silhouette Books

Published by Silhouette Books

America's Publisher of Contemporary Romance

To my mother-in-law, Antoinette,
for her years of love and support...
and for always believing in me.

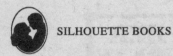 SILHOUETTE BOOKS

ISBN 0-373-80940-9

BEHIND CLOSED DOORS

Copyright © 1997 by Carla Bracale.

All rights reserved. Except for use in any review, the reproduction or utilization of this work in whole or in part in any form by any electronic, mechanical or other means, now known or hereafter invented, including xerography, photocopying and recording, or in any information storage or retrieval system, is forbidden without the written permission of the editorial office, Silhouette Books, 233 Broadway, New York, NY 10279 U.S.A.

All characters in this book have no existence outside the imagination of the author and have no relation whatsoever to anyone bearing the same name or names. They are not even distantly inspired by any individual known or unknown to the author, and all incidents are pure invention.

This edition published by arrangement with Harlequin Books S.A.

® and TM are trademarks of Harlequin Books S.A., used under license. Trademarks indicated with ® are registered in the United States Patent and Trademark Office, the Canadian Trade Marks Office and in other countries.

Visit Silhouette at www.eHarlequin.com

Printed in U.S.A.

Prologue

Reporters and cameramen jockeyed for positions on the courthouse stairs. Police officers bullied and cajoled, attempting to keep everyone behind the tape barrier that created a narrow walkway from the courthouse front door to the street. Overhead the July sun shone, relentless in intensity, adding heat and humidity to the fever of the frenzied mob.

One reporter swiped his sweaty forehead with a handkerchief while a female counterpart applied a fresh coating of lipstick. An air of anticipation electrified the scene, causing the most mundane acts to take on new significance.

The media had traveled from a four state area to Kansas City, Missouri, for this very event. Each and every person would remember what they were doing, what was being said on the morning the witness had arrived in court to present testimony that would put away a serial killer.

A hush fell on the crowd as a late-model black car pulled to the curb. The car belonged to Samantha Whitling, the assistant district attorney. At the same time every morning for the past three years she'd arrived at the courthouse, but never to such fanfare. However, never had she been transporting such an important witness.

As the car came to a halt, Samantha stepped out. No smile softened her stern features. Stone Face, as the press referred to her, walked around to the passenger side of the car, seeming oblivious to the crowd. She walked with military precision, her navy suit unflattering on her sticklike shape.

Samantha Whitling was not a favorite among the press. Not as forthcoming as her predecessor, Samantha maintained a closed-door policy the press resented. Still, there was no way she could have kept a lid on this particular case. Heinous serial murders had a way of being bigger than the best closed mouth.

The hush grew louder as Samantha opened the passenger door and the witness stepped out. Clad in a pink party dress, pale blond hair beribboned with matching bows, the little girl looked as if she were on her way to a birthday party. The only thing missing was a smile. Somber, with her pale eyebrows wrinkled in an unmistakable expression of anxiety, she offered her hand to the assistant district attorney.

Samantha Whitling smiled in encouragement as she took the little girl's hand, and cameras whirred.

Inside the courthouse, from the confines of a small, secured room, the prisoner watched out the window; his eyes narrowed as he watched the child flash a quicksilver smile to the photographers.

Oh yes, smile, little one, he thought. Smile while you can. Anger swelled inside him, pressing tightly against his chest. He closed his eyes and drew in several deep breaths, fighting for control. He had to maintain control, had to maintain patience.

Opening his eyes, he once again focused out the window, watching as the woman and child disappeared from his view. He knew the child's testimony would send him to prison. Ann Carson. Her name was burned into his brain. She'd seen too much, had identified him from three different lineups. Yes, the little brat would send him away, but probably not forever.

He leaned forward, studying the way she walked, memorizing the features of her face. Someday he'd be out again, free to walk the streets. Someday he'd be free to find her, find the little witness. Ann Carson. He'd find her and then he'd make her pay.

Chapter 1

Twenty-one years later

AULD LANG SYNE. I CAN GET YOU ANY TIME. Ann Carson frowned and reread the words of the note she'd just pulled from beneath the wine bottle in her refrigerator. How had it gotten in there? Where had it come from?

A cold breath whispered against the back of her neck, raising the hairs on her nape as the full implication hit her. Somebody had been in her house. At some time during the day while she'd been at work, somebody had been here.

The note fell to the floor as she grabbed the phone and punched in 911. As she waited for the call to be answered, her gaze shot around the room as her heart pounded loudly in her ears.

Was somebody still here? Hiding in the shadows of a closet? Concealed behind the laundry room door? Waning late afternoon light filtered in through the curtains, no longer able to

uminate the dark pockets in the corners of the room…hiding
aces.

"Come on, come on," she breathed into the phone, willing
dispatcher to answer.

"This is 911 emergency," a harried female voice finally
toned.

"I think somebody is in my house. I just got home from
ork and went to get a glass of wine. I found a note in my
frigerator. Somebody's been in here and I don't know if
ey're still here or not." She kept her voice to an urgent whis-
r, her gaze continuing to dart around the room.

"Ma'am…slow down.… Calm down. An officer is on the
ay. You're at 921 Evergreen Avenue?"

"Yes…yes that's right." Ann closed her eyes, trying to calm
e frantic beat of her heart. How could she hear if somebody
eaked up on her with the loud booming of her heart resound-
g in her ears?

"Now tell me your name."

"Ann. Ann Carson." Movement in Ann's peripheral vision
used her to gasp and whirl around. She stifled a scream as
vilight sat down before her and began bathing his sleek fur.

"Ms. Carson. Are you all right?"

"Yes, yes I'm fine. My cat just scared me, that's all."

As Ann answered a round of questions, she hoped an officer
uld arrive before her heart exploded with fear. Slowly, as
e minutes ticked by, the edge of terror waned somewhat. It
emed like forever before she heard a loud knock on the front
or and a voice shouting that it was the police. Hanging up
th the dispatcher, Ann scooped up Twilight and raced to the
or.

He didn't look like a cop. That was her first thought when
e opened the door and saw the man who stood in front of
r. With dark hair that tumbled down on his forehead and a
llsper of a five o'clock shadow darkening his jaw, he looked
ore criminal than crime fighter. The dark blue uniform of the
aceton Police Department reassured Ann that he was, indeed,
cop.

"You think there might be an intruder in the house?" h
asked as he flashed his badge.

She nodded and he pulled her out of the house and pointe
her toward his patrol car. "Wait there. I'll check it out."

As he drew his gun and entered the house, Ann walked dow
to where the car was parked. Leaning against the passenge
side of the car, she felt the first stir of impotent anger.

Somebody had been in her home, invaded her privacy. She'
bought the condo less than a year before after living in a tin
cheap apartment and saving every cent for years. In the pas
eight months her new home had become her sanctuary, he
asylum from her past, a stable, safe place. And now someon
had violated it.

She pulled the belt of her robe more tightly around her wais
grateful she'd put it on over her blue silk pajamas. Picking u
and hugging Twilight close to her chest, she fought agains
another shiver of apprehension.

Had somebody watched her change from her day clothes t
her pajamas? Had the intruder hidden in her closet, watchin
as she'd undressed? Sickened by the thought, she wrapped he
arms around herself.

She straightened up as the officer appeared on her fron
stoop. She started toward him, but hesitated as he held up
hand to stop her. "Just let me do a quick check of th
grounds," he said, then disappeared into the woods at the sid
of the condo.

As the minutes ticked by, Ann's momentary anger died, re
placed once again with a chilling fear. It had been the thic
surrounding woods that had initially sold her on the place. Nov
she saw the trees and brush not as a rustic, beautiful setting
but rather as a plethora of potential hiding places.

The purple shadows of dusk only intensified the dark secre
places in the woods. Overhead the light from a full moon spill
ing down couldn't penetrate the dark heart of the overgrow
area.

"All clear."

Ann jumped and whirled around to where the officer ha

parently completed a full circle around the back of the condo. Let's go inside and you can tell me why you think somebody as in the house.''

She nodded and followed him back into the house. Once side she led him into the kitchen, where he sat at the table d pulled a small notebook and pen from his pocket. "Okay, t's start with your name.''

"Ann. Ann Carson.'' She put down Twilight and sank into e chair across from the officer. The artificial light of the tchen emphasized the harsh, almost brutal lines of his ce…the face of a man who had lived hard with no regrets. And you're…?''

"Clay. Clay Clinton,'' he answered, then resumed his note king. "You live here alone?''

She nodded. "Alone other than my cat.'' Clay Clinton. The me suited him, all hard consonants.

He glanced over to where Twilight had curled up on a oked rug, the feline warily studying him. "He looks like he's d a rough life.''

"He showed up on my doorstep about two years ago, miss- g half an ear and nearly starved. He tolerates my living here ith him.''

"Now tell me why you think somebody was in here. Did u see someone? Hear noises that indicated an intruder?''

"No, nothing like that,'' she replied. "I got home from ork, opened up the patio door and stepped out on the deck r a few minutes. I came in, changed my clothes, then went get a glass of wine.'' She looked around and spied the note here she'd dropped it on the floor before calling 911.

She walked over and picked it up and handed it to him. This was under the wine bottle in my refrigerator.''

He read the handwritten note, a frown deepening the furrow ross his brow. "I know it sounds crazy,'' she continued, "but hoever put the note there also drank the last of the wine.''

"Where's the bottle?''

She pointed to the refrigerator, wishing his dark eyes gave vay his thoughts. He stood up and walked over to the refrig-

erator. As he reached in to grab the bottle, she couldn't help
but notice how the navy uniform emphasized his slender waist
and broad shoulders. Officer Clay Clinton was definitely an
attractive man. She hoped he was a great cop.

"How much wine did you think was left in the bottle?"

"I don't know…I think it was about half empty."

"Have you looked around to see if anything is missing?"
he asked as he placed the bottle on the table between them.

"No," she replied, surprised by the question. She hadn't
even thought about robbery. "I mean, I'm pretty sure nothing
is missing from the living room. But I really wasn't paying
much attention when I first got home."

"Let's go through the rest of the place and make sure our
trespasser isn't a burglar as well."

It took only minutes to go through the house. Despite the
horror of the situation, Ann couldn't help the burst of pride
that suffused her with warmth as she led him through the living
room. Decorated in deep burgundy and hunter green, each
piece of furniture had been chosen carefully.

She'd paid a small fortune in furnishing the house, expensive
items meant to last a lifetime. Furniture that spoke of longevity
and permanence.

There were two bedrooms, a small one devoid of any furniture and the master suite decorated in an explosion of brilliant
colors, the matching bedspread and curtains like a crazed art-
ist's paint palette.

"Nothing is missing that I can tell," Ann said as they returned to the living room.

He looked around the room. "No windows were open? You
have no idea how somebody might have gotten in?"

She shook her head, then frowned. "It's possible the patio
door was left unlocked, but I'm not sure. I've tried and tried
to remember if I had to unlock it when I opened it this evening,
but I just don't remember."

"The front door doesn't show signs of any forced entry. If
you think there's a possibility the back door was unlocked, I'd
say it's a good bet that's how somebody got in."

"But why? Why would somebody do something like this?"
:r gaze sought his.

He smiled for the first time, the gesture smoothing the lines
his face and deepening his attractiveness. "I ask myself that
every crime scene." He sat down on the edge of the sofa.
've got a few more questions to ask you to finish up my
port."

She nodded and sat down next to him, immediately sur-
unded by his masculine scent, a mixture of spicy cologne,
nty soap and an underlying whisper of maleness.

"What about keys? Anyone else have keys to your house?"

She hesitated, unsure whether to mention anything about
eg or not. "Only one, but he wouldn't have anything to do
th this."

"What's his name?"

"Greg Thorton."

"And what's his relationship to you?"

Ann felt the telltale blush that swept across her face. "Noth-
g now. We dated for a while, but it didn't work out. We
oke up about two weeks ago."

He lifted a dark eyebrow. "Who broke up with whom?"

Again Ann's cheeks warmed with a blush. She was a private
rson who rarely shared personal information with anyone,
pecially attractive strangers. "I broke up with him…but I'm
re Greg would never stoop to this kind of cryptic threat and
eaking around."

"Although you've indicated whoever it was might have
und access through the unlocked patio door, it might not be
bad idea for you to get all your locks changed as soon as
ssible."

She nodded. "It's probably one of my students," she said
ore to herself than to him.

He looked at her sharply. "You're a teacher?"

"Yes, I teach freshman English at Northland Junior College.
lso teach a community education course in creative writing."

He shook his head ruefully. "If I had my way, I'd pay all
u teachers hazard pay." He snapped his notebook closed and

put it back into his pocket. "I think you're probably right. Th
smacks of a silly student prank." He stood up and walked
the front door. "I'll file a report on this incident and if yc
have any more problems, don't hesitate to call the station."

"Thank you for getting here so quickly. I'm sure I overr
acted to the whole thing." As she remembered her near blir
panic while speaking to the emergency operator, a surge
embarrassment swept through her.

His dark gaze, which had remained cool and impersonal t
to this point, softened and he reached out and lightly touche
her arm. "Your initial reaction was smart. When it comes
the possibility of an uninvited person in your home, there's r
such thing as overreaction."

Ann fought the impulse to lean into him, force him to ho
her for just a moment. A comforting hug to banish the la
lingering core of icy fear. Instead she wrapped her arms arour
herself. "Thanks again."

"No problem." Saying goodbye, he turned and left.

She watched him until he got into his patrol car and dro
away. When the car was no longer in sight, she closed ar
locked her front door.

Leaning against the door, she gazed around the home she
worked so hard to attain. It frightened her sometimes ho
proud she was of the condo. There were moments late at nig
when she was certain her happiness would be yanked awa
from her.

She walked back into the kitchen, the wine bottle in th
middle of the table a grim reminder. She tossed the bottle
the garbage, then picked up the note that had sent chills dow
her spine. AULD LANG SYNE. I CAN GET YOU AN
TIME.

She was surprised he hadn't taken the wine bottle or no
with him to check for fingerprints or something. Although th
police probably did that kind of thing for more serious crime
After all, nothing had been taken. There wasn't even any i
dication that someone had broken in. Somebody had ju

altzed in her unlocked back door and helped himself to her ine.

A student prank. Surely Officer Clay Clinton had been right. smacked of immaturity. Probably someplace in town one of er students was giggling, recounting to his friends how he'd anaged to get into Ms. Carson's condo, drink a bottle of her ine and leave the note.

She had grown lax about checking to make sure the patio oor was locked. She wouldn't be lax in the future. With a gh of irritation, she crumpled the note into a ball and tossed into the garbage. Even telling herself it was nothing more an a student prank couldn't dispel her underlying unease.

She worried that somehow this was just the beginning, the rst fissure in a widening crack of the happiness and stability e'd worked so hard to attain.

They don't make English teachers like they used to, Clay ought as he drove back to the station. With her big blue eyes d pale blond hair, Ann Carson had looked more like a college udent than a teacher.

He could still smell the scent of her perfume, a clean, floral ent. The entire condo had smelled the same way…pleasant d almost good enough to eat.

Almost, but not quite. Although she was incredibly pretty, e wasn't his type at all. Too cool, too controlled. Even her ldress was off-putting. Secluded and exclusive, the condo had eathed not only of her evocative scent, but also of permae-nce, stability and obligation…all the things he was about to uck from his own life.

Still, something about her had intrigued him. He knew she'd en afraid when he'd first arrived, but she'd hidden it fairly ell. What had drawn him more than anything had been a rkness in her eyes, a darkness that spoke of secrets, of pain.

He shook his head, scolding himself for allowing his imag-ation to take flight. The problem was he hadn't had a date in onths, a fact which made every attractive woman seem vastly triguing.

He wheeled into the station and parked the patrol car. By the time he typed up his report, his shift would be over. An other day done. Forty left to go.

As he entered the Kansas City suburban Graceton Polic Department he was greeted by the usual cacophony of noise Officers shouted back and forth to one another, arrestees pro claimed their innocence, computer printers whirred out report and telephones buzzed with annoying regularity.

Before sitting down at his desk, Clay got himself a cup o coffee from the break room. As usual, the coffee smelled too old and too strong. He carried it back to his desk and sat down Now, if he could just find his computer amid the chaos o papers on the top of his desk.

"Hey, buddy, thought you'd already gone home for th day."

Clay grinned as Raymond Misker clapped him on the back "I caught a late call…possible intruder at the Evergreen con dos. As soon as I type the report I'm outta here."

"So was it an intruder?" Raymond asked as he helped him self to the coffee.

"Somebody had definitely been in the house, but the victim is a teacher. I think it was probably some sort of student ven detta or prank."

Raymond nodded, sipped his coffee, then grimaced. "Whew that's bad." He sat down in the chair next to Clay's desk. "S how many days left?"

"Forty."

Raymond shook his head with a rueful smile. "I still can' believe you're really going to retire."

Clay reared back in his chair. "I figure now is the time while I'm young enough and good-lookin' enough to enjoy it.'

Raymond snorted. "You're definitely young enough, bu certainly not my type."

"Thank God," Clay retorted.

"What are your plans? Going to go into some sort of busi ness for yourself?"

"Ah, that's part of the fun of retirement, not having to hav plans. Right now I've got a one-way ticket to Hawaii waiting for me at home. I figure I'll lie on the beach and contemplate the meaning of life.''

''Yeah, right…and what are you going to do on the second day when you get bored?''

Clay shrugged. ''I'm not planning on getting bored, and if I do, I'll face it when it happens.''

Raymond smiled wistfully. ''Still, sounds like a hell of a nice dream…bright sunshine, tropical breezes and women in bikinis.''

''I intend to make that dream my reality,'' Clay replied.

Raymond shook his head ruefully. ''Ginger keeps telling me I can't ever retire. As long as we've got a mortgage and four kids to put through college, there's no chance of early retirement for me. I'll be lucky if she lets me retire when I'm eighty.''

''And that, my friend, is why I don't have a mortgage, a wife or kids,'' Clay replied. ''Now get the hell out of here so I can type up this report and go home.''

With a good-natured grunt, Raymond stood up and ambled to his own desk across the room. Within minutes, Clay had found the proper form and busied himself inputting the necessary information.

He knew many of his fellow officers envied his having the opportunity to retire at the ripe age of forty-two, but it had been a life plan Clay had never varied from.

As he worked on the form, his thoughts returned to the lovely Ann Carson. Now there was a high-maintenance kind of woman. Whoever she married would not have the luxury of early retirement and living out dreams. He'd be busy paying the mortgage on that fancy condo.

He finished the work on the report, then filed it, along with any further thoughts of the attractive English teacher.

Chapter 2

Ann left her evening class and walked out into the faculty parking lot. Evening had fallen, spreading deep violet hues that washed the surrounding scenery, but brought no relief from the July heat. As darkness spread, the overhead lights of the parking lot cast dark shadows where their luminous beams couldn't reach.

Her heels clicked rhythmically against the hot pavement as she hurried toward her car, not wanting to linger in the nearly deserted parking lot.

She immediately saw the note fluttering beneath her windshield wiper. At first she thought it was a flyer, announcing the latest drama department production, or perhaps an advertisement for tutoring services.

She plucked it from beneath the wiper and opened it, the bold, black marker words all too familiar.

AULD LANG SYNE...SOON YOU'LL BE MINE. I LONG TO HEAR YOU CRY. I'LL WATCH YOU AS YOU DIE.

Her knees weakened and she leaned against the driver door,

her gaze darting around nervously. Dammit. Who was doing this to her? Why was somebody doing this to her?

She frowned as she saw a group of her students from the creative writing class on their way to the student parking lot. They waved at her, their cheerful voices riding on the late evening breeze.

She returned their waves, wondering if one of them had put the note here? She pulled the keys from her purse and got into her car.

Certainly in her three years of teaching, she'd dealt with disgruntled students before. She'd received middle of the night phone calls, nasty notes calling her names, but nothing as threatening as this one.

The handwritten letters seemed to shimmer with malevolence, a hostility far beyond that of a student irritated about the latest grade she'd given.

Starting her car, she decided to take the note to the police station. Even though she might be accused of being an hysterical woman, overreacting to a silly note, she'd feel better knowing the police had some sort of record about the problem.

It took her only minutes to get to the Graceton Police Department, a five-story building whose dirty brick facade made it look much older than it was.

She found a parking space but remained in the car. Leaning her head back against the seat, she closed her eyes. Was she being silly? Running to the police with nothing more than a note? She wasn't accustomed to asking for help for anything, had accomplished everything in her life alone.

She looked at the note once again. It didn't matter if the police thought she was being silly, she'd feel better knowing the police had the note.

Mind made up, she got out of the car and went into the building. Immediately, from all sides, sounds and smells assaulted her senses. The noise level was appalling and the scent of burnt coffee and pungent disinfectant mingled with the underlying odors of sweat, blood and tears.

Two young officers jumped up to greet her, bumping shoulders like Keystone cops as they approached. "May I help you?" They both asked at the same time.

"I'd like to speak with Clay Clinton," she said.

Their eager smiles died. One officer moved back to his previous position and the other one pointed her to the back of the room. "His desk is there in the corner. You can go on back and have a seat and I'll see if I can find him."

Ann made her way to the desk, once again wondering if she was foolish for coming here. The room was uncomfortably warm, but she dismissed the thought of removing her linen suit jacket, aware of the lingering male glances shooting in her direction.

She frowned as she eyed the top of Clay's desk. She hoped he was more organized in fighting crime than he apparently was in his paperwork. Looking up, she saw him approach, a cup of coffee in hand.

"Ms. Carson." He set the mug down amid the mound of papers and offered her a handshake and a pleasant smile. "What brings you here?"

"This." She handed him the note she'd received.

He read it, a frown deepening the furrow of his brow. "Where did you find this?"

"Under the windshield wiper of my car when I came out of evening classes."

He looked at her, his brown eyes exuding an empathy that warmed her. "If this is a student prank, it's not very amusing, is it?"

"I've had nasty notes from students before, but never anything like this. Usually I get them the week after the students have received their final grades, but we're in the middle of the semester right now."

He studied the note once again. "The contents of the first note were easy to dismiss as a bad joke, but this one…this one implies a definite threat." He reared back in his chair and looked at her once again. "Did you get the locks of your house changed?"

She nodded. "Yesterday."

"Good." The front legs of his chair thumped down and he raked a hand through his thick, curly hair. "Look, I'd like to do a little follow-up on all this…get some more information from you, but I have a favor to ask."

She looked at him curiously. "What?"

"How about we go down the street to Maxim's Café and finish our business? The air conditioner is on the blink and it's so damn hot in here it's hard to concentrate. Officially as of fifteen minutes ago I'm off duty for the night and I hate to sit here in this heat a minute longer than I have to."

"It is warm in here," she agreed. Her jacket clung to her with uncomfortable stickiness and the heat was making her a little nauseous. "The café is close?"

"Half a block. During the summers when the air conditioner doesn't work, Maxim's becomes our unofficial annex."

She stood up. "Okay, let's go."

"Can I keep this?" He held up the offensive note.

"I wish you would."

He placed the note in a plastic bag, put it in his drawer, then rose and grabbed his notebook. With a hand to the small of her back, he led her through the squad room to the door where she'd come in.

Ann pretended not to notice the thumbs-up signs and sly winks directed at Clay as they passed other officers, although she felt her cheeks flush hotly at the attention.

"You'll have to excuse the Neanderthals," Clay said as they left the building and walked out into the humid, hot night. "Most of the women they see in the station are hookers or addicts. They don't know how to act when an uptown lady comes in."

"It's all right. I'm not easily offended."

They walked a few moments in silence, Ann double stepping to keep up with his long, confident strides. She felt better already, just knowing the note was in his possession.

"Whew, nothing like summer in the midwest," he said, breaking the silence.

"I've always heard crime rises with the heat and humidity of summer."

He nodded. "It's true. Unfortunately we have yet to figure out a weather pattern that prevents crime."

He opened the door to Maxim's Café and ushered her into the dim coolness within. It was after nine o'clock and whatever dinner crowd the restaurant served was long gone, leaving only a handful of people and plenty of empty tables.

"Hey, Wayne." Clay waved to the man behind the long counter and led Ann to a table in the corner.

The café smelled of rich home cooking and Ann's stomach responded, gurgling to remind her she hadn't eaten in several hours. "Was that yours or mine?" Clay asked as they sat down.

Ann blushed. "I think it was mine. I haven't eaten since noon and then it was just an apple and some crackers."

"My lunch was a hot dog from a street vendor." He pulled out two menus that had been propped behind a napkin holder. "I vote we conduct our business while we eat."

"I second the vote," she replied as she opened the menu.

For a moment they each studied the options. Ann decided on the chicken salad plate, then turned her attention to the man across the table.

She wondered if he was married. She noted the lack of a ring on his finger. Still, she knew that didn't necessarily mean the lack of a life partner. A lot of married men didn't wear rings.

"You mentioned you were off duty. Will your wife be expecting you at home?" she asked.

"Nope. No wife...no significant other, not even a dog to wait up for me." He closed his menu and pushed it aside. "I decided my wife would be my work. Too many marriages don't survive the job. What about you? Ever been married?"

"No. My sole focus has always been my education, then my work."

"So, no reason to suspect an angry ex-spouse left those notes."

She shook her head. "Not a single angry ex-spouse to suspect."

"Hi, Clay." An attractive waitress appeared at the table, flashing Clay a saucy grin, then casting Ann a pleasant smile. The name tag on her tight uniform read Betty. "Air-conditioning must be broken again, you're the fifth cop who's come in here this evening."

"Yeah, someday the taxpayers will approve a bond that will get us a new cooling system for the station…but until that time you're stuck with having our presence whenever the temperature rises above eighty," Clay said.

Betty looked at Ann with a mock pained expression. "The presence of so many cops in here sure ruins our reputation as a dive." She pulled an order pad from her pocket. "So, what's it gonna be, and I don't recommend the daily special."

Once they had ordered and Betty had left the table, Clay opened his notebook and took a pen from his pocket. "Now let's get down to the matter at hand. Tell me again. When and where did you find the note?"

"I was at work…at the college. Tuesdays and Thursdays are my late nights. The creative writing class lasts from seven to eight-thirty on those nights."

"And you found the note when you went out to your car to go home?"

She nodded, then frowned. "But I was at my car earlier, around six-thirty. I'd left the students' papers in the car. I don't remember seeing the note then."

"Would you have noticed it?"

"I think so. It was the first thing I saw when I got to my car later."

"And the first note was left in your home on Tuesday, right?"

"Yes." She eyed him curiously. "Do you think it's somebody in the creative writing class?"

He looked up from the notebook and smiled ruefully. Again she was struck by the warmth that seemed to emanate from his coffee-colored eyes. "I think it's too early to speculate." He leaned forward. "Look, I know this is scary. Usually anonymous notes are the sign of a coward. In the same category of obscene phone callers…a nuisance, but rarely a danger."

"The key word there is *rarely,* right?"

He leaned back once again. "Right. I'd rather err on the side of caution. The first note bothers me because you found it in your home. In that instance a crime has already been committed…trespassing and breaking and entering. This second note bothers me because it's an implied threat to your safety."

"Here we go…" Betty interrupted the conversation, serving their meals and drinks. "Enjoy."

"What happens now?" Ann asked the moment they were alone again.

"We talk. We see if we can figure out who might have an ax to grind with you. Let's start with the boyfriend you told me you recently broke up with…what was his name?"

"Greg. Greg Thorton." Ann didn't want to think of him, let alone talk about him. "Surely this isn't necessary? I'm telling you there's no way Greg can be behind these notes. It's just not his style." Her voice was sharper than intended.

Clay shut his notebook and shoved it aside. "Okay, we won't talk about it." He picked up his hamburger and took a bite. As he chewed, he kept his gaze focused on his plate.

Ann sighed, knowing she couldn't have it both ways. She couldn't ask the police for help, then refuse to answer their questions. "I'm sorry," she offered. "I'm just not accustomed to talking about my personal life." With the tines of her fork, she raked a pattern through the scoop of chicken salad.

"I know this isn't easy, Ann, but if you want me to find the person responsible for these notes, there are certain things you're going to have to talk to me about."

She nodded. "Greg and I dated for about three months before I realized he wasn't what I wanted in my life. A couple of weeks ago I told him I thought we should see other people. He agreed, and that was the end of it."

"And he wasn't upset?"

She smiled and Clay felt as if a fist plunged into his stomach, momentarily taking his breath away. He realized this was the first time he'd seen her smile. And what a smile it was. It lightened the hue of blue in her eyes and brought warmth to her cool, classic features. "Greg doesn't ever get upset. He believes showing emotion is a sign of weakness."

"Not showing emotion is a great way to produce an ulcer," Clay replied, pleased when she not only smiled again, but actually laughed out loud.

"Greg does have ulcers," she admitted, her eyes sparkling as if she and Clay shared a secret.

"What does this strong, ulcer-ridden man do for a living?" Clay asked.

"He's a lawyer with Beatty, Walters and Majors. He's hoping to make partner by the end of the year."

Clay whistled beneath his breath. He knew the firm, one of the most prestigious in the Kansas City area. Still, Greg Thoron being a bright lawyer didn't preclude his having a few loose screws. He made a mental note to stop in and have a little chat with the man.

He took another bite of his hamburger and flipped through his notes. "Auld Lang Syne…what exactly does that mean? I know I sing it every New Year's Eve."

"Old times, that's all it means." Once again she used her fork to make ruts in her salad.

He grinned at her. "My mom used to spank me for playing with my food."

She flushed and took a bite of the chicken. "I'm just sure Greg isn't sending me those notes and what bothers me is I have no idea who might be doing it."

"Probably two things will happen. We'll find out who's guilty and take the appropriate action, or whoever is doing it will tire of the game and move on to another victim." He hoped his words sounded more positive than he felt.

Something about the notes bothered him deep in his gut…in the place that made him a good cop. Instinct, intuition…he wasn't sure what to call it, he only knew how it felt.

"Old times," he mused thoughtfully. "Any other men from your past who might have a bone to pick with you?"

She shook her head. "None that I can think of." She gazed at him curiously, her eyes emanating an intelligence he found sexy as hell. "What makes you think it's a man?"

"I don't know. I suppose it could be a woman, but statistically, the odds lean toward it being a male." He speared a French fry and popped it into his mouth. "Tell me about the people in this creative writing class."

"I've got thirteen students. The youngest is Simon Casmell, he's twenty, and the oldest is Mabel Cornfeld. She's eighty-two."

"If I was to guess, I'd say we can definitely rule out Mabel Cornfeld," Clay said, hoping to see her smile once again. She didn't. Instead she frowned thoughtfully.

"I think we can also rule out Dean Moore. He's an older man in a wheelchair."

Clay nodded. "Okay, tell me the names of the others." Once again he opened his notebook.

As she told him names and small particulars about the rest of the students, Clay once again found himself focused more on the woman herself than on what she was telling him.

There was an intriguing secretiveness about her, a closed-shutter look in her eyes. He had a feeling a man would have to work hard to get to know the real Ann Carson, that what she presented to the world was merely a facade.

He inwardly scoffed at his fanciful notions. It had definitely been too long since he'd had a date, been in the company of an attractive female. Maybe it was time to change that, right here, right now.

He still had thirty-eight days before he left for his retirement dream…over a month of time to spend enjoying a woman's company. Why not Ann? Certainly he wouldn't mind the challenge of getting to know her better.

When she'd finished giving him the names and bits of information about her students, he closed his notebook and signaled to Betty for more iced tea.

"When you aren't teaching classes or receiving disturbing otes, what do you do in your spare time?"

She looked down at her plate, apparently uncomfortable with ne personal turn in the conversation. When she looked up gain, he realized dark shades had fallen over her eyes, disncing her from him. "I don't have much spare time. I carry pretty heavy load at the college and most of my evenings nd weekends are spent grading papers and working on plans or future lessons."

"Haven't you heard that all work and no play makes Ann a ull girl?"

She shrugged and eyed him with a touch of defiance. "Then guess I'm just a dull girl."

He studied her intently. "Somehow I doubt that."

She dabbed her mouth with a napkin. "Well, I'd say I've ken up more than enough of your time." She opened her urse.

"I'll get it," he said, surprised by her abruptness.

"Thank you, but I prefer to pay for my own." She pulled everal bills out of her wallet and placed them on the table etween them.

Clay pulled a business card from his breast pocket. "Here." e held it out to her. "This has the station number and my ome phone number on it. Don't hesitate to use it if something se happens or if you're just feeling scared."

He was rewarded with a small smile. "Thank you. I appreate it." Before he could say another word, she turned and ft the restaurant.

He watched her go, enjoying the sensual sway of her hips eneath the peach-colored skirt. Nice legs…long and shapely, et clad in high heel white pumps.

"She left in a hurry. What did you do? Threaten to arrest er?" Betty plopped down in the booth Ann had vacated and elped herself to the remaining French fries on Clay's plate.

"Nah, guess I just pushed a little too hard."

"I keep telling you that you can push me hard anytime." he winked at him.

Clay laughed, knowing she was all talk. "Betty, you forget, I've met your husband. He's twice my size and knows where I live."

Betty grinned and stood back up. "Want me to put this on your tab?"

"That will work." He stood, his mind recaptured by thoughts of Ann Carson. "I'm heading home. I'll see you later, Betty."

She gave him a jaunty wave as he left the cool air-conditioning and walked back out into the hot summer night. The air smelled of hot pavement, bus exhaust and rotting garbage. Wistfully he remembered the way Ann had smelled, like a floral garden in a rainstorm. Fresh…new…sweet.

Guess he just wasn't her type, he thought as he headed toward his car. She'd certainly backed off in a hurry when he'd tried to take the conversation from business to personal. An odd surge of disappointment winged through him.

Tomorrow was his day off. Maybe he'd take the morning and go have a little talk with Greg Thorton, see what type of man did attract Ann and if the high-power lawyer had anything to do with the notes she'd received.

Ann walked into her home and immediately kicked off her shoes and crunched her toes into the soft carpeting. With a sigh of exhaustion she sank onto the sofa. Twilight peered down at her from his favorite resting place atop the bookshelves along one wall.

"I think he was going to ask me out," she said to the cat, whose tail moved like a metronome, swishing back and forth to an internal rhythm.

She shrugged out of her jacket and placed it carefully over the back of the sofa, then leaned into the cushions, her thoughts consumed with Clay.

He was a nice man…very attractive not only in looks, but in his apparent easygoing personality. She'd felt herself drawn to him, and that's why she'd bolted.

Relationships weren't easy for her and generally she steered

ear of any and all. Relationships demanded sharing and a
vel of trust she'd never been able to achieve.

With Greg it had been relatively easy. Greg was most com-
rtable when talking about himself, his brilliance and his
ork. He'd required next to nothing from Ann. It was only in
e last couple of weeks of their relationship that he'd begun
pressure her for intimacy and she realized she couldn't sleep
th a man she wasn't even sure she liked.

Clay had been much more likable...therefore a threat. She
ghed and rubbed her forehead, where a headache had blos-
med. She was grateful it had been Clay who'd responded to
r initial cry for help, glad it would be him seeing to her case.
it, she had no desire to allow him to be anything but that, a
p on her case.

She wanted him to solve the mystery of the note sender,
en let her get back to her safe life. Safe and lonely, a small
ice whispered inside her head.

"Shut up," she muttered irritably and sat up, startling Twi-
ht who hissed his displeasure. "It's late, Twilight. I'm going
bed."

She was halfway between the master bedroom and the living
om when the phone rang. She raced into the bedroom and
ved for the phone at the side of the bed, at the same time her
ze shot to the clock on her nightstand. Who would be calling
r at a few minutes before eleven?

"Hello?"

Silence. Not the kind of silence that implied an open line,
t rather the thick, pregnant quiet of somebody on the other
d.

"Hello? Who's there?"

She'd been wrong. It wasn't complete silence. She could
ar the low rasp of breathing. She found herself matching her
vn breaths with the sound of the caller's. Ten seconds passed.
teen seconds. Then a click, and Ann knew whoever it was
d hung up.

She hung up as well. A wrong number? Probably. Taking

off her blouse, she yawned, exhaustion settling in full forc
As she stepped out of her skirt the phone rang again.

Once again she picked up the receiver. "Hello?"

Soft breathing. "Who is this?" she demanded. "Stop callir
here." She slammed down the phone.

She had turned out her light and gotten into bed when th
phone rang again....

Chapter 3

he moment Clay walked into the law offices, he knew he'd
derdressed. The law firm of Beatty, Walters and Majors was
used in a downtown fifteen-story building of steel and glass.
atty, Walters and Majors occupied the top floor.

A receptionist greeted him as he stepped off the elevator,
r desk situated to give her complete control over who could
ter the inner sanctum of private offices. "May I help you?"
e asked, her cool gaze disdainful as she eyed his worn jeans
d short-sleeved sport shirt.

"I'd like to speak with Greg Thorton."

"Do you have an appointment?"

"No. I just need a few moments of his time."

Her nostrils thinned as though she smelled something odor-
s. "Sir, Mr. Thorton doesn't see clients without an appoint-
nt."

Clay flipped open his badge. "I'm sure he can work me in.
I just sit over there until he's available." Without waiting
her reply, he ambled over to one of the chairs in a small
iting room across from her desk.

The minute he left her desk, she picked up an intercom phone and spoke briefly, then hung up and studiously ignored Clay.

He leafed through several magazines, the minutes ticking b endlessly. He had a feeling the wait was intentional, a min game of power. No problem. It was his day off, he had nothin better to do. He could wait as long as it took to speak to Gre Thorton.

He was halfway through a travelogue, daydreaming abou his retirement when the receptionist motioned to him. "M Thorton will see you now." She pointed to the door next her desk. "Go through there, down the hall and Mr. Thorton office is the second one on your right."

Clay followed her directions and found the door that held brass nameplate with Thorton's name. He knocked softly, th knock answered by a brisk "Enter."

Greg sat at an impressive desk, his attention focused on piece of paper before him. He didn't even look up as Cla entered. Clay waited patiently and took this opportunity to loo around the office.

Money. The entire room smelled of it, from the leathe bound books in the heavy, mahogany bookshelves to the thic plush carpeting beneath his feet. The scent of expensive co logne hung in the air, overriding the smell of a fresh flor bouquet that sat on the edge of the desk.

"What can I do for you?" He still didn't bother looking u from his paperwork.

Clay held his badge out beneath Greg's nose, close enoug so the jerk could smell it. He flipped his wallet closed ar jammed it back into his pocket.

"Are you selling tickets to the Policeman's Ball, raisin money to take some orphans to the zoo?" He still didn't both to make eye contact with Clay, but continued to peruse th papers before him.

"I'd like to ask you some questions about Ann Carson."

That got his attention. Cold blue eyes met Clay's. "Ann Has something happened? Is she all right?"

Clay eased himself into the chair opposite the desk. "She's fine, but she's been receiving some troubling anonymous notes."

"And she thinks I'm sending them? That's utterly absurd." He closed the manila folder in front of him and folded his hands on the desktop. "Are you accusing me of sending these notes?" His voice remained cool, rather flat in tone.

"Ann doesn't know who's sending them, and I'm not here to make accusations. I'm here to get information." Clay studied the man across from him.

He wore a suit Clay guessed cost more than Clay's entire wardrobe. Greg's sandy-colored hair was expensively styled, the short cut emphasizing his square jaw and strong features.

An attractive man, Clay thought grudgingly. A man who looked accustomed to wielding power. "I understand you and Ann had a parting of the ways a couple of weeks ago," Clay continued.

Greg smiled. A bloodless smile that didn't quite reach the arctic blue of his eyes. "So that's what this is all about? I'm a spurned lover and that makes me the number one suspect in the case of the 'troubling' notes?" He leaned back in his chair, an eyebrow lifted in amusement. "There's only one problem with the scenario. My relationship with Ann was a bit more casual than implied. We weren't lovers."

"But you have a key to her condo." It wasn't a question, but rather a statement of fact. Clay didn't want to think about why the assertion that Greg and Ann weren't lovers pleased him.

Greg's smile didn't waver. "Which is not a crime, the last I heard." He leaned forward and once again laced his fingers together. "Officer...I'm sorry, I didn't catch your name."

"Clinton. Clay Clinton."

"Officer Clinton, Ann and I dated for several months, then decided our relationship wasn't going anywhere. We agreed not to see each other anymore and that was the end of it." He blinked, reminding Clay of a cold-blooded reptile.

"Ann is a fine, intelligent woman, but certainly not the type to inspire the kind of obsessive passion that would warrant my sneaking around leaving her notes." He reopened the file folder on his desk. "And now if you'll excuse me, I have work to do." He picked up a sheet of paper, effectively dismissing Clay.

Clay bridled, unaccustomed to being summarily discharged. "If you don't mind, I have just another question or two."

A flash of impatience crossed Greg's features, there only a moment then gone beneath a smooth facade. "Yes?"

"Do you know of anyone who might want to give Ann some grief? Friends, family members?"

"Ann doesn't have any family that I know of. Nor does she have any friends that I met during the time we dated. She's a very private person and if you want to know any more about her, I suggest you ask her."

"Thank you for your time, Mr. Thorton."

Clay left the office building, grateful to be outside, despite the July heat. Although the law office had been cool, Clay had felt stifled by the excessive display of wealth and the cold, passionless Greg Thorton.

He'd never had a particularly high opinion of lawyers, considered them a necessary evil in the world. But Greg Thorton definitely pushed his hot buttons.

His head told him the man was too cool, too dispassionate to be the note writer, but Clay had been around the block more than once. He knew that sometimes a calm exterior hid a cauldron of seething, raging emotions.

As he drove home, he replayed the interview in his head, wondering vaguely if his dislike of Greg Thorton had nothing to do with what the man did for a living or his cool personality, but rather with the fact that Ann had chosen to date the cold fish.

He frowned, irritated by his own thoughts. The last thing he needed in his life right now was a relationship. In thirty-seven days he'd be on a beach in Hawaii, living the life of a single retired cop. No problems, no hassles, nobody to answer to or support. Just sand, beach and sun.

Pulling into the apartment complex where he lived, he shoved all thoughts of Greg Thorton and Ann Carson out of his head. Instead, he focused on what he needed to accomplish today. Today he started packing up, throwing out and getting organized for his life of leisure.

His apartment was a small, one-bedroom unit, more a place to eat and change clothes than a real home. He'd lived in the same space for the last ten years. The rent and utilities were low and he didn't spend enough time here to get depressed about the smallness of the place or the lack of attractive decor.

The small apartment, the old, but reliable car...all had been a part of his master plan. The plan of saving as much money as possible, taking retirement as soon as possible, then living out his dream. The plan had been born on the night of his father's death ten years ago.

He'd just finished packing up a box of winter clothes for charity when a knock fell on his door. "Hey, Raymond," Clay greeted his buddy and ushered him in through the living room and into the kitchen. "What are you doing here?"

"You forgot." Raymond's smile fell. "I knew I should have called and reminded you."

Clay snapped his fingers, suddenly remembering exactly why Raymond was here. "The ski equipment."

"Have you changed your mind? I mean, maybe you'd rather store it instead of just giving it away."

"I'm not going to have much use for snow equipment in Hawaii. Have a seat, all I have to do is go downstairs to the storage area and get it." Clay grabbed his keys off the table. "Help yourself to a beer, or whatever. I'll be right back."

It took Clay only minutes to find the ski equipment he intended to give to Raymond. When he got back to the kitchen Raymond had popped the top on a brew and was munching some peanuts from a can Clay had forgotten he had. "Here you are, skis, poles, boots and a snowsuit you'll never manage to get your beer gut into." Clay placed the things in the corner, then went to the refrigerator and grabbed a beer for himself.

"Don't make fun of my gut. I've worked long and hard to

attain it," Raymond said as he patted his protruding stomach. He took a deep draw of his beer. "Hey, that was some nice-looking woman who came into the station to see you last night. Business or pleasure?"

"Business, although I wouldn't mind a little pleasure," Clay said wryly. "Her name is Ann Carson. She's the possible intruder call I answered the other night at the Evergreen condos. She received another note…this one more threatening."

"You know, I read about a case where a woman was getting threatening notes and horrible things in the mail. Her dog was killed and left on her front porch…graffiti was sprayed on her house. The cops went nuts trying to find the perpetrator."

"What happened?" Clay asked.

"They discovered the woman was doing it all herself."

"You're kidding? Why?"

Raymond shrugged. "I guess for attention. Who knows why women do the things they do?" Raymond swallowed another slug of beer and belched. "Maybe the attractive Ann Carson is writing notes to herself."

"I can't imagine that," Clay replied. "She doesn't seem the type who would do anything to seek attention."

Raymond finished his beer and crushed the can. "Just a thought. At least you aren't working a murder case or anything serious that would play havoc with your retirement."

"I don't intend to allow anything to play havoc with my retirement. Besides, the chief is keeping my caseload light in anticipation of my leaving the force."

"Lucky you." Raymond tossed his crumpled beer can into the wastebasket in the corner and stood up. "Guess I'd better get out of here. Ginger wants me to paint the shutters, and I've been promising her to get to it and it looks like today is the day." He gathered up the ski paraphernalia.

"I don't envy you that job in this heat," Clay replied, also rising and walking with Raymond to the front door.

"Ah, but Ginger has promised me a decadent reward for my hard work in the heat." Raymond mugged a leer, then grinned. "I'll see you at the station tomorrow. Thanks for the ski stuff."

"Enjoy it," Clay said, then closed the door and went back to the kitchen. He sank down at the table and grabbed his beer and a handful of peanuts. Popping the peanuts into his mouth, he chewed thoughtfully.

Was it possible Ann Carson had written those notes? Was it some sort of psychotic plea for help or attention? He just couldn't imagine such a thing. Or was he allowing a stab of personal interest in the woman to cloud his professional shrewdness?

She'd certainly done nothing to indicate any culpability, but that didn't necessarily mean anything. Still, he found it difficult to seriously entertain the idea that Ann had written the notes to herself.

Maybe he'd take a ride over to the college later that afternoon, tell her he'd spoken with Greg Thorton, see what kind of a reaction she'd have to that bit of information. He refused to dwell on the pleasure that coursed through him as he thought of seeing her once again.

Ann sat at her desk, grateful this was her last class of the day and the students were doing a reading assignment that required nothing from her.

Checking her watch, she decided to give them ten more minutes, then use the last fifteen minutes of class time to go over some of the finer points of Poe's prose.

A headache pointed with sharp intensity just behind her eyes, an old familiar sign of lack of sleep. She rubbed the bridge of her nose, seeking relief but knowing only a good night's rest would banish the cursed ache.

Thank goodness it was Friday. No classes, no students for the next two days. Hopefully she could catch up on some much-needed sleep over the weekend.

The classroom door opened and she looked up to see Clay come in. Surprised, and oddly pleased to see him, she started to rise. He indicated he'd wait for the end of the class and she sat back down.

He found a chair at the back of the room and slid into it,

his posture a relaxed sprawl. He looked perfectly at ease and Ann would bet he'd spent most of his high school years slouched in a desk at the back of the room.

Without his uniform, clad in a pair of worn, tight-fitting jeans and a navy T-shirt, he looked younger, even more vital than he had on the previous occasions she'd seen him.

She tried to focus on the paperwork in front of her, but found it next to impossible with him watching her. She felt his gaze lingering on her, as if he knew that beneath the pale blue suit she wore a completely frivolous lacy camisole.

Of course he knows no such thing, she berated herself. Wondering if lack of sleep had addled her brain as well as given her a headache, she arose to complete the last ten minutes of class.

As the last student left the classroom, she walked back to where Clay sat. "You look like you belong in the back of the room," she said.

He grinned, the warm smile that stroked Ann with an unexpected heat. "It definitely brings back memories of high school days. I was what you teachers refer to as an underachiever."

She smiled. "Most kids are underachievers in high school. It's what you do with your life that counts and I'd say you've achieved just fine in that aspect." Her smile faltered slightly. "Any news for me? More questions? What brings you to my turf?"

Clay stood up and took a step toward her, bringing with him the evocative scent of minty soap, bright sunshine and an underlying whisper of maleness. "I went to Greg Thorton's office this morning and had a little chat with him."

A group of students entered, their laughter filling the room. "We can't talk here. Another class is going to start soon."

She hesitated a moment, her head pounding with almost nauseating intensity. "Why don't you follow me back to my place? We can talk there." She really didn't want to go anywhere but home…home where as soon as they finished talking she could go to bed.

"Okay. I'll meet you there."

Together they walked out of the classroom and into the early evening twilight. They parted ways on the sidewalk, Ann heading for the staff parking lot and Clay going in the opposite direction.

As Ann hurried toward her car, she was thankful the day was over and hoped she could sleep undisturbed tonight.

"Ms. Carson."

She looked around, seeking who had called her. She smiled as she saw Dean Moore heading toward her, his electric wheelchair covering the space between them with an audible hum. "Dean. I didn't know you were taking other classes besides my creative writing course."

He nodded, the silver strands in his hair shining in the waning golden sun. "Taking classes helps pass the time," he said. He shuffled through some paperwork and held out several sheets. "I wrote another short story and want you to critique it. I think I fixed a lot of the mistakes I made when I wrote the last one."

"Great, I'll look at it and bring it to class Tuesday night." She tucked it among her other papers. "Now, I've got to get out of here."

"And I've got to get to class." With a wave, he pushed the button that moved his chair forward. "See you next Tuesday," he called over his shoulder.

Ann continued to her car, wondering what malady had struck Dean Moore to put him in the wheelchair. The stories he'd written so far had been filled with barely veiled bitterness, tales of what might have been for him if not for the inconvenience of being confined to a wheelchair.

Making a note to herself to read the story over the weekend, Ann got into her car and headed home. As she drove, her thoughts again turned to Clay Clinton.

It bothered her just a bit, how his very presence evoked a warm river of pleasure inside her. Surely it was just because he was a policeman. The notes had frightened her, once again given her a taste of victim mentality. It was only natural that a policeman would make her feel safe and banish the bitter taste of being victimized.

Certainly her pleasure at seeing him had nothing to do with the breadth of his shoulders or the way his jeans fit his slender hips. Surely it had nothing to do with his coffee-colored eyes that radiated a lively sense of humor and the smile that seemed to caress her like a touch.

She didn't want a relationship of any kind, didn't feel mentally ready to share intimately with a man, either on a physical or mental level. Her failed relationship with Greg merely supported her belief that relationships just didn't work for her.

As always when she pulled into her driveway, a sweet peace rushed through her as she eyed the place she called home. Home. She'd lived her life dreaming of being in one place, waking up each morning and knowing exactly where she was and that nobody could take it away from her.

Clay's car was already parked by the curb. As she turned off her engine, he appeared at the side of her car. "Thanks," she said as he opened her door and took her papers and books from her arms.

"If I'd thought, I'd have brought you an apple."

She smiled. "Don't worry about it. I'm not grading your performance as a policeman and you aren't in my classes."

They paused at the front door as she unlocked it. Pushing it open, she ushered him inside. "You can just put that stuff on the end table. Would you like some coffee?"

He shook his head. "No, thanks. I'm fine." He sank down on the sofa, then jumped in surprise as Twilight leapt up next to him.

"Twilight, get down," Ann scolded.

"He's all right." Clay scratched the big tomcat behind his ears.

Ann watched in surprise as the cat curled up next to Clay, closing his eyes in utter contentment as Clay continued to scratch him. "I'm shocked. Normally Twilight is quite anti-social."

"That's me, loved by animals and small children." He flashed her a quick grin.

"I'll be right back. I've got to get a couple of aspirin." She escaped from the living room into the kitchen, disconcerted by the fact that Clay looked so at ease, so like he belonged in her living room. She opened her cabinet and took out a bottle of aspirin. Shaking two out in her palm, she thought with amazement how easily Twilight had accepted Clay.

In all the time Twilight had shared her living space, Ann had never seen the cat cuddle up next to anyone, except for herself. Twilight, like Ann, had always seemed to enjoy solitude. Slow to trust, wary of closeness, they had that in common.

She got a glass of water and swallowed the aspirins, then went back into the living room, where Clay was still petting the purring cat. "Headache?" he asked.

She nodded, realizing she'd been rubbing her forehead. She sank down in the chair opposite him. "I had a night of phone calls. The phone rang every fifteen minutes from the time I got home from work until five o'clock this morning."

"I don't understand." He stopped petting Twilight and leaned forward. "Who was calling?"

"I wish I knew. The caller doesn't say anything...just breathes for a moment or two, then hangs up."

"You didn't take the phone off the hook?"

She shook her head. "I'm embarrassed to say I didn't think about it until this morning."

"Is your number unlisted?"

"No, but if this continues, I'll get an unlisted one."

"What about an answering machine?" he added. "Most people tire quickly of machines taking their calls."

"I know it sounds silly, but I feel like the notes and the calls are related...that somebody is watching me, enjoying the fact that they're scaring me." She shivered, the thought of somebody spying on her, watching her every movement chilling her to the bone.

Again she had the feeling that the happiness and security

she'd finally managed to build had been constructed on the shifting sands of a beach. Any moment a wave would appear to carry it out to sea.

Clay frowned, obviously musing over the situation. "Maybe the calls are the work of the note writer, but if you were being watched and the caller intended to harass you again, he'd have seen you come home and the phone would be ringing now."

"And he would have seen you, too." She offered him a shaky smile. "I'm probably being far too paranoid. I just hope the caller got tired last night, because I'm exhausted and don't want another night of interruptions."

"If the calls continue, let me know and call the phone company. They have ways of dealing with that kind of harassment."

She nodded. "And if the calls continue tonight, I'll definitely unplug my bedroom extension." She tucked her hair behind her ear. "You said you went to speak with Greg this morning. Do you think he's responsible?"

"I don't know. He's definitely a hard man to read." He opened his mouth as if to say something, then snapped it shut, apparently changing his mind.

"What?" she asked. "What were you going to say?"

He grinned, looking like a mischievous boy. "Something distinctly unprofessional. Greg Thorton struck me as an arrogant jerk...I'm just wondering what attracted you to dating him." Clay no longer looked boyish. His gaze was all man, filled with a man's curiosity and an attention that whispered of something sexual and intimate.

She felt her cheeks warm beneath the scrutiny, an answering interest stirred in her. "Now that I'm out of that relationship, I've asked myself that a dozen times."

"Any answers?"

She shook her head and offered him a rueful smile. "I have yet to come up with any logical explanation." She squeezed the bridge of her nose once again. "I still can't imagine him being behind the notes and phone calls. It's just not his style."

"I should get out of here and let you get some rest," Clay

said. "We can talk some more another time. You look exhausted and I can see the pain of your headache in your eyes." He stood and gave Twilight a final scratch on his belly.

Ann also got up and walked with him to the front door. Her headache pounded with each step she took. She thought longingly of her bed. Hopefully there would be no calls tonight. She opened the door and leaned against it. "Thanks, Clay."

"For what?" He smiled gently. "Don't thank me yet, I haven't done anything."

She shrugged. "I just feel better knowing you aren't dismissing the notes as a prank and are actively working to find out what's going on."

"And I'll feel better knowing you're getting a good night's sleep and having pleasant dreams." He reached out and touched her cheek. A warm, momentary touch, then he dropped his hand. "'Night, Ann." He turned and left, his long strides carrying him across the lawn and to his car.

She watched him go, the feel of his soft touch lingering on her skin. Reaching up, she touched her cheek thoughtfully. She suddenly knew why she'd chosen to date Greg. He'd been safe, nonthreatening...everything Clay Clinton was not.

She had a feeling Clay would demand give-and-take in a relationship, that he'd want to know a woman's secret fantasies, deep yearnings and hidden past.

As his headlights disappeared from view, Ann closed and locked the front door...and the phone rang.

Chapter 4

"Hey, man, that's a heavy frown you're wearing. What's going on?"

Clay looked up as Raymond sank down in the chair next to his desk. "I just got back the lab report on the last note Ann Carson got."

"And let me guess...the only fingerprints on it are hers."

"No, mine are on there, too." Clay sighed and set the report aside. He'd hoped there would be another set of prints; even if they were unidentifiable, they would have attested to a third person being involved. "Besides the notes, she told me last night when I was over there she's also been getting a lot of hang up phone calls."

Raymond frowned. "While you were there did she get any?" he asked.

"No...but that doesn't mean she's lying about them." It irritated Clay that he felt the need to defend her.

Raymond grinned. "You know what I think?"

Clay swallowed a sigh. "No, but I'm sure you're about to tell me."

Raymond leaned toward Clay. "I think you've got hot pants for the nice teacher and that's coloring your professional judgment."

"Don't be ridiculous," Clay scoffed, then smiled ruefully. "Okay, I'll admit I have a touch of a thing for her, but that doesn't mean I'm not looking at all sides of the case."

"All I know is when a man's got hot pants, it constricts the blood flow to the brain, making rational thought difficult." Raymond scratched his belly and eyed Clay affectionately. "Just keep an open mind. It's possible your lady teacher has got some personal problems."

"I've got an open mind and she's not my lady teacher," Clay retorted.

Raymond smirked and stood up. "Whatever. I just hope you get this out of your system before you take off for Hawaii. It would be tough lying on those sun-kissed beaches yearning for a mainland lady."

Clay laughed. "Don't worry about me. Once I get on that beach, you and the rest of this life will be just a distant memory."

He watched as Raymond went back to his own desk, then focused his attention back on the lab report. The lack of fingerprints other than his own and Ann's bothered him. It implied something more insidious than a disgruntled student dashing off a nasty note to the teacher

Whoever had written it had taken care not to leave fingerprints. They'd probably worn gloves. Or Ann wrote the note herself, a small voice whispered inside his head.

As much as he hated to admit it, he knew Raymond was right. He couldn't dismiss the possibility that Ann herself was responsible just because he didn't want it to be so.

Clay had been a cop long enough to know the various psychological profiles of criminals, knew that according to Greg Thorton, Ann had no family, no friends to speak of…facts that fit one particular profile and furthered the vague possibility of her being responsible.

"Officer Clinton?"

He looked up to see a small, white-haired woman, her face wrinkled beneath the heavy rouge that spotted her cheeks.

"Yes?"

"That man over there said I should talk to you. I want to make a missing persons report."

Clay looked over to see several officers watching him and her, faces schooled but not quite hiding roguish grins. He looked back at the old woman, wondering why his fellow officers looked so damned guilty and so amused. "A missing person report?"

She nodded and sank down into the chair next to his desk, the heavy scent of roses wafting with her movement. "My Harry is missing."

Clay shuffled through the files on his computer and pulled up the appropriate form. "And Harry's relationship to you?"

"Harry's my husband. Our fifty-fifth wedding anniversary is next week." She pulled a purse the size of a small suitcase onto her lap and opened it. She withdrew a framed picture. The photo was a portrait of herself and the missing man. Harry appeared to be a big man, with massive shoulders and a barrel chest. He was looking at his wife, and the smile on his face spoke of a man contented and still in love despite the passing of youth.

"How long has your husband been missing?"

"Forty-eight hours. I knew I couldn't make a report until he'd been missing for over twenty-four." She snapped her purse closed once again.

"Okay. Let's start with some names. What is your name?"

"Gloria Woninski."

Bells went off in Clay's head. He'd heard about Gloria, a familiar visitor to the station, but he'd never had any personal dealings with her.

He typed her name on the form even though he knew there would be no follow-up on this particular case. "And when was the last time you saw your husband?"

She frowned and pursed ruby lips. "Two nights ago. That's when they came for him. I woke up to the bright lights and they were singing 'Up, Up and Away,' and they were little men with big heads. They lifted Harry in their arms and they all went up to the mother ship.''

Her eyes radiated complete belief in her own words and with a perfectly straight face Clay typed in what she'd said. ''Actually, I think this should be considered a kidnapping,'' she continued. ''I know my Harry. He'd much rather be here with me than with them, but I think they're holding him against his will.''

Once again she opened her purse, this time to pull out a tissue. She dabbed teary eyes and drew in a tremulous breath. ''You have to find my Harry. I miss him so much, and he didn't take his heart pills with him. He needs those pills.''

''We'll do what we can, Mrs. Woninski.''

She leaned over and patted his hand. ''You're a nice man to listen to an old woman.''

''Do you have any children, ma'am?''

She shook her head, a coquettish smile curving her lips and for a moment Clay saw the whisper of the young, flirtatious woman she had once been. ''My Harry never wanted children. He always told me I was all he needed to be happy.'' The smile crumpled and she was once again an old, bewildered woman. ''You've got to find him. I'm all alone and I need him.''

''I'll make sure this report gets put at the top of the stack,'' he assured her despite the fact he knew the report would be filed away in their crackpot file.

''And you'll call me the minute you find him? You'll bring him home where he belongs?'' She stood up, the huge purse clutched against her chest.

''I promise when we find him, we'll bring him home to you,'' Clay replied.

''Thank you.'' Dabbing one last time at tear-filled eyes, she turned and left.

The minute she was gone from the squad room, Raymond ambled over, his shoulders shaking with laughter. ''We figured before you retire you had to have the experience of Gloria.''

He hiked a hip onto Clay's desk. "What was it this time? Alien abduction? Kidnapping by gypsies? Her stories are always good for a few laughs."

Clay eyed his friend in disgust. "Sometimes, Raymond, you're a callous man."

"What are you talking about?" Raymond exclaimed in surprise. "The woman is a nutcase…a crazy. Once a month, for the past two years, like clockwork she's in here filing another missing husband report."

"And if I recall the facts, her husband has been dead for two years. She's all alone and can't accept it. I don't find that amusing, I find it pitiful."

"Clay Clinton, defender of the nuts of the world." Raymond stood up and shook his head ruefully. "Better watch it, that kind of compassion can make you insane in this job."

"That kind of compassion is what's made me good at this job for twenty years." Clay also stood, unsure why an edge of anger had reared its head inside him.

He drew in a deep, steadying breath and placed a hand on Raymond's shoulder. "Sorry, I didn't mean to snap," he apologized. "Guess I just don't find Gloria Woninski's suffering as amusing as the rest of you do."

"You're right," Raymond conceded. "We all feel bad about the old woman, but you've also been around here long enough to know that black humor is what gets us all through the tough times."

Clay nodded and flashed his friend a conciliatory smile. "I know. Don't mind me. I've just got a lot of things on my mind."

"Take her to bed, that will ease some of your tension."

Clay frowned. "Gloria Woninski?"

Raymond laughed. "No, your teacher. You've been too long between women and you're losing your sense of humor."

"Ha ha," Clay retorted dryly as Raymond went back to his desk.

Too bad mental illness and lack of coping skills wasn't as easily spotted in others as they were in Gloria Woninski, Clay thought. If Ann had talked about spaceships and aliens he'd know he was dealing with a woman in crisis. But Ann had seemed well-adjusted and worked at a respectable job requiring intelligence.

What was she? A victim receiving notes from an unknown perp, or a victim by her own design, writing notes to herself and making up phone calls in a bid for attention?

One thing was definitely true. She was occupying far too much of his mind in relationship to the lack of severity of her case. He'd spent more time thinking about her, wondering about the notes, speculating on her than he had most of his other, more serious cases.

Raymond was right. Clay had the hots for her. Although his interest in her was not bound solely by a physical desire. No, it went deeper than that. There was something about the sadness in her eyes that pulled him, something about the infrequency of her smiles that made him want to bring her happiness.

Damn. Irritated, he put the lab report away and instead pulled up the files on an armed robbery he'd been working on for several weeks.

"Hey, Clinton. The chief wants to talk to you," one of the other officers yelled across the room.

Clay raised a hand in acknowledgment. Probably some leftover paperwork to sign or discuss concerning his retirement. He got up and made his way to the stairs that led to the chief's office.

Chief Walter Zolinni answered Clay's knock. "Clay, come in, come in." He motioned Clay to the seat in front of his massive desk, then eased himself down into his own chair.

Clay waited patiently while the Chief lit one of the three cigars he allowed himself per day. Once it was lit, Walter leaned back in his chair and studied Clay for a long moment. "You still set on this retirement nonsense?"

"Yes, sir."

"What are we down to? A little over a month?" Clay nodded and Walter continued, "And there's nothing I can say to change your mind?"

"No, sir."

Walter puffed thoughtfully. "Too bad. I was going over your file this morning. Lots of good stuff in there...accolades and letters of community support. You're a good man, Clay. The department hates to lose you."

"Thank you. The job has been good to me."

"So, tell me about this Ann Carson thing."

Clay looked at his boss in surprise. It was rare that the chief got involved in actual casework, especially in something so benign. "She's an English teacher at Northland Community College. She's gotten a couple of threatening notes, one inside her refrigerator in her condo...."

Walter sucked on the cigar, blowing the smoke out the side of his mouth toward a wilted, browning plant in the corner. "I got a call this morning from Mayor Walker. Seems you've managed to step on some toes."

"Step on toes?" Clay frowned and leaned back in his chair. "I'm not sure I understand. Whose toes?"

"Mayor Walker is golf buddy with the senior partners at Beatty, Walters and Majors. Seems they complained to him that you've been harassing one of their up-and-coming stars."

"I didn't harass anyone. I questioned one of their lawyers because he and Ann Carson recently broke off a relationship."

"I figured as much." Walter dabbed the cigar, forcing ashes to fall into a pristine ashtray. "Just do me a favor, if you have to speak to this lawyer again, tread easily. The mayor was upset and when he's upset his foot always manages to connect with my butt."

"I'll do my best not to ruffle feathers," Clay agreed.

"Thanks." Walter stood up and walked with Clay to the door. "You're a good man, Clay. An excellent cop. We're all going to miss you when you leave."

"Thank you, sir."

As Clay walked back down the stairs to his desk, his mind whirled. So Thorton had complained about him. Not just in-

nocuous grumbling. He'd gone to his powerful friends to get
Clay's butt chewed. An interesting reaction for a man who
presumably had nothing to hide.

Perhaps it wouldn't hurt to check out Greg Thorton a little
more thoroughly. He could be discreet, make sure the worm
didn't even know Clay was around.

Ann left the movie theater and walked out into the darkness
of the night. She'd escaped her house earlier in the day, driven
out by the incessant ringing of the phone. After shopping at
the mall, she'd finally decided to relax for a couple of hours
in the cool quiet of the theater. She hadn't realized the movie
would run so late and the mall would be closed and the parking
lot nearly deserted when she emerged.

Her car was a mere dot in the distant parking lot and the lot
itself looked ominously dark, with light poles sparse and half
the bulbs burned out.

She pulled her keys out of her purse before advancing. With
her purchases in one hand, the keys in the other, she took off
walking toward her car.

She'd hoped the movie theater would provide a nice quiet
environment and that she'd be able to lose herself in the story
unfolding on the screen. She hadn't realized that Saturday
nights the mall belonged to bands of teens.

The movie had been slow, the theater noisy and she now felt
no more relaxed than she had when she'd gone in. She did feel
good about one thing. First thing that morning she'd run to a
nearby discount store and bought an answering machine
equipped with caller identification.

If the phone had rung while she was out, she'd not only
have a record of the call, she'd have a record of the caller's
number as well.

Against one wall of the mall structure, a group of young
teenagers stood, laughing and joking, apparently waiting for a
parent to come and pick them up. Someday, she told herself.
Someday she'd have children…a family. It was a promise to
herself, the dream of a future filled with love and security.

She was halfway between her car and the mall when she heard the sound of a car engine racing. She turned to see a car heading toward her. Gaining speed, the bright headlights nearly blinded her. She froze, watching as the car came faster and closer. Like a deer in the middle of the road, half mesmerized by the brightness of the lights, she watched unmoving until the car was nearly on her.

With a cry of horror, realizing the driver wasn't swerving away, she ran. With a whoosh, the car passed by her so close she felt the engine heat, smelled the hot tires. The car whizzed by her, then turned around and faced her once again.

Like a bull pawing the ground and snorting steam, the engine once again raced, tires smoking as the rpms increased. Frantically, Ann realized the driver intended to chase her again. She looked around for help, for a place where she could run, but the near empty parking lot made her a helpless target.

With a squeal of tires, the car came again. Ann fought the impulse to turn and flee, knowing there was no way to beat out the speeding car. The best she could do was outmaneuver it.

Pulse pounding, she waited until the car was practically on top of her, then threw herself to the side, gasping in stunned disbelief as she hit the pavement and skidded on the rough ground.

In relief she saw the taillights of the car continuing on toward the parking lot exit. A sob tore through her and she sat up.

"Hey, lady...are you all right?" One of the teenage boys who'd been standing against the buildings ran toward her. "Jeez, I've never seen anything like that. It looked like he was trying to run you down." Helplessly he stood over her, afraid to touch her yet obviously wanting to help. "Are you okay?"

"I'm all right," she finally managed to say. Although she wasn't. Her palms were bloody, her hose shredded from her facedown ride against the asphalt. Still, it wasn't the physical wounds that bothered her. Icy fear crept through her, making her shake uncontrollably.

"My buddy is calling the police," the kid said. "They should be here any minute."

She nodded. She knew she should stand up, that by doing so she'd make the teenager feel better. But, she couldn't. Fear kept her immobile. If she tried to rise to her feet, she knew her trembling legs wouldn't hold her.

"Did you see what kind of car it was?" she asked as she picked up the keys she'd dropped.

"Nah. It was too dark. I couldn't even tell what color it was."

Could this be coincidence or was this connected to the notes? But who? Hysteria bubbled up inside her. Who was doing these things? Paper threats were one thing…but this was something else. Had she not flung herself out of the way, the car would have killed her.

With a sigh of relief, she heard the distant sound of a siren, signaling the approach of help. A minute later a patrol car pulled up, the red and blue lights atop the cab swirling a measure of comfort.

Ann pulled out the card Clay Clinton had given her and handed it to the officer. "Call him," she said. "I want him here."

He handed the card to his partner, who returned to the car, then he helped her up. "What happened? The 911 call was a report of a hit-and-run."

The teenage boy looked sheepish. "I told him to say that so you'd come quicker. It was an almost-hit-and-run and we saw the whole thing."

For the next several minutes, the officers took statements from the kids while Ann leaned weakly against the side of the patrol car.

The first policeman had just finished questioning the kids when Clay pulled up. In a single movement, he turned off the engine and bounded out of the car, immediately approaching Ann.

"You all right?" he asked, his eyes radiating a concern that washed over her like a soothing balm. She nodded and he walked over to where the other two cops were still speaking with the group of kids.

Ann closed her eyes, trying to shake off the hysteria that tried to gain control. She felt better with Clay here, knew it was important to maintain continuity so that one officer had all the facts of everything that had been happening to her.

"Ann." She snapped her eyes back open. "Why don't you give me your car keys?" Clay suggested. "I'll have one of the officers take your car home and you can ride with me."

She nodded, relieved she wouldn't have to drive, wasn't sure she could with her hands still shaking so badly. She handed him the keys, surprised when he grasped her hand and looked at the raw, bloody palm.

For a split second, all warmth disappeared from his eyes and she saw the cold, hard gaze of a cop…a cop angered by the hurt inflicted on her.

When he looked at her again, the warmth was back, washing over her, infusing her. "Come on, let's get you home."

Every time he thought of the vision of her in the beam of his headlights, a burst of laughter bubbled to his lips. It had been a freeze-frame of terror, her mouth in a perfect O, her eyes widened in abject fear.

He could have killed her. Right then and there he could have hit her and she'd be dead. But he didn't want that. Not yet.

A quick, easy death was too good for her. Before he killed her he wanted her to suffer. He wanted her to know the same kind of fear he'd felt for twenty long years. Every morning he'd awakened with a lump of terror in his throat. Each night he'd gone to bed wondering if he'd awaken the next morning. Prison had been hell, and he wanted Ann to suffer hell before she died.

He'd thought he'd fixed her before, thought he'd killed her before. He'd spent weeks terrifying another Ann Carson, had finally killed her, then discovered when he'd read the obituary that she wasn't the one he sought after all.

Pulling the van into his garage, he frowned, remembering

the rage that had swept over him when he realized he'd killed the wrong one. Although all her friends had called her Ann, her real name had been Anntoinette and she'd moved to the Kansas City area only months before from back East.

He was certain now he had the right one. She was the only other Ann Carson in the phone book, and he knew she'd grown up in the Kansas City area.

Besides, the memory of those pale blond pigtails was burned in his head, as was the blue of the little girl's eyes. The same blue eyes...the same blond shade of hair belonged to the woman he'd nearly run over. No mistake this time.

He smiled. He hoped she was frightened. He hoped she had nightmares. He'd had them for twenty years. Now it was her turn.

Chapter 5

Clay drove silently, gazing at Ann every few seconds, unsure what to think about the night's events. It was without dispute that somebody had tried to run her down, or at the very least scare her to death. But, was that somebody the same person leaving notes and making phone calls, or had it simply been a carload of teenagers generating a little Saturday night excitement for themselves?

Coincidence…or another event in a string of escalating threats? He looked at her once again, amazed by how quickly she'd managed to completely put her fear behind. Her features were schooled in an expression of calm and she seemed to have distanced herself from the events that had just happened. It was as if she were afraid to share her fear, reluctant to share any part of herself with anyone.

He frowned and tightened his grip on the steering wheel, irritated with his fanciful meandering where she was concerned.

"Weren't you able to see what make or model the vehicle was?" he asked, breaking the silence.

"Afraid not. I was too busy trying to stay out of its path.

She drew in a deep breath and rubbed her palms, where the blood had dried. ''All I saw were headlights pointed at me and all I heard was the racing motor.'' She shivered and Clay realized her grip on control was more tenuous than he'd initially thought.

He fought the impulse to reach over and pull her close against his side, knowing he was dangerously close to losing all objectivity where she was concerned.

Something about Ann Carson pulled out protective instincts, alien emotions he'd never felt before. It bothered him, confused him and exhilarated him all at the same time.

''You'll never be able to find who it was, will you?'' She turned and looked at him.

He wanted to say yes. He wanted to assure her they'd catch the person who'd tried to run her down, punish him within the structure of the law, but any assurance he gave to her would be a lie.

''I doubt it,'' he finally answered. ''We don't have a description of the make or model, we don't even know the color. The kids weren't sure if it was a Jeep or a van, although they all agreed it was bigger than a car. Unless we find another witness who might have more answers, I doubt we find out who it was.''

She nodded. ''Thank you for being honest with me.'' She rubbed her palms once again and winced. ''I just don't understand this. I don't understand any of this. I'm not sure what's worse, not knowing who is doing it, or not knowing why.''

''It's possible this thing tonight is just a coincidence,'' Clay said. ''You know, not related to the notes or phone calls at all.''

''Do you really believe that?''

He sighed. ''Not really.'' He pulled into her driveway, unsurprised to see another patrol car waiting. Ann's car parked in the driveway. ''Hang on. I'll be right back.'' It took him only a moment to get Ann's keys and send the other officers on their way

"Let's get you inside and get those hands fixed up," he said as he unlocked her door and ushered her inside.

She flipped on light after light, as if seeking safety in a blaze of illumination, then stopped in front of the answering machine and frowned. "Not a single call the whole time I've been gone." She looked up at Clay, the blue of her eyes darkened. "It's as if he knows when I'm home and when I'm not. He didn't start the phone calls last night until after you left, then he called off and on all night until I finally took the phone off the hook so I could get some sleep." She sank down in a chair, her hands palms up on her lap. "I've felt so safe here…and now somebody is destroying it all."

"Come on, first things first. We can talk after we get your hands cleaned up." He took her by her wrists and led her into the bathroom. She sat docilely on the edge of the tub while he ran water in the sink, turning first the hot, then the cold until he had it the temperature he wanted. Once satisfied, he gestured for her to rinse her palms. "Do you have a first-aid kit?"

She shook her head. "There's peroxide and bandages and such in my bathroom under the sink."

"You keep rinsing," he instructed, then left her to get the required items.

Although the bright bedspread neatly covered the bed, the moment Clay walked into the room he got a sudden vision of Ann beneath the covers…her shoulder-length hair erotically pale against the colorful pillowcase, her lithe body naked against the crisp sheets.

He shook his head to dispel the image and went directly into her bathroom. This room breathed an intimacy that stoked the fires of his imagination. A midnight blue silk nightgown hung on a hook near the door and a lacy camisole rested on the edge of the tub.

The air smelled of her, the whisper of sweet flowers and femininity. He wondered if it came from one of the bottles on the countertop, or emanated naturally from her pores? Opening the cabinet beneath the sink, he grabbed the necessary items and left, hoping to leave his fanciful erotic images behind.

Ann stood where he'd left her, palms held beneath the spray of lukewarm water. He shut off the faucets and carefully dabbed the wounds with a clean washcloth. As he worked to make certain the cuts and scrapes were clean, he tried not to notice how warm her body was next to his, how her scent eddied in the air. He tried not to imagine how that blue silk nightgown would hug her curves, display the creamy skin of her throat and chest.

When he'd finished and had placed a bandage on each palm, her fingers closed around his hands. "Thank you," she breathed softly. "I'm not accustomed to having somebody take care of me." Her eyes plied him with gratefulness and something deeper...more compelling.

He stepped away from her, afraid of getting in too deep, not wanting to care about this woman, and yet finding it impossible not to. He pointed to her knees, where her hose hung in shreds and blood speckled each kneecap. "Why don't you get out of those clothes and take care of your legs? While you're doing that I'll make us a pot of coffee." He escaped without waiting for her answer, needing to be away from the heat of the small room, her unnerving closeness and sweet scent.

In the sterile atmosphere of her kitchen, it was easy to regain his composure. It took him several minutes to find the necessary things to get a pot of coffee going, then while the dark brew bubbled through the machine, he sat down at the kitchen table. Twilight appeared seemingly from nowhere and rubbed against his leg.

"Hey, cat." He leaned down and rubbed along the gray fur of the cat's back. Twilight arched in pleasure and closed his eyes as he began a noisy purr.

They both jumped as the phone rang, the discordant jangle breaking the relative silence.

"Want me to get that?" Clay yelled.

"No, let the machine pick it up," she replied from the bedroom.

He got up and walked into the living room where the machine sat next to the phone on a polished wooden table. On the third ring, the machine answered and Ann's voice filled the room. After a brief greeting message, the tone beeped and whoever was on the other end of the line breathed noisily. After a moment, a soft giggle replaced the breathing. "Close call tonight, sweet Ann. Next time I might not miss." Click.

A gasp pulled Clay's attention from the machine to Ann, who stood in the doorway, face pale and a hand at her mouth.

Although he knew she was frightened, relief flooded him. At least now he knew, now he had proof. He wasn't dealing with a lonely, half-psychotic woman writing herself threatening notes. He was dealing with attempted murder.

"That's the first time he's talked," she finally said.

"Does the voice sound familiar?"

She walked over to a chair and sank down. "No...no it didn't sound familiar at all." Her eyes were so dark they appeared nearly black.

"Let me play it again. Concentrate and see if you recognize the voice." Clay hit the Play button and the voice resounded in the otherwise silent room.

"No. I don't recognize it." She swallowed audibly. "He tried to kill me. Who is he? Who is he?" Her voice rose slightly and she leaned back and swallowed again, as if fighting hysteria. "Wait...there's a caller identification box." She jumped up and hit a button on the answering machine. Her shoulders sagged. "Of course. He called from a pay phone."

Clay took the tape from the machine and placed it in his pocket. "You have another tape for this thing?"

She nodded and opened a drawer. She pulled out another tape and handed it to him. "What are you going to do with the other one?"

"Give it to the lab...listen to it over and over again...see what clues we can get off it." He smiled gently. "We'll get him, Ann. Whoever he is we'll find him." He touched her arm. "Come on, let's go get some coffee."

Clay poured the coffee as she sat down at the table. She'd changed from her torn, dirty clothes to a soft peach-colored, floor-length dress. Although Clay knew little about women's clothing, he guessed it was some sort of lounging thing and not something she'd wear outside. The peach color did nice things to her complexion and made the blue of her eyes deeper.

Setting their cups down, he sank into the chair next to her, tugging his thoughts from personal observation to professional matters. "Ann, are you certain there's nobody from your past who might think they have a reason to do these things to you?"

She tucked a strand of shining hair behind her ear. "I can't imagine who it might be."

"Old boyfriends? Lovers?"

Like a chameleon, her face took on the hue of her gown, cheeks pinkened in obvious embarrassment. "There was only one man before Greg. It's been a couple years since I've seen or heard from him. I don't even know where he is anymore."

"What's his name?"

"Mark. Mark Livingston. We were in college together, had a fairly typical college romance. But once school was over it just didn't work out. The last I heard he was living on the south side of town and dating a former Miss Missouri contestant." She wrapped her bandaged hands around her coffee cup. When she looked back at him, her eyes were the exact hue of the gown he'd seen in her bathroom. "I'm scared."

The simple words, spoken with little emotion tore through him. He wanted to take her in his arms, make her feel safe and protected, hold her until the fear passed. Instead he reached out and touched her arm. "I know and I wish there was something I could do to make you feel not scared, but right now there's nothing." He drew his hand back and took a drink of his coffee. "You have any family here in town? Or a friend you could stay with for a little while?"

"No. I don't have any family and although I have lots of casual acquaintances, I'm not close enough to anyone to feel comfortable asking to stay with them." She raised her chin a fraction of an inch. "Besides, I won't be put out of my home by some creep."

"Okay, then what you need to do is be cautious. Don't go places alone, don't linger in parking lots after dark. Use your common sense and don't put yourself in dangerous positions. Until we know who's behind all this, you're at risk.''

"Clay…'' She looked down into her coffee cup, as if unable to meet his gaze. "I know this is asking a lot, but could you stay here tonight? Sleep on the sofa?'' Her hand trembled as she reached up and once again tucked her hair behind her ear. He had a feeling she rarely asked for favors, wasn't accustomed to needing anyone. As she raised her gaze and looked at him, he saw the fear still darkening her eyes. "I just…I just don't want to be alone tonight.''

"Sure, I could bunk on the sofa for tonight if it will make you feel better,'' he said after only a moment of hesitation. She wasn't asking him to sleep with her, she wanted him there because he was a cop, nothing more, he reminded himself.

"Thank you.''

She seemed to relax somewhat. For a moment they sipped their coffee in silence. Twilight sauntered into the kitchen and curled up on the hooked rug in front of the sink and the ice maker in the refrigerator clunked and spewed new cubes.

Despite Clay's desire to maintain a professional distance, he found himself studying her, curious about what kind of a woman she was. A woman without a best friend was an anomaly to him. Every woman he'd ever dated had a close friend to confide in, share experiences with. No family, no friends. He couldn't help but be intrigued and somehow saddened.

He stood up and poured them each another cup of coffee. "Did you grow up here in Kansas City?'' he asked as he eased back down.

"Yes, I've always lived in this general area,'' she said, looking relieved at the change of topic. "What about you?''

"Born and raised here.''

"Is your family still here?''

"My mom is, my dad passed away ten years ago.''

"Are you close to your mother?'' she asked.

He grinned at thoughts of his mom. "Yeah, we're close. She gets mad if more than a couple of days pass and she doesn't hear from me. She also expects and demands I take her out to dinner at least one time a week.''

She smiled, and again Clay felt as if he'd been gifted. The gesture warmed her eyes, and made her features come alive with a vibrancy that nearly took his breath away. ''That's nice,'' she said. ''So you're an only child?''

''That's right. My mother is fond of saying that I was such a cranky, fussy baby she didn't dare have another one.''

Ann's smile increased. ''I find that hard to believe.''

He shrugged. ''When I was five I had a make-believe brother. His name was Charlie and he was bigger and smarter than me. I drove my mother crazy with Charlie, made her set a place for him at each meal, kiss him good-night and comb his hair. Charlie had lots of hair.''

Ann laughed, the color of her eyes lightened as the fear receded beneath his silly story.

''You were an only child, too?'' he asked.

She nodded. ''Although I didn't have enough imagination to dream up an invisible sister or two.'' She stood up and took her cup to the sink. ''If you don't mind, I think I'll get some blankets and a pillow for you to use, then I'm going to try to get some rest. I'm exhausted.''

Clay looked at the clock on the oven, surprised to realize it was after eleven o'clock. ''Of course you're exhausted,'' he said, adding his cup to hers in the sink. ''You've had a horrendous experience and I've kept you up talking about silly imaginary brothers.''

''I'm glad you told me about Charlie and thank you for agreeing to stay the night. I know it's above and beyond the call of duty. I just feel that if I can get one good night's sleep then I can face whatever tomorrow brings.''

''At least for tonight you have nothing to worry about,'' he assured her.

It took only minutes for her to make up a bed for him on the couch. ''Twilight, get off,'' she demanded as the cat jumped up and snuggled amid the sheets.

"He's all right," Clay replied and sat down next to the ragged tomcat. "The sofa's big enough to share."

Ann shook her head. "I can't get over how he takes to you. Normally he doesn't trust anyone." As if to further prove her wrong, the cat rolled over on his back and bared his furry tummy to Clay.

"We'll be fine, won't we, tough guy?" Clay stroked the cat, causing him to purr in contentment. "If the phone rings, I'll get it," he said. "Unplug the extension in your bedroom for the night. Hopefully you can sleep in and get some needed rest. I'll probably be gone when you get up, I've got to be back at the station by eight."

She frowned. "I hope this isn't too big of an imposition. I probably shouldn't have asked..."

"Ann, go to bed," he said gently.

"Yes." She turned to leave, then hesitated and looked back at him. "Thanks again." She disappeared down the hallway and into the master suite. He heard the sound of her door closing, then a small click as she locked it.

For a long moment Clay sat on the sofa, thoughtfully stroking Twilight's fur. He had a feeling her thank-you had come hard, that she wasn't accustomed to asking for help, and therefore was unaccustomed to giving thanks. And she'd locked her bedroom door. She trusted him enough to have him stay here, but apparently not enough to keep her door unlocked. Another intriguing piece in a puzzle he shouldn't even be contemplating putting together.

He sat scratching Twilight until he was certain Ann had had enough time to get settled in for the night. Then he got up and took off his uniform pants and shirt and tossed them onto the chair. He placed his gun on the table next to the sofa where he'd have easy access in case of an emergency.   Clad only in his T-shirt and briefs, he turned out the light and got beneath the sheets. He knew the odds were good that nothing would happen tonight. Ann had changed her locks and she probably would have been safe for the night without his presence.

His sole purpose for staying was to ease her mind, allow her to rest in the sleep of the protected. He tried to tell himself he would have done it for any woman under the circumstances, tried to convince himself it had nothing to do with Ann personally.

Still, with Twilight a warm ball at his side, visions of Ann in a sexy midnight blue nightgown danced in his mind as sleep overtook him.

Ann sat straight up, gasping for breath. Nightmare images danced in her head, familiar images from nightmares that had haunted her for years. She squeezed her eyes tightly closed, willing herself to breathe deeply, evenly.

When the last vestige of the dream fell away, she reached over and turned on the lamp next to her bed. Her alarm clock read just a few minutes after two.

''Damn.'' She covered her face with her hands, despair overwhelming her. She'd thought the nightmares were finally behind her, had hoped she'd never suffer through another one again. She hadn't had one since moving to the condo and now they were back.

Even if her tormentor never did another thing to her, he'd managed to shatter her security, he'd brought back her nightmares.

She swung her feet over the edge of the bed, knowing from experience that it would be some time before she could go back to sleep. What she needed was a cup of tea, her remedy for nightmares.

She left her room and turned on the hall light. She didn't remember Clay's presence until she walked into the living room and saw him there.

She froze in the doorway, her gaze captured by the sight of the half-dressed man sprawled on her sofa. He lay on his side and with the light filtering in from the hallway she could see he was sound asleep, his features softened with whatever dreams he entertained.

Twilight was curled up next to his chest. He gazed at her

lazily, his eyes glowing incandescently, but didn't budge from his position.

Her cheeks warmed as her gaze traveled down the length of Clay, taking in the width of his shoulders, the slim hips and the long, muscular legs that were covered with a fine dusting of dark hair. He looked so masculine, so capable.

For a moment she wished she could curl up next to him, feel the strength of his arms surrounding her, protecting her. That would be the perfect panacea for a nightmare, to be soothed and caressed until all memories of the dream fell away.

She silently passed him and went into the kitchen. Instead of turning on the overhead light, she switched on only the small light above the sink, then quietly set about to make a cup of tea. The microwave hummed as it heated water and as she unwrapped one of the tea bags the sound of the paper crumpling seemed magnified.

Finally she sat down at the table, the hot drink before her. She rubbed her forehead wearily and thought of the dream that had awakened her. Always the same. She was in bed in a dark, strange place. Frightened. Alone. She calls for her mama, needs her mama to come and tell her it's all right. A door opens and a man comes in…a faceless stranger, a monster in the dark.

"You all right?"

She jumped and yelped. "Oh, you scared me."

Clay walked into the kitchen, his hair tousled and his eyes still soft with sleep. He'd pulled on his slacks and held his gun in his hand. "Sorry. I woke up and heard somebody in here." He set the gun on the countertop and slid into a chair at the table. "Can't sleep?"

"I had a nightmare."

"Probably stress. Stress is supposed to cause people to have all kinds of weird dreams." He raked a hand through his hair, only managing to increase the dishevelment. "Wanna talk about it?"

She shook her head. "No, it's all right. It's an old, recurring nightmare from my childhood." She flashed him a smile. "I'm fine, really. Want a cup of tea?"

He frowned his distaste. "No, thanks. My mom always made me drink that stuff whenever I was sick. Now that I'm an adult I refuse to drink it."

Ann looked down in her cup, finding it easier to stare at the tea instead of at him in his undershirt. "This is a special blend, it's said to help induce sleep. I'm not sure exactly what's in it…lavender and orange peel and some other natural herbs."

"Sounds nauseating."

She laughed. "Yes, I suppose it does." She gazed down at her cup again, disturbed by the setting and the man next to her.

The dim kitchen created an atmosphere that produced intimacy. Outside the window darkness reigned, reminding her it was the middle of the night and in other houses people were cuddled together in sleep.

Clay's body radiated a sleepy warmth that made her want to lean against him, curl up and let his warmth suffuse her. She looked back up at him and for a moment their gazes locked. She wondered if he could read her thoughts, knew she wanted his arms around her.

His gaze swept over her and she suddenly became aware of the provocative nature of her nightgown. Although the blue material covered her, the lace edging at the low neck emphasized the swell of her breasts and the silk clung intimately to her skin. It was a gown designed for seduction, although she had bought it simply because wearing it made her feel good.

"Guess I'll go back to bed," he said abruptly. When he looked at her, she saw a spark of something breathtaking in his eyes. Desire. Fiery and strong, it radiated from his gaze. Her heart thudded in a foreign rhythm. She wanted him to go back to bed…she wanted him to take her in his arms and love her. Confusion swirled in her.

He stood up and the emotion she'd seen in his eyes was gone, making her wonder if she'd only imagined it in the first place.

"You sure you're all right?" he asked.

"I'm fine. I'll just finish this tea and go back to bed."

"Good night, Ann." He turned and left the kitchen.

Ann drew in a deep breath, grateful he was gone, sorry he was gone. His very presence had chased away the residual fear from the nightmare. The kitchen suddenly felt dark and cold.

She drained the last of her tea and placed her cup in the sink, then turned out the light and made her way back through the living room. As she reached the doorway he called to her. She turned to face him.

"I hope the rest of your night is filled with pleasant dreams."

"Thanks." She turned and fled to her bedroom. If she dreamed, she had a feeling her dreams would still be disturbing, although in a very different way.

Chapter 6

Sleep was a long time coming for Clay once he got back on the sofa. The vision of Ann in that damnable nightgown tormented him. In reality she'd looked much sexier in it than he'd originally imagined. It had hugged her curves to perfection, the dark color setting off the creamy richness of her skin and the pale lustre of her hair. She'd looked breathtakingly sensuous, achingly touchable.

He tossed and turned until just after dawn, then decided to get up. He could shower and dress and be out of here before Ann woke up.

As he stood beneath the shower, he berated himself for staying the night. He was in danger of losing his objectivity and spending the night at her house, smelling the sweet scent of her and having erotic visions of her filling his head wouldn't help him as a cop.

Although he'd love to have an intense, physical relationship with her, he definitely wasn't interested in anything more. He didn't want any emotional entanglements to screw up his plans. It would take a hell of a lot more than an attractive blonde in trouble to keep him from his future dreams. He had a one-way ticket to Hawaii and he wasn't about to let anything or anyone get in the way of his plans.

Once he'd showered and dressed, he went into the kitchen and made coffee. He hoped Ann slept late, knew she needed the rest after the turmoil of her life the past couple of days.

Twilight meandered into the kitchen and toward his food bowl, which was empty. The cat sat down and stared at Clay, as if by willpower alone he could force the human to do his bidding. It worked. Clay dug around in the cabinets until he found a can of cat food.

"Okay, buddy, it's coming," he said as he opened the can then spooned the smelly concoction into the dish.

As Clay drank his coffee, Twilight finished his meal, then sat on the rug and groomed himself. The early morning sun streamed into the window, portending another hot day and for just a moment Clay felt a curious contentment.

Something about the sun-kissed kitchen and the sated cat, the taste of the good coffee and the thought of Ann sleeping peacefully in the next room, filled him with a strange serenity.

He frowned and looked at his watch. Seven-thirty. Time for him to get moving. He washed the cups in the sink, reminded of that brief middle of the night sojourn with Ann. Funny, how in the conversations he'd had with her, he'd learned very little about her. She'd expertly steered the conversation so that he had talked about himself and they hadn't talked about her.

He'd just finished rinsing the last cup when the doorbell rang. He hurried to the door, not wanting the noise to awaken Ann. He opened it to see Greg Thorton.

"Well, well. What a surprise." Greg smiled in cool bemusement. His pale blue gaze swept down the length of Clay, obviously taking in the partially buttoned shirt and the beltless slacks. "I didn't know the Graceton Police Department took such personal interest in their cases."

"Greg?"

Both men turned to see Ann standing in the doorway. Although she had thrown a robe on over the sexy nightgown, with her eyes half-closed and her hair tousled carelessly, she looked as if she'd just been completely, thoroughly loved.

"Ann." Greg stepped past Clay as if Clay were nothing more than an irritating butler. He took Ann's hands in his. "Your friend here told me you've been getting nasty phone calls and that somebody had been in your home. I decided to stop by on my way to the office this morning to make sure you're all right."

"You work on Sundays?" Clay asked.

"I often work seven days a week," he answered without looking at Clay.

"And where were you last night?" Clay asked, surprised to discover he didn't like Greg touching Ann in any fashion.

Greg dropped Ann's hands and turned back to Clay. "I was at home all evening. Why?"

"Somebody in a car tried to run Ann down in the parking lot of the mall last night."

"And I suppose you want to know if I can substantiate my alibi?" Greg's smile didn't reach the coolness of his eyes. "Officer...what was your name again?"

"Clinton. Clay Clinton," Clay answered although he knew Greg remembered his name perfectly. People who complained to the mayor rarely forgot the name of the person they'd complained about. "Is there somebody who *can* substantiate that you were at home all evening?"

"No one that I can think of offhand." He turned back to Ann. "I really just stopped by to make sure you're all right."

"I'm fine, thank you." Ann belted the robe more tightly around her waist, obviously discomfited by the tension radiating between the two men.

"Is there anything I can do to help?"

Ann shook her head. "No, it's in the hands of the police and I'm sure they'll take care of it "

"I'm sure," Greg said thinly. "You'll call me if you need anything...anything at all."

"Yes. Thank you." Ann's voice was strained, and Clay had

the distinct impression she wasn't necessarily pleased to see Greg.

Clay's instincts went on alert. Was it possible there was more to their breakup than the amicable split they'd both maintained happened? He made a mental note to further check out Mr. Greg Thorton.

"Thank you for stopping by, Greg," Ann said as she led him back to the front door. "I appreciate your concern."

He paused in the doorway. "You know no matter that we no longer date, I do care about what happens to you." With a curt nod to Clay, he turned and left.

Ann closed the door, leaned against it and expelled a deep breath. "Being around him always makes me feel like I'm not getting enough oxygen."

"What do you mean?" Clay asked.

"He's too focused, too confident...too...too everything. Whenever he's around I feel like an insubstantial leaf blowing in his wind."

"Is that why you broke up with him?"

She shrugged and wrapped her arms around herself. "One of several reasons." She ran fingers through her hair. "You want some breakfast?"

"No, thanks." Clay looked at his watch. "I've got to get out of here and get to work. Would it be possible for you to come down to the station some time this afternoon? I need you to fill out some report forms on what happened last night."

"Any particular time?"

"Let's say about two."

"Okay." She walked with him to the door. "Clay...I want to thank you again for last night, for staying here."

"You going to be all right today?"

She nodded. "Everything looks better in the light of day. I'll be fine."

Unable to stop his impulse, he reached out and softly touched her cheek with the back of his hand. "Don't open your door for anyone, no matter how well you think you know them.

Don't let anyone in. If anything happens, if you get frightened, call the station."

Before he could follow through on any other impulses, he turned and left the house.

Ann closed and locked her door, disturbed by Greg's visit, even more disturbed by Clay's effect on her. Add in the trauma of the last four days of her life, and she should be a neurotic basket case. Thank God she wasn't. Instead she was confused, angry and frightened.

She peeled off the bandages on her palms, aware that the best thing for the cuts and scrapes was fresh air. Besides, the wounds looked better this morning.

A chill danced through her as she remembered that moment in the parking lot, facing a car attempting to run her down. Never could she remember being so terrified. And what scared her more than anything was trying to anticipate what might happen next.

Going into the kitchen, she thought again of Greg's surprise visit. She'd told Clay the truth when she said Greg always made it hard for her to breathe.

He'd come into her life with an overwhelming force, certain that she would make an appropriate wife for him. After all, she worked at a respectable job, lived in an exclusive area of the city. He'd decided she would make the perfect wife for an up-and-coming high-powered lawyer and he'd pursued her with a single-mindedness she'd found overpowering.

He'd spun a fantasy that she'd desperately wanted to believe in, the fantasy of a happily-ever-after. But, just as Cinderella had her evil stepmother, and Snow White had the wicked queen, there was a dark force in their fairy tale. And that dark force was Ann's past.

The closer she'd felt to Greg, the more she shared with him and the more of herself she'd shared with him, the greater distance she'd felt from him. His fantasy of the perfect, refined wife shattered and when Ann realized that, she'd broken off their relationship.

She'd made a cardinal mistake. She'd trusted him. Trust had

always been difficult for her and it had been painfully ironic that the first man she chose to trust hadn't been able to handle it, was incapable of the kind of love she needed.

As she wandered back into the living room, she thought of Clay and those moments they'd shared in the kitchen the night before. He'd helped banish the lingering effects of her nightmare with his silly stories of childhood...a childhood that had seemed wondrously normal and sane. She wondered what it would be like to be loved by a man like Clay, a man who seemed to have little baggage in his background, a man who appeared sensitive and loving. Still, she'd be wary to trust again, to tell any man the secrets of her background, the horrors of her past.

Stifling a yawn, she sank down on the sofa. Clay's scent surrounded her, trapped in the sheets where he'd slept the night before. It was the smell of clean maleness mingling with a whisper of his enticing cologne.

She thought of that moment in the middle of the night, when his eyes had flamed with the fires of desire. She'd wanted to melt into him, let their combined desire sweep away the terror of the past four days, she wanted to dwell in the safety of his arms just for a little while.

Why not? a small voice whispered inside her head. They were both consenting adults and were responsible for their own actions. She had a feeling if she showed the least bit of interest in him, Clay would take the initiative and sweep her into his passion.

She stretched out on the sofa, burrowing into the sheets that still seemed to retain some of Clay's body heat, an essence of him that was comforting.

It had been so long since she'd given herself physically to a man. Not since her college days with Mark Livingston had she indulged in an intense physical relationship.

How nice it would be to give herself completely to somebody, not worry about the tomorrows or the forevers, just live in the moment of being consumed by the fire of passion. How wonderful it would be to allow herself to be possessed physically, know the joy of intimate union with a man who she suspected would be a tender, sensitive lover.

With this thought in mind, she closed her eyes and fell into pleasant dreams of making love to Clay.

"Close call tonight, sweet Ann. Next time I might not miss."

Clay punched the Stop button and rewound the answering machine tape, then played it again. "Close call tonight, sweet Ann. Next time I might not miss."

Once again he hit the Stop then Rewind button. He'd listened to the tape about a hundred times, trying to discern any background noise, anything that might glean a clue to the identity of the caller.

The first thing he'd done upon arriving at the station was make a call to the phone company to find out what pay phone had been used. He hadn't been surprised to find the phone wasn't far from Ann's residence, a drive-up phone in front of a convenience store.

Clay had driven there and checked it out. Gathering fingerprint evidence was useless as when he got there a teenage boy was using the phone, having a fight with his mother about curfews. There was no way to know how many other people had used the phone since the call had been made to Ann's.

Besides, he had a feeling the caller was too smart to leave behind fingerprints. As with the note, Clay suspected gloves would probably have been used, some sort of care would have been taken not to leave behind any incriminating evidence.

He'd gone back to the station from the phone booth, unsettled by the way disturbing events were unfolding in Ann's life. From notes to phone calls to a personal attack…an escalation of danger that implied worse to come. Was he dealing with a killer? Or a deranged nut who got his kicks from frightening helpless women? Would the attack with the car last night be the end of it or was there more to come? More terror for Ann, terror that would culminate in another attempt on her life?

And who was responsible? Clay's instincts told him it was

somebody Ann knew, a student, an old lover…somebody from her past. Her past. She'd had very little to say about her past, only that she had grown up in the area.

Was it possible she had an idea who might be behind this assault on her? Mark Livingston? Greg Thorton? After arriving back at the station, he'd spent the next few minutes finding the address for Mark Livingston.

"Hey, Clay." Raymond approached Clay's desk. "The lieutenant just assigned me to help you with the Ann Carson case. He told me she had some more trouble last night," he said as he sat down.

"Somebody tried to run her over. Unfortunately it was too dark for any of the witnesses to get a color or model of the vehicle. The witnesses stated it was either a van or a Jeep." Clay quickly filled Raymond in on the events at the mall the night before, then grabbed the tape player once again. "She also received this on her answering machine after the incident." He played the brief message for Raymond.

"At least we know now for sure that the threats are legitimate."

"I knew they were all along," Clay replied.

"Let me hear that tape again."

As Clay replayed the message, Raymond frowned with concentration. Clay wasn't surprised the lieutenant had assigned another man to Ann's case. Clay had filled the senior officer in that morning on the latest events. With Clay's retirement looming, he suspected the powers that be wanted somebody else on the case should it not be resolved before Clay left the department.

"The way he says 'sweet Ann' seems to me to hold a familiarity," Raymond said.

Clay nodded. "I felt the same way. I also think some sort of instrument must have been used to disguise the voice. Although it's obviously a man, it doesn't sound quite human."

"Sounds like he used a voice synthesizer. You can buy cheap ones at any toy shop. One of my kids has one."

"So even if Ann knows this man, it's possible she wouldn't recognize his voice."

Raymond grinned. "I wouldn't recognize my own mother's voice if she was using one of those things." He reared back in his chair and eyed Clay thoughtfully. "Where do we go from here?"

"I've got Ann coming in at two to fill out a report. In the meantime I thought I might take a drive and talk with Mark Livingston. He's an old boyfriend of Ann's."

"Let's go."

Within minutes the two men were in Clay's car and headed toward Mark Livingston's residence. "Did you hear there's a new guy coming over from homicide?" Raymond asked, focusing one of the air conditioner vents so it blew directly on him.

"Yeah, I heard he's been working mostly the Kansas side of the city. He's coming in the next couple of weeks, as I go out."

Raymond shook his head. "I still can't believe you're actually going to follow through on this retirement nonsense."

"It isn't nonsense," Clay protested. "I'm not going to make the same mistake so many people do, working all their lives, growing old under the burden of providing for a family, dreaming of the day of freedom. I'm grabbing my freedom now."

"Funny, I've never considered taking care of Ginger and the kids a burden. If it is, certainly the benefits far outweigh the hassle."

Clay grunted, wondering if all men managed to somehow rationalize the daily grind. Certainly as death approached, his father had, although Clay had sensed the disappointment of dreams left unfulfilled, adventures not explored. Clay wasn't about to be trapped by the same oppressive life-style. He didn't intend to wait until he was too old, too sick, too tired to enjoy retirement.

He looked back at Raymond, wondering if he liked being married, having the same woman to come home to each night, the same woman to make love with…it was a concept…the happily-ever-after.

Clay sometimes wondered if he was missing out. Missing out on what? an inner voice asked. Working his butt off to pay for a mortgage and a wife and kids? Spending his spare time painting shutters to please a wife?

Still, there were occasional moments in the night when a wave of loneliness swept through him and he wondered what it would be like to have a woman by his side, perhaps a baby to look at him with sweet, innocent eyes.

Clay didn't think the benefits would outweigh the burden. He'd watched his father grow old and sick, dreaming of the time he could retire and go on a month-long Alaskan fishing trip. He'd died before he'd gotten the opportunity. Clay refused to make the same mistake.

He pulled his thoughts outward as he spotted Mark Livingston's residence. He parked in the double wide driveway and together he and Raymond got out of the car. "How do you want to play this?" Raymond asked. "You want me to ask the questions, or you?"

"You question, I'll take notes," Clay said, knowing how his partner loved to do interrogation. Raymond had perfected the Columbo bumble and Clay never tired of watching him work. He only hoped Raymond could get them some answers.

An hour later they were once again in the car and headed back to the station. "What do you think?" Raymond asked.

Clay frowned thoughtfully. "I think he's telling the truth. He hasn't thought about Ann in years."

"Yeah, I got the impression he was telling the truth, too. He seemed like a nice guy."

Yes, Mark Livingston had appeared to be a very nice guy.

Tall, with dark hair and an open, boyish face, he'd expressed genuine concern for Ann, and a fondness that came from past memories. He'd also mentioned he was getting married in two months time, making the theory that he was obsessed with Ann less viable.

"Looks like we've hit a brick wall," Raymond observed.

"Yeah, I'm not sure where to go from here," Clay admitted. "I can't help but feel certain whoever is bothering Ann knows her personally, that this isn't some sort of stranger obsession. But right now I can't even be certain about that." He sighed in frustration.

"It's like chasing a phantom," Raymond said.

Clay nodded. "Except I have the feeling this phantom is dangerous and smart, and that's a combination I don't like."

"Amen," Ray agreed fervently.

The radio crackled and the dispatcher's voice filled the airway. "911 possible intruder call. Any units in the area respond to 921 Evergreen Avenue."

Clay hit the switch on the siren, setting it wailing as he stepped on the gas.

"What are you doing?" Raymond asked, bracing himself as Clay maneuvered the car in a sharp right turn.

"Responding," Clay said tersely.

"Why? I'm sure there are other cars closer to the address than we are."

"Yeah, but that's Ann's address."

Chapter 7

Two patrol cars were already parked in front of Ann's drive-way when Clay pulled up. Ann stood on the porch while two officers spoke with a husky, dark-haired young man.

As Clay got out of the car, Ann ran toward him. "Are you all right?" he asked.

"Yes...yes. I think it was a false alarm."

"Who is the guy in the red shirt?" he asked.

"Barry Namath. He's a student in my creative writing class."

"Let me go find out what's going on." Clay left Ann standing by his car and he and Raymond walked over to where the two cops were talking to the kid.

"I'm telling you, I just came by to deliver some papers for somebody," the man exclaimed. "Jeez, I didn't know it was against the law to do somebody a favor."

"What's going on?" Clay asked.

"We got a call from Ms. Carson about somebody sneaking around the place. When we pulled up, this guy was skulking around the backyard," one of the officers explained.

"I wasn't skulking…I was looking for a place to put these papers so Ms. Carson could get them."

"In the backyard?" Raymond asked in disbelief.

"I knocked on the front door and nobody answered. I figured I'd put the papers on the back porch, then write a note to tell Ms. Carson they were there."

Clay took the papers from Barry. Up close, he realized Barry wasn't as young a man as he'd first thought. Although he had the build of a healthy teenage wrestler, he appeared to be closer to midthirties or early forties. There also seemed to be a coiled intensity about the man, a wariness that spoke of a familiar interaction with the police.

Clay thumbed through the papers. It appeared to be a short story. "Is this your work?" he asked.

Barry shook his head. "No. Dean Moore asked me to bring them by. He's crippled and in a wheelchair, so I told him I'd do him the favor." Barry's features twisted angrily. "It's the last damn favor I'll ever do for anyone."

"What kind of a record have you got, Barry?" Clay asked, working on sheer gut instinct alone.

Barry's eyes flashed defiantly. "What has that got to do with anything?"

"Just answer the question," Raymond said with all the authority he could muster.

Again Barry's eyes snapped with suppressed anger. "Maybe I shouldn't say anything else unless I have a lawyer."

Raymond shrugged. "That's certainly your right, but we can get this all settled right here and right now if you'll just answer our questions."

Barry's nostrils flared as he blew out air like a deflated balloon. "Breaking and entering, assault and battery…but it was a long time ago. I've been clean for a long time."

"Check it out," Raymond said to one of the other officers, who immediately went to his car and radioed in.

"Clay."

He turned as Ann approached, her forehead furrowed in a worried frown. "I'm sure this is all just a simple mistake."

Her cheeks flushed prettily. "After everything that has happened, I...I just overreacted." He could tell she was embarrassed, both for herself and for Barry. "He has Dean's papers. I'm sure he's telling the truth. I was in the shower and apparently didn't hear the doorbell. I saw a man in the backyard and panicked."

Clay fought an impulse to caress the furrow from her brow. "You did exactly what you should have done," he assured her.

"Are you going to arrest me or what?" Barry asked angrily.

The officer who'd radioed in walked over to Clay. "No outstanding warrants, no record of arrests for the past five years," he said.

"I told you I was clean," Barry exclaimed.

Clay nodded to the other two officers. "Let him go."

Barry didn't wait around to say thank you. With a scowl still darkening his features, he shot toward his car, muttering a string of epithets that would make a sailor blush.

Within minutes the responding officers had left as well, leaving Clay, Ann and Raymond standing in the front yard. "I think it would be wise if we kept an eye on good old Barry," Raymond said.

"I agree. When we get back to the station I want to dig a little into his record, find out the details of his prior arrests."

"Do you think he's the one?" Ann asked.

"I don't know, but even if it is him, we can't do anything about it without some substantial evidence." Clay looked at his watch, surprised to realize it was already after two. "How about you ride with us down to the station and fill out that report, then I'll bring you back here?" Clay suggested.

"Okay," she agreed. "Just let me get my purse and lock up the house."

"Well, what do you think?" Raymond asked when Ann had gone inside and left the two of them standing on the driveway.

"You mean about Barry? I'm not sure what to think. Granted he acted suspiciously and had a chip on his shoulder, but he obviously didn't want us to know about his past arrests." Clay frowned. "When we get to the station, we should get a list from Ann of all her students in her classes. At least it's a place to start.''

"What about Greg Thorton and Mark Livingston?" Raymond asked.

"I think we can cross Mark off our list of potential suspects. Thorton is another story. Something about that man bothers me." Clay didn't want to admit that he wasn't sure if his dislike of Greg was personal or based on his cop's intuition.

They both turned as Ann came back out of the house. "I can't find Twilight," she said. "He must have gotten out during all the excitement."

"Should we look around for him?" Clay asked.

"No, he'll be fine. He's used to being outside for much of the day, although he always comes home when it starts getting dark."

"An alley cat afraid of the dark?" Clay asked teasingly.

She smiled. "That's why I love him so much."

Lucky cat. Clay bit back the words before they verbalized, irritated by their very presence in his head. "Come on, let's get down to the station and file some reports."

As Clay drove, Raymond small-talked with Ann, commenting on the weather, city politics and favorite television programs.

Clay listened absently, wondering if it was possible Barry Namath had an ax to grind with Ann. Had he really been at Ann's on an innocent mission for a friend, or had that just been a ruse in case he got caught. Only one way to find out. Clay made a mental note to check with Dean Moore, see if he'd asked Barry to deliver the papers.

As Ann laughed at something Raymond said, a flood of warmth swept through Clay. God, he loved the sound of her laughter. She had the kind of rich laugh that could pull a responding smile from a corpse.

He frowned, wondering if he could keep Ann from harm. Somebody seemed to be enjoying tormenting her. He made another mental note to check the files they had on male stalkers. Perhaps they already had a file on the responsible perp and all

Clay had to do was match the elements of Ann's torment to another case.

He should have done that after the first note, but at that time he hadn't realized he was dealing with a stalker. He looked in his rearview mirror, catching her reflection.

He supposed if he were a crazed obsessive type, Ann would certainly be the kind of woman it would be easy to get obsessed about. She was quite lovely, with a light in her eyes that whispered of untapped passion, haunting secrets and unfulfilled dreams. He wondered what it would be like to be loved by a woman like Ann Carson?

He tightened his grip on the steering wheel, irritated with his thoughts. The reality was loving or being loved by a woman like Ann would mean sacrificing his dreams. She wasn't the type of woman to chuck her earthly goods, her job security and luxurious life-style to follow a man to a sandy beach.

Of course, he wasn't about to fall in love with her, so it wasn't a problem. All he wanted to do was find out who was giving her problems, give her back the safety of her life, then move on with his plans for his future.

By the time Ann and Clay filled out reports concerning both the incident in the mall parking lot and the intruder call that afternoon, it was almost seven.

"Why don't you let me buy you some dinner since we kept you so long?" Clay suggested as he walked with her out of the station.

"I've got another idea. Since you're taking me home anyway, why don't you let me whip something up for us?"

Clay grinned at her. "Are you a good cook?"

She nodded. "I'm a good cook, not a *great* one." She knew she shouldn't be pursuing anything with him and yet couldn't seem to help herself. As they drove to her house, she shot a surreptitious glance his way.

Something about Clay Clinton intrigued her, drew her to him as if she were cold and he were a blanket. She liked him, and it had been a long time since she'd liked a man. She was also physically attracted to him in a way she hadn't felt about a man in years.

Still, there was no way she intended to trust a man with the secrets of her past...not for a very long time. The relationship with Greg had left a bad taste in her mouth, and she refused to fool herself that Clay would be any different. However, the thought of sharing an intimate physical relationship with him appealed to some small part of her.

She glanced at him again, noting his hands on the steering wheel. He had nice hands, ones that looked capable of strength, ones she knew capable of tenderness. She remembered the feel of his hand against her cheek before he'd left her house that morning, how often in the brief time she'd known him his hands had touched her casually, but with exquisite sensitivity.

The thought of his strong arms surrounding her, his lips claiming hers, filled her with a delicious heat. She'd almost forgotten that she was capable of feeling desire but something about Clay had definitely awakened latent hormones.

"You cool enough?" he asked as he redirected one of the air vents toward her.

"I'm fine," she assured him, glad he couldn't read her thoughts. "I just wonder if this heat wave is ever going to break." She tried to concentrate on the weather outside and not on the heat storm raging inside her when she taunted herself with thoughts of making love with Clay.

"I heard the weatherman say we might get a break in the next day or two. Rain is supposed to be moving in."

Ann leaned her head back against the seat and sighed. "Good, I like rainy days. There's something nice about being safe inside your home while rain patters against the window." She frowned. "I just hope I feel safe again soon."

"You will," he said with conviction. "We're going to find this nut, Ann, and when we do he'll never bother you again."

"I feel so ridiculous about overreacting this afternoon when Barry came by." She wrapped her arms around herself, stifling a shiver as she remembered seeing him in her backyard. "I just panicked."

"You did exactly what anyone should do when a strange man is in her yard," Clay replied.

"Yes, but I don't want the police department to think of me as the boy who cried wolf."

"Ann, that's not going to happen. There's enough documented proof that nobody is going to dismiss your cries for help."

Again she sighed. "The worse thing about all this isn't so much the fact that I'm afraid. It's that I feel like my life is out of control and there's nothing I can do to regain control. I'm reacting instead of acting, and I'm not accustomed to doing that."

Clay smiled. "So you like being a woman who captains her own ship."

"I've never thought about whether I necessarily like it or not. It's just been a fact of my life. When you're all alone in the world, you pretty much have to be the captain of your own ship."

"Consider this a squall you have to ride out. I promise you'll be in tranquil waters again soon." He wheeled into her driveway and turned off the engine. "In the meantime, I'm eager to see if the captain can really cook and if she'll accept help in the galley."

"All galley help not only welcomed, but actively encouraged." She laughed, glad she'd invited him to stay for dinner. When she was with him she somehow managed to forget the fearful incidents that had first brought and now kept him in her life. She enjoyed his company, his quick smile and warm gaze.

They got out of the car and walked toward her front porch. As they walked, Ann looked around the yard, wondering where Twilight might be hiding. Dusk was falling and usually the cat could be found at the front door when night approached.

"I wonder where Twilight is," she said as she unlocked the door, then took one last look around the yard.

"Want me to take a look around?" Clay offered.

"No. He'll probably turn up in a few minutes. He never stays outside at night for long."

"You mentioned that before. I can't believe you have a cat afraid of the dark."

Ann smiled softly, thinking of the cat who'd appeared on her doorway early one morning, half dead from hunger and missing an ear. "I think he was terribly abused before finding me. Whatever he suffered the night before I found him was horrible enough to drive him to overcome his suspicion of people. I feel like it's my job to keep him safe from a world that hasn't treated him very well." She flushed and laughed in embarrassment. "Sorry, I'm in danger of getting on my soapbox. Cruelty to helpless animals and innocent children, it makes me crazy."

"Me, too," he agreed.

"Come on, let's go see what I can find to fix us to eat." She went into the kitchen and flipped on the light against the approaching darkness. She motioned Clay to a chair at the table, then looked inside the refrigerator. "What about omelets? I've got cheese and mushrooms, scallions and ham."

"Sounds great," he agreed.

She began setting items out on the countertop, trying to think of topics for casual conversation. She'd never had to worry about talking when she was with Greg, since he didn't really care for conversation as much as he enjoyed his own monologues.

She jumped as Clay joined her at the counter. "I'm a great chopper. Just give me a knife and cutting board and I'll do the honors on the ingredients."

"It's a deal," she agreed.

Within minutes Clay was busy chopping as Ann made coffee and toasted bread. "You enjoy being a policeman, don't you?" he asked as they worked together.

"It's been a good career, but it's almost over."

She looked at him in surprise. "Almost over? What do you mean?"

"I'm retiring in a month."

"Retiring? Surely you're kidding. You aren't old enough to retire."

He grinned. "I'm almost forty-two. I've put in twenty years with the department. My goal has always been to retire before I got too old to enjoy it."

Ann looked at him searchingly, still finding it hard to believe that a man as vital, as youthful as Clay intended to retire. "But, what are you going to do? I mean, do you have another career in mind?"

"Nope. I've got a ticket to Hawaii and a plan to spend some time lying on the beaches and exploring the islands." He flashed her a boyish smile. "It's been a dream I've worked toward for years. I want to live the life of a beach bum."

Ann stared at him. "But where will you live? Are you going to buy a house?"

"No way." Clay sliced the mushrooms with an expert flourish. "I don't want any financial commitments, I'll sleep on the beach or in a rented room. Perhaps I'll be a vagabond, going where the wind and my whims take me."

Ann buttered toast and placed two more slices of bread into the toaster. "Sounds like a nice way to spend a vacation, but I wouldn't want to live that way for any length of time." She fought against a wave of fragmented memories, distant painful remembrances from her past. "Personally, I need a home base, a place of safety that belongs to me."

"Different strokes for different folks, I guess," he said, finishing with the mushrooms and beginning to chop scallions.

"You must have started in the department when you were young," Ann said.

"I started in the academy on my twenty-first birthday. I always knew what I wanted to do with my life. What about you? What made you decide to teach?"

"When I was in high school, I had a wonderful English teacher who challenged me and encouraged me. She made such a difference in my life, I knew I wanted to emulate her and become a teacher." Ann smiled at the memory of Mrs. Johnson, the teacher who'd taken the time to see beyond the frightened young girl she'd been and had encouraged Ann to develop dreams and go after them. "I love my job," she finished simply.

"It's nice to like what you do. My mother thinks I'm crazy to retire," Clay admitted. "Do you think I'm crazy?" He set the knife down and looked at her with his warm, brown eyes.

Ann smiled once again. "I'd be crazy to make any kind of a value judgment on how you want to live your life. I believe each one of us has to follow our dreams, and if that's your dream then you aren't crazy."

He finished with the onions and washed his hands in the sink. "So, tell me about your dreams. What do you want out of life?" he asked as he dried his hands then moved to sit down at the table.

"You'll think my dreams are terribly boring," she protested as she busied herself pouring the omelet mixture into the awaiting skillet.

"Who am I to put a value judgment on your dreams?" he asked, teasingly giving her words back to her.

She laughed. "Okay, someday I'd like to get married and have a family. That's my dream for the future."

He nodded. "And it's a very nice dream, just not for me."

Ann cut the omelet and slid half onto each plate, then set the plates on the table. "If you don't mind, why don't you pour the coffee while I check to see if Twilight is waiting at the front door."

"Sure," Clay agreed easily. As Ann left the kitchen, Clay felt a twinge of relief. There had been something almost too compelling, too intimate in sharing dreams with a woman in the comfort of a kitchen while night fell outside the windows. At least he'd told her about his imminent retirement plans.

He couldn't deny there was some sort of chemistry between them, a spark of sexual energy both exciting and confusing. At least if anything got out of control, she couldn't fault him for not being truthful. She knew in a month's time he'd be gone. If she wanted a relationship of any kind with him, she knew it would be a brief one.

"He's still not there," Ann said as she returned to the kitchen, a frown marring the smooth skin across her forehead.

"You want me to go out and take a look around?" he offered.

"No. Let's go ahead and eat before it gets cold. I'm sure Twilight will show up by then."

As they ate, Clay tried to keep the conversation light, regaling her with stories from his youth. Although she laughed at the right places, kept up her end of the inane conversation, she occasionally tilted her head as if listening for something and he knew she was worried about the cat.   He offered several more times to go looking for the feline, but she protested, insisting he eat and that Twilight would be grounded for missing curfew.

"Every time I missed curfew, my mother would make me clean the whole house the next day. I thought it was the worse punishment she could inflict on me."

Ann laughed. "It was probably good for you, although I have to admit, I hate to clean."

Clay looked at her incredulously. "But this place is spotless."

"I have a woman who comes in to clean once every two weeks. It was the first gift I gave myself when I bought the condo." She smiled ruefully. "In fact, she's due next week, so don't look too closely at things. Who knows what kind of dust bunnies you'll find."

"Dust bunnies I can handle. It's the dust monsters that live under my bed that worry me." Clay made a mental note to check out the cleaning lady.

She laughed and again he felt a warm burst of pleasure sweep through him at the deep, throaty sound. She was a woman meant to laugh. The expression of merriment lifted the shadows from her eyes, banished the darkness he sensed resided inside her.

"So tell me, what dire ways did your mother punish you when you were bad?" he asked.

She closed up. Her smile faded and she seemed to turn inward. "My mother wasn't much of a disciplinarian." She flashed him a tight smile. "Besides, what makes you think I was anything other than a perfect child?" She started to rise from the table.

"Sit still," he commanded. "You cooked, I'll clean up." She settled back in her chair and he poured her a fresh cup of coffee, then began to clear the table.

"Why haven't you ever married?" she asked, then flushed. "I don't mean to be personal, I'm just curious."

"It's all right, I don't mind answering, although I'm not sure have a good answer." He carried the last of the dishes to the sink, then turned back to her. "I guess I've never met a woman could imagine spending the rest of my life with. Besides, I knew from a pretty young age that I wanted an early retirement and family commitments would make that particular dream a little more difficult to achieve."

"Don't you ever get lonely?"

He shrugged. "Sure, but not often." He turned back to the sink, unwilling to confess to her that whenever he got lonely all he had to do was think of his dad's death, and the dreams his father had never experienced. His father had sacrificed his dreams for his family, and Clay wasn't willing to do the same thing. "Besides, whenever I get really lonely, I just go sit for a few hours at my mom's. She believes every silence should be filled and it doesn't take very long before I'm not lonely anymore."

"She sounds like a delight. You're lucky to have her." Her voice held a slight wistfulness.

"When did you lose your parents?" he asked as he put the dishes in the dishwasher.

"I never knew my father and my mom passed away when was fifteen."

"Tough break. Where did you go when she died?"

"Oh, it's a long, boring story." She stood up and carried her cup to him. "I'm going to check for Twilight again."

As she left the room, Clay once again realized he'd learned next to nothing about her past. Throughout the entire dinner,

she'd adroitly turned the conversation away from herself. Wha
he couldn't decide was if she'd done it intentionally or if sh
was merely a woman unaccustomed to talking about herself.

"I can't understand it," she said as she walked back int
the kitchen. "It's pitch-dark outside and Twilight has neve
been out this late."

"Let's go outside and hunt," Clay said, knowing sh
wouldn't relax until the cat was inside safe and sound.

"Are you sure you don't mind?"

"Of course I don't."

The air outside was redolent with the scent of flowers an
dew-laden grass. Thick humidity made it almost difficult t
breathe and overhead clouds chased across the face of a fu
moon.

"Here kitty," Clay called softly, listening for taletell rus
tling. Nothing. He heard nothing but the whisper of a nigh
breeze through the trees and Ann's voice echoing his call.

They moved from the front yard to the back, where the fo
liage was thicker and more difficult to search. "Come on, Tw
light. Where are you hiding?" He started on the left side c
the porch, hunting under bushes, looking up in the tre
branches. Nothing. No sign of the bedraggled alley cat.

He moved to the right side of the patio, where the light didn
quite reach and shadows hung deep. It was there he foun
Twilight.

The cat lay on his side, not moving, foam ringing his mout
A can of tuna was on one side of him, a note tucked just und
his hindquarters. "Oh God," Clay breathed. He leaned dow
and gently pulled the note free and read it. REVENGE I
SWEET WHEN IT'S LONG IN COMING. BE CAREFU
WHAT YOU EAT, SWEET ANN.

Clay's hand shook with suppressed rage. "You bastard," h
muttered. "I'll get you, you sick bastard, if it's the last thin
I do."

"Clay? I didn't find him anywhere." Ann said as she walke
out on the patio. "What about…" She froze, her gaze follow
ing Clay's to the cat. With a heartrending cry, she fell to he
knees.

Chapter 8

Ann crawled on her knees to Twilight, her pain too great to verbalize, her loss too intense for tears. Someplace in the back of her mind, she knew what had happened. The tuna can and the foam told her that Twilight had been poisoned, but it all seemed surreal. She felt as if she were swimming in a dream fog, and if she could just wake up, Twilight would be fine.

She crouched over the cat. "Oh, baby," she said softly. With the gentleness of a mother, she gathered Twilight in her arms. "Why, Clay? Why would somebody do this?" She tangled her fingers in the warm fur. Warm. The fog dissipated. "Clay...I think he's still alive."

With three long strides Clay reached her side. "Are you sure?"

Ann placed her palm against Twilight's chest, adrenaline surging through her as she felt a faint, but discernible heartbeat. "He's alive, Clay. He's alive." Temporary joy raced through her, coupled with a dreadful anxiety.

"Get him to the car, I'll lock up the house. We've got to

get him to a vet." Clay grabbed the tuna can, then took off toward the door.

"Grab my purse," Ann yelled after him, her heart aching as if broken as she gently picked up the limp cat.

Within minutes they were in the car, headed for an emergency animal clinic Ann knew was open all night. "Come on baby, hang on," she whispered to Twilight.

The tears she'd been too stunned to shed earlier now trekked down her cheeks. Twilight had been her family, a waif like herself. She stroked his ear, the gray fur above his eyes, despair making her feel hollow inside. Losing Twilight would be like losing a part of her soul. "Turn left at the next light," she instructed Clay, relieved the animal clinic was just another block away. "It's the second building on the right."

Clay pulled into the lot. The moment he shut off the engine they exited the car on the run.

"May I help you?" A young female receptionist greeted them. Her eyes widened as she saw Twilight in Ann's arms. "Come on back." She motioned them through a doorway and into what appeared to be an exam-operating room. "I'll go get Dr. Turwell."

Dr. Turwell took one look at the cat and asked Clay and Ann to go back to the waiting room. Clay handed the doctor the tuna can he'd brought along. "This probably contains whatever poison he ate," he explained. As they left, the doctor began giving Twilight oxygen.

Ann and Clay sat down on the worn love seat in the waiting room. "Oh, God, I don't know if he's going to make it or not." Ann's hand trembled as she looped a strand of her hair behind her ear.

She felt sick and knew it was grief that caused her stomach to ache and her heart to hurt. Not Twilight, please God, no Twilight.

"Twilight looked like a pretty tough cat to me," Clay replied softly.

She nodded. "Yes, he looks tough, and he's had a tough life, but really he's quite fragile." She closed her eyes, willing back a renewed burst of tears as she remembered how Twilight would curl up at her feet at night, how he purred his contentment when he'd cuddle close to her chest and she'd stroke his fur. For so long, Twilight had been husband, child and parent to her. He'd been a friend who offered unconditional love.

She drew in a deep breath. "You probably think I'm crazy to be carrying on so for a cat. A lot of people don't understand the bond that can grow between somebody and their pet."

Clay's fingers touched her chin and he turned her head so she was looking into his warm, brown eyes. "Ann...I've never had a pet, but I do understand about love and loss." He stroked her cheek and again she was struck by the gentleness and empathy in his touch.

He put his arm around her shoulders and she leaned into him. Strange, how shared grief became somehow easier to handle. She'd spent so much of her life grieving alone, surviving fate's hits.

It felt good to have Clay's arm around her, as if somehow he could shelter her from any more fear or pain. Although she knew it wasn't true, she allowed the fantasy to wash over her, the fantasy that somehow Clay could shield her from anything life threw at her. For the moment, it was enough to keep her from losing her mind.

The minutes ticked by, agonizingly slow as they waited to find out if Twilight would make it or not. Ann alternated between praying and crying and Clay remained a pillar of strength, holding her and occasionally murmuring soothing words.

It was nearly midnight when Dr. Turwell finally emerged from the operating area and joined them in the waiting room. "We finally got him stabilized."

"Thank God," Ann breathed.

"Although he's not completely out of the woods yet," the doctor continued. "We'll monitor him for the rest of the night. You can call in the morning and we'll see where we are."

"Thank you, Dr. Turwell. I'll call first thing in the morning,'' Ann said. He nodded, then left the waiting room and returned to the private back area.

''Let's get you home,'' Clay said, his arm still warm around her shoulders.

The ride back to her house was less frantic. The adrenaline that had kept Ann going through the long wait in the clinic was gone, leaving behind exhaustion and the seeds of a growing anger.

''Do you think the person who poisoned Twilight is the same one who's been bothering me?'' she asked.

''I know it is,'' Clay answered, a tic working overtime in his lower jaw. He reached into his pocket and pulled out a piece of paper and handed it to her. He turned on the interior light so she could read the note.

As she read, her anger exploded. ''Dammit. Why is this happening? Who is doing these things to me?''

Clay turned out the light and reached for her hand across the seat. ''I told you we'll find him.''

Ann pushed his hand away. ''When? When will you find him? You've been telling me that for a week and now Twilight was almost killed. What next? How long do I have to endure this terrorism?'' She drew in a deep breath, realizing she was venting her anger at the wrong person. ''I'm sorry. I shouldn't yell at you.''

''That's right. You shouldn't yell at me. I'm on your side.'' He offered her a tentative smile.

''I am sorry, Clay.'' She grabbed his hand and gave it a squeeze. ''I know you're doing all you can to try to find out who's responsible for this. I'm just frustrated...and frightened.''

This time he squeezed her hand reassuringly, then let go and once again grabbed the steering wheel. ''Ann, I want a list of all your male students. I'm going to run their names through the computer and see what I come up with.'' He raked a hand through his hair, frustration evident on his features. ''I have to confess, initially, I thought maybe the notes and the phone calls were from some creep and he'd grow tired of the game and move on to somebody else.''

"Then he tried to run me over in the mall parking lot,'' Ann said.

"And now this.'' Again his hand raked through his hair. "We're checking all the known stalkers in the area, to see if we can match what's happening to you with anyone else. We're doing all we can, Ann.''

"I know.'' She wrapped her arms around her shoulders, chilled despite the warmth of the car.

"But you've got to do what you can to help us. If you think of anyone…a teenage boyfriend, a hotheaded co-worker, anyone who might have something against you, you've got to tell me.''

"I've thought and thought, and I can't come up with anyone who would have any reason to seek revenge on me.'' Tell him, a small voice niggled inside her head. Tell him about the lost years.

She frowned and rubbed her forehead, a battle waging inside her brain. Why, what difference would it make? Surely those dark distant years of her life had no bearing on what was happening to her now.

Besides, she'd finally gotten the courage to tell Greg and had watched him turn away from her. She'd tell Clay if she thought any of it would help, but she didn't think it would.

He pulled into her driveway and whatever anger had surged inside her died once again, leaving only the despair. She couldn't imagine going inside and knowing Twilight wouldn't greet her with a cranky meow. He wouldn't curl up at the foot of the bed and keep her feet warm through the night. A sob hiccupped out of her.

"Come on, let's get you settled in for the night, then I'll get out of your hair.'' Together they got out of the car. He placed his arm around her shoulders as they walked to the front door. She fought the impulse to lean against him once again, knowing leaning on Clay could become a habit.

Once inside, she sank down on the sofa, again nearly overwhelmed by anguish. Twilight was her family, her baby. She felt as if the cat had been a gift, a survivor like herself in need of nurturing.

"How could somebody harm an innocent animal?" she asked Clay through tear-blurred eyes. "What kind of person could do such a thing?"

He sat down next to her and with his thumb swiped an errant tear from her cheek. "A monster. But unfortunately this world is full of monsters disguised as human beings. In my twenty years on the force I've met a million."

"Is that why you're retiring? Chucking it all?" she asked curiously. "I'm sure you get tired of dealing with the worst of human nature."

He shrugged. "Sure, I see a lot of bad, but I also see the best human nature has to offer. It's rewarding work. I've always felt like I make a difference, help keep the monsters at bay for good people."

Without thought, she reached up and placed her palm against his cheek. She could feel the whisker stubble that darkened his jaw, and beneath that the warmth of his skin. "You're a good man, Clay Clinton," she said softly.

"No, I'm not," he countered. "If I were a truly good man, I wouldn't be thinking about kissing you right now."

Ann's breath caught in her throat as a thrill shivered through her. Although she knew it was probably a mistake, knew she was too fragile at the moment to make rational decisions, she couldn't stop herself. "What I want to know is why you're just thinking about it and why you aren't doing it."

His eyes flared with fiery intensity and Ann leaned toward him, wanting to immerse herself in the flames. His mouth claimed hers hotly, hungrily. There was nothing tentative about the kiss. It was as if he'd been preparing for it for a long time.

As he deepened the kiss, his tongue meeting hers, his arms wrapped around her and pulled her closer. She melted against him, wanting to conform herself to his broad chest. Her fingers played in the thick hair at the nape of his neck, as she marveled at the silkiness of the strands.

Still the kiss went on, breathtaking yet life giving. Warmth suffused her, chasing away the cold core of heartache. Her body felt electrified and shivers of delight continued to work up her back. She knew he was just as affected by their kiss. His breathing had deepened, become irregular and his hands moved up and down her back in slow, sensual strokes.

When he finally broke the kiss, he disentangled her arms from around his neck, then leaned back and drew in a ragged breath. "Whew," he finally said. "I'd better get out of here before caution gets thrown to the wind."

He started to rise, but paused as Ann held on to his arm. "Clay...please. Let's throw caution to the wind." She couldn't believe the words had fallen from her mouth, but the minute she spoke them she realized it was exactly what she wanted. She dropped her hand from his arm.

"Ann..." He stood up. "I don't want to take advantage of you. You're shaken up and in an emotional frame of mind." Despite his words, she saw the want in his eyes, knew he desired her as strongly as she desired him.

"I'm a grown woman, Clay. You aren't taking advantage of me." She stood and moved so she stood mere inches from him.

"Yes, but..."

"Shhh." She placed a finger over his lips. "I know. In a month's time you're going to Hawaii. Tomorrow doesn't matter. All that matters is the here and now. Stay with me tonight, Clay. Make love to me."

She gasped as he drew her to him once again. His mouth claimed hers in another mind-reeling kiss. His hands went to her hips and he pulled her intimately against him, allowing her to realize the extent of his arousal.

When the kiss broke, she took his hand and without a word led him down the hallway and into her bedroom. She'd never had a man in here before, although many nights she'd slept alone and dreamed of passion, and strong masculine arms holding her tight.

She didn't turn on the lamp. The illumination from the hallway spilled into the room, creating a soft, penumbral light. She stood by the edge of the bed, eager yet afraid of appearing too brazen.

He seemed to sense her fear. He unbuckled his gun belt and placed it on the nightstand, then approached her. With a soft smile he kissed her on the cheek, then began to unfasten the buttons of her blouse. Once he had them all unbuttoned, he slid the blouse off her shoulders, kissing first one, then the other as the blouse fell to the floor.

He started to unsnap her slacks, but she stopped him, wanting to be an active participant in their foreplay dance. Her fingers trembled as she undid his shirt. It had been so long...so very, very long. As his shirt fell away she leaned forward and pressed her lips against his hot flesh. He hissed inwardly and tangled his hands in her hair, pulling her up so their lips could meet again.

Within minutes they had divested themselves of the rest of their clothing. Ann pulled down the bedspread and together they got into bed beneath the sheets.

Flesh against flesh, warmth against warmth, Ann felt drugged from the tactile pleasure of Clay's body wrapped around hers. His lips moved from her mouth to the hollow of her throat, blazing a trail of fire each place they lingered. The slight wisp of whiskers only intensified her pleasure and she gasped aloud as his mouth moved from the base of her neck to the turgid tip of one of her breasts.

Moans welled up in her throat, moans too powerful to keep inside her. Deep and throaty, they escaped her as his mouth continued to trek down her stomach and across her inner thighs.

Teasing, maddening, he caressed her with his hands and mouth, exploring her inch by inch, loving her in increments that made her want to scream.

Every nerve ending felt electrified beneath the magic of his touch. She sobbed his name as he carried her closer and closer to fulfillment. When she finally reached it, she clung to him, crying with joy.

"Wait...I've got to catch my breath," she finally gasped.

He smiled and kissed her cheek. "You are so beautiful," he whispered.

She rolled over on top, straddling him, her eyes gleaming with renewed fire. "And you are a very generous lover. But, now it's your turn."

She leaned forward and kissed his cheek, at the same time touching the tips of her breasts to his chest. The light spilling in the bedroom doorway loved her, imbibing her skin with a rich golden hue. Her pale hair spilled onto his chest as she moved her mouth down the flat of his abdomen.

As he had done to her, she explored his body with gentle touches and sweet kisses, exhibiting a passionate nature that both surprised and enthralled him.

It didn't take long before Clay realized his control was about to fail. She felt too good. Her lips were too hot. With a low moan he rolled her over on her back. He braced himself above her, gazing into her dazed dark blue eyes. For just a moment it was as if he were no longer looking at her, but rather into her, seeking her soul, seeking the very essence of her.

The moment was lost as he entered her warmth. She wrapped her legs around him, pulling him deeper. He closed his eyes, overwhelmed by sensation. He wanted it to last forever, but knew he was rushing toward the brink and couldn't stop it.

He wanted to tell her to wait just a minute, to stop moving so sweetly, so seductively against him. He wanted to tell her to lie still so he could regain a little bit of control, but she met him thrust for thrust, making it impossible for him to speak, impossible for him to do anything but love her.

He cried out her name as he reached his peak, vaguely aware of her crying out at the same time. In that moment they seemed to melt together, become a single entity through an incredible form of osmosis. It was as if not only their bodies had bonded, but for a brief space in time their souls had touched as well.

When they were finished, Clay rolled off her, but kept her enfolded in his arms. They didn't move but instead waited for heartbeats to slow, for their breathing to return to normal. She moved so her head rested on his chest and he stroked her hair, enjoying the sweet fragrance of the silky strands.

"Clay?" She didn't look at him.

"Hmm?"

"Thank you."

He emitted a burst of laughter. "Sweetheart, I should be thanking you. That was…" He sought words and realized all that came to mind seemed inadequate to describe what he'd just felt. "It was very special."

She looked at him, her eyes dewy and her lips slightly swollen from his kisses. "Yes, it was special." A small frown appeared across her forehead. "Clay,…I just want you to know… I don't sleep with every policeman I meet."

He smiled. "And I don't sleep with every attractive damsel in distress I meet." Clay felt himself stir, desire once again swirling through him. Even now, so soon after being sated, he wanted her again…and again.

"Will you stay here for the rest of the night?" she asked.

"Okay," he agreed, tamping down his rising desire as she stifled a yawn with the back of her hand. "But I'll have to leave early in the morning."

She nodded. "Just hold me through the night."

Once again she lay her cheek against his chest and he resumed caressing her hair. Her sweet scent filled the air and her silky skin seemed to surround him. He could feel the press of her soft breasts against his side, and beneath the warm flesh the resounding beat of her heart. A sense of incredible peace stole through him.

He was grateful he'd told Ann about his pending retirement and plans to leave the mainland, so there could be no mistake about what he had to offer her. He didn't want to hurt her, and as long as she understood his future plans there could be no misunderstanding, no misconceptions about what they had just shared.

Still, he couldn't deny that he felt something for Ann aside from his enormous physical attraction. She intrigued him. He found her a curious mix of contradictions. Controlled, yet with passionate streak. Strong, yet oddly vulnerable. A loner whom he sensed was lonely. Definitely intriguing.

He closed his eyes, knowing sleep was only moments away. He'd just about fallen into slumber when Ann moved out of his arms. "Wha…what's wrong?" he asked as she crawled out of bed.

"Nothing. It's okay. I just need to do something." She walked over to the bedroom door and closed, then locked it. "Now I can sleep," she murmured as she got back under the covers and cuddled against him.

Immediately she fell asleep. Her breathing grew deep and regular and her body seemed to melt against him in complete and utter surrender.

He frowned, his gaze going to the door she'd closed and locked. It bothered him that the outer doors being locked up tight was not enough, that she also had to lock the bedroom door to feel safe. The night he'd slept on her sofa, he'd heard her lock her bedroom door and had assumed she'd been locking him out. Now he realized that hadn't been right. She'd been locking herself in.

Was it only the events of the last week that had her so frightened or had she always been afraid? Clay couldn't imagine living with such fear. He touched her hair and looked at her features in the moonlight streaking through the window.

He hoped he could find the crazy man causing her grief, prayed he could find him before anything else bad happened. More than anything, before he retired from the force, he wanted to give her a sense of security, a feeling of safety to last her a lifetime. Most of all, he wanted her to be able to go to sleep without feeling the need to lock her bedroom door.

Chapter 9

Clay woke up with the dawn, for a moment disoriented b[y] the strange surroundings. The faint glow of light danced on th[e] brightly colored bedspread and immediately he remembere[d]. He was with Ann.

At some point in the night they had separated, each seeki[ng] their own side of the bed. He turned over and looked at h[er] his heart expanding at her beauty even in sleep. She was curl[ed] in a fetal ball, her hands folded beneath her cheek. Her h[air] was a curtain of pale silk fanning out across the pillow.

Before his hormones could fully awaken, he slid out of be[d] not wanting to disturb her sleep. He dressed quickly, the[n] kissed her softly on her cheek. Her eyes fluttered open at h[is] touch and her lips curved upward in a smile.

"I'm leaving. I'll lock you in and call you later this mor[n]ing," he said.

She nodded and before he was out of the room she was on[ce] again asleep. He locked her bedroom door and closed it behi[nd] him, then carefully locked the front door when he left.

The early morning air once again hung thick with humidi[ty]

ortending storms in the near future. He wouldn't mind a little
ain to ease the heat wave they'd endured for the past two
eeks.

As he got into his car his mind whirled with all the things
e needed to do. He wanted to follow up on Barry Namath,
ake sure the man had been telling the truth about what
rought him to Ann's house yesterday morning.

Nasty notes, harassing phone calls, a near hit-and-run and a
oisoned cat. "And no clues," he murmured aloud with a
own. Again he had the feeling of escalating danger, but didn't
now how to stop it without knowing who was behind it.

All he knew for certain was that it was somebody with in-
mate knowledge of Ann's life, somebody who knew where
e lived, knew her love for her cat. A student? Greg Thorton?
r just a nut who'd focused his obsession on Ann?

He was determined to crack this case before he left the de-
rtment. The thought of leaving his job and handing Ann's
se to another officer who knew little or nothing about it both-
ed him. He needed to know she was safe before he left.

From Ann's place he drove to his apartment. Once there, he
owered and dressed in clean clothes. As he left for the sta-
on, he wondered how Twilight was doing. He hoped the cat
d made it through the night, would continue to be all right.
nn's grief over the cat had touched him deeply.

As she'd cradled Twilight in her arms, murmuring words of
couragement and love, for a moment Clay had been able to
agine what kind of a mother she'd make. He had a feeling
y child would be lucky to have her as a mother.

If he had any regrets about his future plans, the fact that he'd
ver have children was one. He liked kids, enjoyed playing
cle to Raymond's brood. He would have liked to have a few
his own, but had never met a woman whom he felt com-
lled to marry. Now it was too late. Retirement wasn't the
ne to start thinking about having a family.

As for Ann, eventually she'd find a nice man to marry and
obably have a couple of kids. Whomever she married would
rk to help her pay for the luxury condo, keep her and the

kids in nice clothing. She and her husband would live an uppe
middle class life...and endure all the stresses that life-styl
brought with it.

"Not me," he said firmly as he wheeled his car into a park
ing space at the station. He thought of the plane ticket insid
his bureau drawer. Less than a month and he'd be warmed b
the heat of a tropical sun with no worries or responsibilities t
clutter his mind. But first he wanted to fix Ann's life...an
time was growing short.

Entering the station, the first person he met was Raymond
carrying a cup of coffee in one hand and a donut in the othe
"Hey, partner," Raymond greeted him.

"I see you're still on a diet," Clay said wryly and looke
pointedly at the donut.

"I think Ginger is trying to kill me. Every night for dinne
all she feeds me is lettuce and fat-free stuff. It's gross."

"Yeah, well last night somebody tried to kill Ann Carson
cat. Fed him poison."

"You're kidding me." Raymond hurried to catch up to Cla
who'd continued toward his desk. "Is the cat all right?"

Clay reached his desk and sat down. "As of last night h
was stable. If we'd found him a minute or two later, he'd b
dead."

Raymond sank down in the chair in front of Clay's des
"What kind of a creep does something like that?"

Clay pulled out the note that had been left beneath the ca
He'd bagged it at his house, although was certain no finge
prints would be found on the sheet of paper. He placed it
front of him, where Raymond could read it.

"Where do we go from here?" Raymond asked.

"Did we get back anything on Barry Namath? I want hi
checked out thoroughly. It's some coincidence that yesterd
morning he was caught in her backyard, and last night I fou
her cat half dead on the back patio."

"The report came through earlier. It's on my desk."

Raymond left to retrieve it. He returned a moment later a
handed the report to Clay.

"Barry Namath...forty-four years old. Two prior arrests. Breaking and entering and assault and battery. He served eighteen months." Clay frowned and read further. According to the report, Barry Namath had broken into his girlfriend's house while she was at work. He'd waited for her to return, then had beaten the hell out of her.

"Not a nice guy, huh," Raymond said, stating the obvious.

"Not a nice guy," Clay agreed. "He told the officers he was doing a favor for a fellow student by delivering some papers to Ann. Maybe we should talk to this fellow student, make sure Barry's telling us the truth."

Raymond finished his donut and licked his blunt fingers. "Let's go." He stood up.

Clay pulled out his notebook and checked to find the name of the student Barry had mentioned. Dean Moore. "Hang tight, I need to find an address." He grabbed a phone book and thumbed to the *M*'s.

Within minutes he and Raymond were headed toward Dean Moore's residence. "You think this Barry is the one tormenting Ann?"

"I don't know what to think," Clay admitted. "All I know is whoever is after Ann is smart and evil and that's a combination that worries me."

"I still say whoever it is, he's somebody from Ann's past. That last note you showed me said something about revenge being sweet when it's long in coming."

"Yeah, but it's all relative, isn't it? I mean, long in coming could be years, or in the mind of a madman, it could be mere days." Frustration ate inside him and Clay hit the steering wheel with the palm of his hand. "Dammit, I keep feeling like there's something we're missing."

"Hey, buddy, take it easy. It's just another case. We can only do what we can do."

Clay drew in a deep breath. Just another case? Somehow, someway in the past week, it had become more than that. Watching Ann get out of bed to lock her bedroom door last night had twisted something inside Clay's soul, had touched him in a place he'd never been touched before.

"I warned you about losing your objectivity," Raymond said softly.

"I haven't lost my objectivity," Clay protested vehemently. "It's just, you know, this is my last case. I want to walk away from this job with all the ends tied up neatly. I don't want to leave the department with this case not solved."

"Then we'll solve it," Raymond replied, then shot a sly glance at Clay. "Of course, if we don't in the next couple of weeks, you could always put off your retirement plans. Hawaii will still be there no matter when you decide to go."

"No way. I'm not going to let anything stand in the way of my plans. I watched my dad put off and postpone his dream of a fishing cruise for years until finally it was too late for him. I'm not going to make the same mistake."

He steadfastly refused to dwell on the sweetness of making love to Ann the night before, the thought of walking away from her knowing she would still be in danger while he lounged on a distant beach.

Although he felt a certain emotional bond with her based on their physical union the night before, he presumed he would have felt that same bond with any woman he'd slept with. It had nothing to do with love and he certainly wasn't about to sacrifice himself and his dreams because he'd enjoyed a night of lovemaking with her.

He was grateful when they spotted Dean Moore's address on the front of a neat, small bungalow. Time to get his thoughts back to the matter at hand.

Dean Moore lived only a couple of miles from Ann's condo, but that meant little. Most of the students in her class were from her general area of the city.

As the two officers approached the house, Clay saw the front curtain lift momentarily, then fall back across the window. Somebody was home.

They walked up the stairs to the porch. Clay knocked on the door and it was immediately answered. Dean Moore sat tall in the wheelchair, his silver-shot hair glistening in the sunlight that shone through the doorway. "May I help you?" he asked, his wheelchair blocking their entrance into the house.

"I'm Officer Clinton and this is my partner, Officer Misker. Can we come in? We'd like to ask you a few questions about Barry Namath."

Dean smiled and nodded. He rolled backward, allowing them inside. "I figured somebody might be contacting me. This is about yesterday, right?" He motioned them to a worn sofa. "Please, make yourselves comfortable. Barry called me yesterday afternoon, screaming and cussing for getting him into trouble."

"So you asked him to go to Ann Carson's place?" Raymond asked.

Dean nodded. "I have a lot of time on my hands and writing has become my passion. Ms. Carson has been kind enough to tell me she'll critique whatever I turn in, but sometimes getting the work to her is difficult for me. Yesterday morning I called Barry and asked him if he would mind dropping off some papers at Ms. Carson's house."

Dean folded his hands in his lap and shook his head. "I had no idea Barry would get into any trouble. He's not in trouble, is he?"

"Not unless he was the one who poisoned Ann Carson's cat last night," Raymond exclaimed.

Dean's dark eyes widened. "Somebody poisoned her cat? Ms. Carson must be heartbroken."

"Luckily, the cat didn't die," Raymond returned. He stood up and shot a glance at Clay, indicating as far as he was concerned their work here was finished.

Clay also rose, frustration winging through him. It would have been so easy had Barry been their culprit, had they been able to prove that he'd been at Ann's for nefarious reasons.

"Thank you for your time, Mr. Moore," Raymond said as they walked to the door.

"Certainly, glad to help. I just hope you find whoever is

responsible for the attack on Ms. Carson's cat. She's such a nice lady.''

''Thanks again, Mr. Moore.'' Together Clay and his partner left the house and got back into their patrol car. As Clay started the engine, Raymond turned to look at him. ''You got awfully quiet.''

''Frustration.'' Clay frowned. Something niggled at the back of his brain, something he sensed was important. But, he couldn't quite grasp what it was.

He thought again of Ann leaving the comfort and warmth of her bed to lock the bedroom door. In that single act, she'd raised the stakes for him, made herself more than just a case.

When they got back to the station, Clay called her, wanting to check to see what she'd found out about Twilight's condition.

''Dr. Turwell says he's doing as well as can be expected,'' she said. ''He wants to keep him for another day or two just to be on the safe side.''

''How are you doing?''

She hesitated a moment before answering. ''Okay, I guess. I never realized how much company Twilight was for me, how often I spoke to him. The house seems very quiet without him here.''

Again Clay felt an unexpected tug on his heart. His mother had expressed the same kinds of sentiments right after his father had died. The quiet of the house, the loss of a companion, the knowledge that when she spoke, nobody was in the house to hear her. ''I'm taking my mom out for dinner tonight. Why don't you come with us.'' The invitation was purely spontaneous, without any thought other than it might do her good to spend a few hours away from the house.

''Oh, Clay, I don't want to intrude on your time with your mother.''

''You wouldn't be an intrusion,'' he protested. ''Besides, my mom would love to share dinner conversation with somebody other than me. I aggravate her. You'd be doing both of us a big favor by coming along.''

She laughed and he could easily imagine the sparkle of her eyes. "How can I say no when you put it like that?"

"Good. I'll pick you up about six, okay?"

"I'll be ready."

Clay hung up, wondering if he'd just made an enormous mistake. Usually he tried to keep his dates very separate from his mother, who had a tendency to matchmake for her poor, misguided, unattached son.

Oh well, it was done now. Surely if Ann could survive a near hit-and-run by a car with a madman at the wheel, she could survive an evening with Rosemary Clinton.

Ann had been rather nervous all afternoon anticipating her evening with Clay. She'd barely been awake when he'd left that morning, thankfully missing the morning-after small talk and awkwardness.

She'd found herself daydreaming through her afternoon classes, replaying the entire night with Clay in her mind. Just as she'd suspected, he'd been a caring, giving lover. For a brief moment in time, while he'd held her, she'd been able to forget the darkness of her past, the uncertainty of her future and just dwell in the glow of being with him.

At least with Clay she knew exactly where she stood. In less than a month he'd be gone. They could enjoy each other's company until he left, but there would be no commitment, no future with him.

Rather than make her feel bad, this knowledge relieved her. She would never have to tell him about her past, never have to bare her soul. She would enjoy what he had to offer her, the time they had together, then they'd both move on to the rest of their lives.

It was exactly six o'clock when he knocked on her door. She opened it and smiled at him in surprise. "Do you know this is the first time I've seen you in regular clothes?"

He grinned and ran a hand down the front of his gray sport shirt. "I get so used to wearing my uniform, I sometimes forget how to dress like a regular guy."

Ann glanced at his shirt, the black slacks and loafers. "You look very nice," she replied with a touch of shyness.

"And so do you." He eyed the pale apricot-colored dress she wore, creating pinpoints of heat each place his gaze lingered. He cleared his throat. "We'd better get out of here. I told Mom I'd pick her up about six-fifteen."

Ann locked her front door and together they walked to his car.

"Did you have a good day?" Clay asked once they were on the road to his mother's house.

"Yes, what about you?"

He sighed. "Raymond and I spoke with Dean Moore this morning. He confirmed that he'd asked Barry to deliver those papers to you. We're running background checks on the list of names you gave me, but it all takes time. You've got a lot of men in your writing class. That struck me as unusual."

"The college put a male-appeal spin on the class description, indicating we'd be doing action-adventure and science fiction writing among other genres." She looked at him in appeal. "Let's not talk about the case tonight. I don't even want to think about any of that for the rest of the evening."

"It's a deal," he agreed. "Let's talk about you instead."

"Me?" She looked at him in surprise. "What do you want to know about me?"

"What's your favorite color?"

Ann relaxed at the benign nature of his question. "Yellow," she answered without hesitation.

"Why?"

"Why? I don't know, I guess because to me it implies warmth, dawn...hope." She laughed uneasily. "Is this some sort of a test?"

"Not at all. I just realized after last night I know your body intimately, but don't know much else about you."

Ann felt her blush warm her cheeks. "I could say the same thing about you," she replied, her mind filled with a vision of his nakedness. Yes, she'd learned intimate secrets of his body...the mole that decorated the inside of his thigh, the swirl of hair that covered his chest, the faint appendectomy scar that slashed across his lower abdomen. "What's your favorite color?" she asked, shoving the erotic image out of her head.

"I don't think I have one," he said, then shot her a wicked heated glance, "although at the moment I think my favorite color is orange."

Her blush grew hotter as she realized he was talking about the color of her dress. "You are a tease, Clay Clinton."

"Yeah, I guess I am," he agreed easily.

He pulled into an apartment-complex parking lot and swerved to the curb in front of one of the units. "Wait right here, I'll get Mom."

She watched as he got out of the car and walked up the sidewalk. She would miss him when he left. She'd miss his easygoing demeanor, his quick smile and the desire that lit his eyes when he gazed at her.

Still, she was glad he'd be leaving, that there would be no chance of her seeing his eyes darken with revulsion. She'd never have to tell him about her lost years, never have to confess the black void that was her childhood.

As Clay and his mother came out of the apartment, Ann looked at Mrs. Clinton curiously. With her dark, curly hair and bold features, she looked like an older, feminine version of her son.

Clay opened the back door for his Mom. "Ann, this is my mother, Rosemary. Mom, this is Ann Carson."

Ann turned in her seat and smiled at the older woman. "It's nice to meet you, Mrs. Clinton."

"Please, make it Rosemary. Whenever anyone calls me Mrs. Clinton I look around for my mother-in-law, God rest her soul."

Clay got into the car and slid behind the wheel, then took off. "We're going to my Mom's favorite Italian restaurant."

"Manconni's," Rosemary said to Ann. "Have you ever eaten there?" Ann shook her head. "Oh, the food is to die for. They have the best lasagna I've ever eaten." Rosemary leaned forward. "So, how did you and my son meet?"

"We met through my work, Mom," Clay answered.

"You're a police officer?" Rosemary asked.

"No, I'm a teacher. I teach creative writing," Ann explained.

Rosemary frowned. "The police are taking writing classes? My son, the writer?"

Clay laughed. "No, Mom, Ann isn't teaching writing to the police. She teaches at the community college. I met her because she was having some problems with somebody leaving her anonymous notes."

"Ah." Rosemary patted Ann's arm. "Don't you worry, my son is a good policeman. He'll find whoever is bothering you."

Ann smiled first at Rosemary, then at Clay. "I'm counting on it," she replied.

The rest of the ride to the restaurant was filled with pleasant conversation. Rosemary asked her about her job, they spoke of the weather and before Ann knew it Clay was parking in Manconni's lot.

The interior of the restaurant was dim, tables and hanging greenery arranged for maximum intimacy. They were led to a corner table, upon which a candle burned in the center, creating an inviting, golden glow.

Clay sat next to his mother and across from Ann. Their knees bumped beneath the table and he grinned at her, as if telling her with his gaze that he enjoyed the inadvertent brief contact.

Almost immediately a waitress appeared at their table to take their orders. "Do we need more time?" Clay asked the two women.

"I don't," Rosemary exclaimed. "I know I want the lasagna."

"That sounds good to me," Ann agreed.

Clay ordered for the three of them and the waitress left. Throughout the meal, the pleasant conversation continued. Rosemary kept up a steady stream of talk, regaling Ann with stories of Clay's youth, memories of her husband and humorous descriptions of her bingo buddies.

"My mother is almost as addicted to bingo as she is to talking," Clay said, an amused affection lighting his eyes.

Rosemary cuffed him on the shoulder. "I am not." Her dark eyes, so like Clay's, twinkled merrily. "I like to talk a lot more than I like playing bingo."

As mother and son went back and forth, Ann found herself envying Clay his relationship with his mother. Their intense love for each other was apparent, but beyond that there was also a genuine affection and respect that spoke of a healthy familial connection.

Ann wished she'd had that with her mother. She shoved away thoughts of the sad, dysfunctional woman who'd given her birth, not wanting thoughts of that distant past to taint her pleasant evening with Clay and his mother.

Over coffee, Rosemary turned to Ann. "Has my son told you his plans for retirement?"

"My mother doesn't approve of my plans. She thinks I'm a fool," Clay added.

"That's not true," Rosemary protested. "I know you aren't a fool and that's why I don't understand your foolish plans." She looked at Ann once again. "What do you think of his plans?"

"I think Clay should follow his heart," Ann replied.

"She's just mad because I won't be around to take her out to dinner every week," Clay said.

"That's ridiculous," Rosemary scoffed. "You think you're the only male around who will pay for my dinner?" She smiled coyly, then sobered. "You're too old to be a teenage beach bum, and too young to sit idle for the rest of your life."

"What other male will pay for your dinner?" Clay asked, turning the subject back to her.

Again a coy smile curved her lips. "I have several gentlemen friends who enjoy my company. Unlike you, I don't enjoy living my life alone." Rosemary looked at Ann once again. "Now, dear, tell me about these writing classes of yours."

An hour later, after dropping off his mother at her place,

Clay drove toward Ann's house. "Your mother is wonderful," she said.

He grinned. "She's irrepressible, could talk the ear off an elephant, and is far too meddling, but I love her."

"Does it bother you that she's apparently dating?"

"Not at all. In fact, I'm pleased for her. Dad has been gone a long time and I know she's been lonely. I'll feel better taking off from here knowing she has some other people in her life."

"I imagine your mother doesn't have problems finding friends. She appears to be a very warm, very amicable person."

Clay smiled again. "No, she doesn't have problems making friends. She has a group of women she plays bingo with, another gang who plays bridge. The one thing my mother doesn't lack is friends."

"Thank you for inviting me along this evening," she said as he pulled into her driveway.

"No, thank you for coming." He shut off the engine and turned to her. "If you hadn't been there, I would have had to listen to an hour-long lecture on my ridiculous retirement plans."

"Your mother made it pretty clear she doesn't approve of your plans."

Clay winced slightly. "No, she doesn't. If she had her wish, I'd be married and have half a dozen kids for her to spoil."

"But the nice thing is you know she's going to love you no matter what you do."

"That's true," he agreed. "Come on, I'll walk you to the door."

When they got to her door, Ann fought the impulse to invite him in. She knew she couldn't become too dependent on him, yet wished she could spend another night in his arms, another night of lovemaking. "Good night, Clay. Thanks again."

"You going to be all right for the night?"

She nodded. "I'll be fine."

He leaned forward and kissed her, a kiss of gentleness. "Sweet dreams," he said, then after a lingering touch to her cheek, he turned and went back to his car.

Ann waved to him, then slipped inside her house and locked the door. For a moment she leaned against the door, her mouth still holding the imprint of his lips.

He'd given her a perfect opening for inviting him in. She knew she'd done the right thing in not inviting him to stay with her. It would be far too easy to grow too dependant on him and in a few weeks he would be gone.

She'd never needed anyone before, had never had anyone in her life to be dependant on. She wasn't about to change now; she couldn't afford to care about Clay.

She shoved herself away from the door and went into the living room, a smile curving her lips as she thought of the pleasant evening she'd just shared. She couldn't remember the last time she'd had such a good time. Rosemary had been an absolute delight. Ann felt as if the loving and caring that existed between Clay and his mother had somehow spilled over on her, bathing her in a warm glow.

Stifling a yawn, she headed for the bedroom, but paused as the telephone rang. Without thought, bathed in the residual glow of the evening, she picked up the receiver.

"Ann."

The familiar, yet unfamiliar voice caused a wave of shivers to overtake Ann. "Who...who are you? Why are you doing these things to me?"

"You know who I am, Ann."

"No, I don't. Who are you? For God's sake, what do you want from me?" Ann screamed.

"I just wanted to remind you that your cat has nine lives, but you, sweet Ann, only have one."

Ann sobbed, realizing he'd hung up, and she, too, slammed down the receiver. For just a little while this evening, she'd been able to forget about him and his threats. For several hours she'd felt normal, sane...safe.

Now the horror was back. She moved to the front window and pulled the curtain aside just an inch. She peered out, her heart thudding with painful intensity.

Someplace out there was a madman who wanted her dead.

Chapter 10

Silence can be as terrifying as a scream, Ann thought over the next couple of days. There were no calls, no notes, nothing from her tormentor. Just silence…and a dreadful anticipation of what might come next.

Thursday morning she lay in bed, listening to the sound of raindrops pinging against the window. The rain had begun sometime in the night, a welcome relief after the hot spell of the last several weeks.

Maybe he's gone away, a small voice spoke inside her head, bringing with it a burst of hope. Maybe the ordeal was finally over. Three days of utter silence.

Perhaps the poisoning of Twilight had been the final act of a madman who'd now turned his demented sights to somebody else. Although she hated the thought of another woman having to deal with the madness, she wanted it out of her own life.

A faint scratching sound came from under her bed, and she knew Twilight was waking up. Since she'd brought him home on Tuesday, he'd spent most of his time hiding beneath the bed, obviously traumatized by his ordeal.

It would take time and love to bring him back, to teach him to trust once again. In the meantime Ann had infinite patience when it came to her furry friend.

As she showered and dressed for her day of classes, she remembered it was Tina's day to clean. She'd need to leave a note for the young woman, explaining about Twilight and telling her not to worry about vacuuming beneath her bed.

Driving to the college, the burst of optimism that had greeted her first thing that morning renewed itself, warming her like meeting a long lost friend.

She didn't know whether it was the three days of silence or the sweet, fresh rain that rejuvenated her feeling that perhaps it was all finally over. The rain had brought with it a pleasant drop in temperature, and the scent of a world washed anew.

It was hard to hold on to terror, hang on to fear for an extended period of time. The human spirit could only sustain fright for so long before rebelling. She steadfastly refused to dwell on fear today, instead embracing her feeling of optimism and pulling it into her soul.

Her students seemed to respond positively to the cooler weather and soothing rain. Classes seemed more relaxed, the students in good spirits despite the dreariness of the skies outside.

She let the students of her last class before her dinner break go fifteen minutes early. It was an English Lit class and they had all done their work and turned in their papers. As they left the classroom, she gathered up her things, eager to grab something to eat before her creative writing class began.

"Ms. Carson?"

"Yes?" She looked up to see that the room had emptied and Barry Namath had entered. "Barry." She tried to still the sudden rapidity of her heartbeats. She hadn't seen him since the scene at her house. He hadn't come to class on Tuesday night.

"Can I talk with you for a minute?" he asked, advancing toward her.

She took a step backward, uncomfortable as he moved close

enough to invade her personal space. "What can I do for you?
she asked, refusing to give in to the fear that suddenly winge
through her as she realized how alone she was with him.

"I heard about your cat. I just wanted you to know I ha
nothing to do with that." His features pulled into a tight scow
"I might be capable of doing lots of things, but I could neve
poison no cat."

"I never thought you were responsible, Barry."

"Yeah, well the cops think I did something. Somebody cam
sniffing around my work, checking me out. I just wanted yo
to know I'd never do anything to hurt you."

"Ann."

Both Ann and Barry turned toward the doorway, where Cla
stood, a pulsating tension radiating from him. "Everything a
right in here?" he asked.

Barry stepped back from Ann, his eyes flashing thunderhead
to rival the black clouds outside. "Everything is just fine.
Without waiting for any reply, he turned and left the classroon

"You sure you're all right?" Clay asked, moving closer.

She nodded reassuringly, unsurprised to discover that sh
didn't mind him invading her personal space. "Barry was ju
telling me he had nothing to do with poisoning Twilight." Sh
picked up the last of her papers. "What are you doing here?

"I was in the neighborhood on another call, so thought I'
drop in and see if I could take you to dinner."

Warmth spread through Ann. She hadn't seen him since th
night she'd gone out with him and his mother. Although h
had called her every day, the calls had been brief. "I only hav
about a half an hour before the creative writing class. We coul
get a sandwich in the student union."

"Great, just lead the way."

The rain had slackened to a fine mist as they left the Englis
building and headed for the nearby student union. He walke
with long, confident strides, seemingly unaware that she hurrie
to keep up with him. She could smell his cologne, a wonder
fully familiar scent that mingled with the fresh odor of the rai

nd recalled the sensory pleasures of the night they'd made ove.

She blushed, realizing he'd asked her a question and was vaiting for her answer. "I'm sorry?"

"I asked if you'd heard from the creep again."

She shook her head. "Nothing. Not a word since the night e left the message about Twilight."

They entered the student union and went through the cafe- eria line. Ann grabbed a tuna salad sandwich and Clay chose roast beef. They both got sodas, then made their way to one f the tables that crowded the room.

"I'm beginning to hope that maybe he's moved on," Ann aid, picking up the thread of their conversation as they sat own.

"That would be nice," he replied.

"But you don't think he'll move on."

Clay smiled at her. "I don't know, Ann. I wish I could give ou some answers, but we know nothing about this guy, have o clues as to what makes him tick. It's very possible he'll nove on and you'll never be bothered by him again. Or, it's ossible he'll keep on until—"

"Until?" She swallowed hard against the lump that grew in he back of her throat.

"Until we catch him." He reached across the table and ouched her hand. "Everything else okay? You sleeping all ight?"

She hesitated, then decided to be truthful. "Not really. I've een having nightmares." She looked down at her sandwich, nen back at Clay. "I hate him for bringing back my night- nares." She averted her gaze from him, instead focusing on ne occupants on a nearby table. "It's hard to believe he might e somebody right here, right now in this room."

Clay followed her gaze to the table where several of her reative writing students all sat. Dean Moore was there, along vith Barry Namath and several other men Clay didn't rec- gnize.

"Who's the young blonde?" he asked, noting the skull ta
too decorating the youth's upper arm.

"Warren Taylor. He's a good kid. His mother is a fello
teacher." Ann chewed a bite of her sandwich thoughtfully, the
added, "I like to think that whoever this man is, I don't kno
him personally. He's not one of my students or anyone who'
ever been in my life. He's just some crazy man who saw m
in the grocery store or at the dry cleaners and fixated on m
for some reason."

"Maybe you're right," he agreed easily. "It's very possib
you don't personally know him. We won't know for sure unt
he makes a mistake."

"Will he make a mistake?"

He smiled, his gaze warming her. "They always do, An
Sooner or later they all make mistakes."

Again hope buoyed inside her, like a sailboat refusing to gi
in to a storm. "I think it's over," she said. "It's been fo
days since anything has happened. I think he's moved on, c
grown tired of his sick game."

"I hope you're right. It would be nice to know your life
once again your own when I leave the department."

His words reminded her that she shouldn't get too dependa
on him, couldn't allow him to crawl into her heart. She woul
only be hurt and life had handed her enough hurts already. Sh
certainly didn't intend to set herself up for another one.

She finished her sandwich then looked at her watch. '
should get going. Class starts in ten minutes and the studen
are accustomed to me being there a little early."

He nodded. "I've got to get moving, too. The chief hande
me another case this morning, a shooting that's hot wit
leads." He stood. "I'll walk you to your class."

"I'm glad you stopped by," she said as they walked bac
the way they had come.

"Phone checks are all right, but I wanted to see for myse
that you were doing okay. Make sure you get somebody t
walk with you out to your car after class. I don't want yo
walking alone after dark."

"Tuesday I got campus security to escort me out after class."

"Good. Even though you think things might be over, it's not time to let down your guard."

They paused just outside Ann's classroom. The rain had momentarily halted, although no stars peeked out of the thick clouds overhead. "Thanks for supper," she said.

"You're a cheap date," he returned with a smile. As always, he reached up and touched her cheek, his fingertips warming her skin. "I'll call you later, okay?"

"Okay."

He dropped his hand and left. Ann watched him go, a curious bereavement slicing through her as he disappeared around the corner of the building.

"Careful girl," she whispered to herself. "Hang on to your heart." She had a feeling Clay had purposely reminded her that he was leaving, wanting her to understand yet again that there would be no future, no commitment, no happily-ever-after between the two of them.

Still, was it wrong for her to enjoy his company for as long as he was here? Was it wrong for her to want the comfort, the passion that his embrace inspired? Surely she deserved that, a few weeks of being happy.

Her feeling of optimism continued after class when she got to her car and discovered no note, no threatening message under her windshield wipers.

As she drove home the rain began again. Soft and soothing, it pattered against the windshield in a near-hypnotic rhythm.

Ann had always liked rain. Rainy nights had sometimes brought the only normalcy Ann had ever known in childhood. Rain kept people at home...including mothers.

She shook away thoughts of her past, refusing to be drawn back in time, back to those dark years of fear. She'd survived so much. She was strong and would survive whatever fate threw her way.

The moment she walked into her house the scent of lemon oil and pine cleanser greeted her and she remembered Tina had been there to clean that day. A rivulet of pleasure danced through her. Nothing better than coming home to a sparkling house, knowing she wouldn't have to do any of the cleaning herself at least for a couple of days.

She walked through the living room and into her bedroom where she immediately pulled up the dust ruffle and peered beneath the bed.

Just as she'd expected, Twilight was curled up in the corner his eyes gleaming iridescently from the dark shadows. "Hi baby," she said softly and reached a hand out. He crawled a few inches toward her, licked her extended hand, but refused to budge from his hiding place. "I'm going to put some food out for you. Maybe later you'll feel like coming out and eating."

She stood up and kicked off her shoes. Weariness tugged at her shoulders. It had been a long day and with the gentle rain pattering against the windows, she hoped to get a good night' sleep.

It took her only minutes to change from her day clothes into her nightgown. As the sleek blue silk caressed her body, she thought again of Clay.

Despite the fact that their bodies had seemed made for each other, that he made her smile and she enjoyed his company the fact that he had apparently lived his life so far solely for the purpose of following some dream to live every day as an adventure spoke of how different their goals were in life.

She'd had all the adventure she wanted as a child and what she needed and wanted now more than anything was the security of her home, the knowledge that every morning she'd wake up in the same safe place.

She started to get into bed, then remembered she needed to put out food for Twilight. She left her bedroom and padded into the kitchen.

She turned on the kitchen light, surprised to see Tina's cleaning supplies in the center of the table. That's odd, she thought Why would Tina leave her things here?

As she started around the corner of the island, she saw feet

Tina's familiar red-and-white sneakers. Ann froze. She blinked rapidly, the significance of what she stared at not making sense, refusing to pull into comprehensive focus.

Dread…deep abiding dread she'd never felt before surged inside her. She didn't want to look any further, yet knew she had to.

"Tina?" The name croaked out of her, a whispered plea, an anguished cry. Maybe Tina had passed out, Ann thought. Perhaps she needed help.

The moment Ann stepped around the island, she knew Tina was beyond help. Sprawled stomach down on the floor, the back of her head was bloodied and her face was turned toward Ann. Her eyes were wide open, her features frozen in eternal surprise.

Ann backed away, bile rising in the back of her throat. The sound of harsh breathing and deep moans filled the kitchen and it took a moment for Ann to realize the noises came from her.

Stumbling backward, she ran into the bedroom and grabbed the phone. It wasn't until after she'd made the emergency call that she allowed her screams to escape. And once she started, she wondered if she'd ever stop.

Clay was on his way home from work when he heard the call. Adrenaline pumped through him as he turned around and headed toward Ann's place.

"No," he exclaimed as he screeched around a corner. The call had been a homicide code. It couldn't be Ann. There had to be some sort of mistake. It had to be a mistake, any other thought was unacceptable.

He felt his heartbeat pounding at his temples as he remembered her relaxed features as they'd eaten the sandwiches in the student union. She'd thought it might be over, that the crazy person haunting her might have moved on. Her eyes had shone with a compelling hope, a need to believe that the past three days of silence was a good sign.

"Dammit." He hit the steering wheel, stinging his palm with

the force of the blow. It had to be a mistake. Ann had to be safe.

When he pulled up to her house, the tension increased as he saw the bevy of patrol cars that had already arrived. His heart banged painfully against his ribs as he recognized one of the cars as belonging to the medical examiner.

In one swift motion he parked, left his car and raced to the front door. An officer from his division met him there. "What have you got?" Clay asked tersely.

"Some lady got smacked in the back of the head with a blunt instrument. The medical examiner is in there with her now."

Visceral pain rocked through Clay as he shoved past the officer and into the house. Police officers were everywhere, the sound of their voices aching in Clay's head. He ignored those who greeted him, unable to speak around the lump in his throat.

Instead, on legs that trembled he walked through the living room and into the kitchen. He smelled death before he saw it. The acrid, coppery scent of spilled blood, the odor of life departed, once smelled the odors stayed with you forever.

Her face was turned away from him, but as he saw the spill of blond hair now matted with blood, a moan issued from deep inside him. At that moment he realized just how much he'd grown to care about Ann.

"Clay?"

He turned at the sound of the achingly familiar voice, shock riveting through him as he saw Ann standing in the doorway. "Ann?" Her name came out on a choked, hoarse breath.

"Oh, Clay."

In an instant she filled his arms, warmly alive, sobbing against his chest as her arms clung tightly around his neck. For a moment Clay didn't respond, couldn't make the transition from grief to joy, felt as if he were functioning in a euphoric dream and when he awakened Ann would be dead on the floor.

If it was a dream, he didn't want to wake up. He enfolded her close against his chest, absorbing her sobs into his soul, feeling the warmth of her body that radiated through the nightgown and robe she wore. The sweet scent of her hair filled his senses and he wanted to tangle his hands in it, bury himself in her very aliveness.

A touch on his shoulder brought him back to reality. Ann might be alive and well, but there was a dead woman on her kitchen floor. He disentangled her arms from around his neck and turned to see Ray, face drawn with the familiar look of a cop who had seen too much death.

"Ms. Carson, why don't you come into the bedroom? We need to talk," Ray suggested.

Together Clay and Ann followed Ray to the master bedroom. "Who's the victim?" Clay asked once they were inside the quiet room.

"The cleaning lady," Ray answered.

"Tina. Her name is Tina Mathews." Ann sat down on the edge of the bed and pressed a fist against her mouth. She drew in an audible breath and released it on a tremulous sigh.

"Time of death?" Clay asked his partner.

"The ME says she's been dead at least three to four hours, possibly as long as six," Ray explained. He looked at Ann. "You up to some questions?"

She hesitated, then nodded. Clay sat down next to her. He took her hand in his, unsurprised to find it icy cold. She clung to his hand desperately, as if it were her lifeline to sanity. "I…I'm fine. What do you want to know?"

"What time did you get home this evening?"

"About eight-fifteen…right after my class at the college."

"And what did you do when you got home?"

Ann frowned, as if her memories had all been wiped clean in the moment she'd seen Tina's lifeless body. "I came into the bedroom…changed clothes and got ready for bed. Then I remembered I needed to put some food out for Twilight and I went into the kitchen. That's…that's when I saw her." She closed her eyes, as if to ward off the horror of the vision.

"Did Tina have any relatives?" Ray asked gently.

"An ex-husband, no children. I don't know whether she had a boyfriend or parents." Ann looked at Clay, her eyes hollow and dark. "He thought it was me. He killed her because he thought she was me."

Clay looked at Ray for confirmation. Ray nodded. "He left a message on the answering machine. Called from a pay phone not far from here."

"I want to hear the message," Clay said. His fear for Ann's safety had left him, as had the joy in discovering her alive. Now a simmering rage filled him, a rage directed at a nameless, faceless man who'd stolen a life.

"Why don't you wait here while I play the message for Clay?" Ray suggested. "We'll be back in just a minute or two."

Clay followed his partner back into the living room. "Clay, you've got to help us out here," Ray said. "I think your lady knows more than she's telling."

"What makes you think so?" Clay asked curiously.

"Listen to the message." Ray punched the Play button on the answering machine.

The voice that filled the room could barely be described as human. Deep, crazed with rage, it sent chills up Clay's spine as he listened.

"It's your fault, bitch. I thought she was you. It was supposed to be you. I owe you, and I'll get you. You deserve to die for what you did to me. You hear me? You're going to die. You destroyed my life...now I'm going to take yours."

"See what I mean?" Ray asked as he pushed the Stop button. "This isn't some nut fixated on a stranger. This is a man seeking revenge against Ann because of something she did to him. I'm telling you Ann has the answer to who this guy is, but for some reason she's not telling."

"I'll talk to her," Clay said. "Give us a few minutes alone."

Ray nodded and Clay walked back toward the bedroom, wondering exactly what Ann knew and why she was reluctant to tell.

Chapter 11

Alone in the bedroom, Ann got up from the bed and walked over to the window. She pulled back the curtain and stared into the blackness of the night, a blackness as deep, as profound as her despair.

Tina is dead. Tina is dead. The words reverberated in her head in sharp tones of outrage. How had this happened? Why had this happened?

Tina was dead because she was approximately the same size and shape and had the same shade of hair color as Ann. "It should have been me," she whispered, a new colder breath of horror whispering up her back.

She turned as the door to the bedroom opened and Clay came in alone. "I thought it was over," she said, her voice scratchy from her initial screams and subsequent tears. "I came home so happy because I actually thought it was over. God, how stupid."

He took her hand and led her to the bed where they sat down once again. "Did you listen to the answering machine message?"

She nodded. "I heard it. I'll never forget it. There's so much hatred in his voice." She shivered and drew a deep breath.

"Ann, he says he's paying you back for something you did to him. This is not a stranger fixation or obsession stalking. He's doing these things for revenge. You must know who he is."

She shook her head first slowly, then more vehemently. "But I don't know...I can't imagine." She closed her eyes and drew in a another shuddering breath.

"Ann." He took her hand once again and she looked at him. "You've got to think, you've got to remember anyone in your past who might have some sort of vendetta against you. It could have happened a year ago, five years ago...ten. You might have been a child, a teenager...whatever happened, you have to remember."

She pulled her hand from his and stood up. Belting her robe more tightly around her waist, she walked once again to the window. He had no idea what he was asking.

She'd spent most of her adult life shoving childhood memories to the back recesses of her mind where they could no longer be recalled without enormous effort. Was it possible that buried someplace beneath the dark mist of those memories was the motive for her murder?

Pressing two fingers to her forehead, she turned back to Clay. "If I remembered anything, I'd tell you. I just can't think of anything right now. Every time I close my eyes to think, all I see is Tina sprawled on the floor, staring at me. Her eyes...her eyes..." She swallowed a sob, knowing if she gave in to the despair she'd be lost, would go stark, raving mad.

Clay walked over to her and pulled her to his chest, as if sensing the tenuous grasp she had on sanity. For a long moment she stood in his embrace, her head resting against his broad chest. Neither of them spoke; it was as if both knew no words of comfort could ease the horror.

Ann was vaguely aware of her bedroom door opening, then closing once again. When she finally pulled away from Clay's arms, she saw Raymond standing just inside the door. Dread coursed through her as she saw the tautness of his blunt features.

"Ms. Carson, I've got a dead young woman out there in your kitchen and a message from a man who believes he owes you for something you did to him. I need some answers from you." Raymond's eyes held none of the empathetic light that Clay's did.

"I don't have any answers for you," Ann said, wrapping her arms around herself, wishing herself far, far away from this place.

"Maybe you'd better try harder." Raymond's voice held an edge of harshness. "Somewhere along the line, you've made somebody very angry with you...angry enough to commit murder. You hold the keys to the lock."

Ann closed her eyes, wanting to remember, needing to remember. She owed it to Tina, owed it to the officers who had no other clues but what might be shrouded in the darkness of her past.

She concentrated as hard as she could, but gasped as once again the only image that came to mind was Tina's lifeless body and her wide, staring eyes.

Tears once again burned and oozed down her cheeks. She looked first at Raymond, then at Clay. "I can't...I just can't do this right now. I...I can't think...."

"That's enough for now," Clay said. He placed an arm around Ann once again. "She's had enough for one day," he said firmly to Raymond. "Ann, change your clothes and gather up some things. You can't stay here tonight."

Once again Ann had the feeling she was swimming in a sea of thick, deep liquid, functioning in a foggy landscape where reality was slightly skewed. Nothing seemed real. Nothing felt real. She knew it was shock flirting with her, but she fought against it as she packed a suitcase.

Clay and Raymond left the room and she changed from her nightgown and robe into a pair of slacks and a blouse, then threw the nightgown into the awaiting suitcase.

She'd bought this condo wanting a home to call her own, a

place where she'd always feel safe and secure. Now the safety had been breached, the ugliness and insanity of the world had crept in and she knew this place would never be home again.

A soft knock fell on the door. "That it?" Clay asked as he came back in.

"Except Twilight." She snapped the suitcase closed. "It might take me a minute or two to get him out from under the bed." She bent down and tried to coax the cat out from his hiding place, but Twilight refused to budge.

"Let me try," Clay suggested. He leaned down and talked softly to the cat. To Ann's surprise, within minutes he had Twilight out from beneath the bed and in his arms. He handed her the cat, then picked up her suitcase and looked at Raymond. "I'll let you know in the morning where she is," he said.

Raymond nodded curtly. "We need some answers, Clay. This isn't just about nasty notes anymore."

"He's angry with you," Ann said as they left the house.

"Nah, he's frustrated and when Raymond gets frustrated he gets a little testy."

"Clay, I want to help. I really do...I just can't think right now. Everything is muddled in my head."

He took her arm and guided her toward his car. "It's okay, Ann. You've had a bad shock. Give yourself a little time."

He opened the passenger car door and ushered her in, then went around to the driver door. "Where are you taking me? A hotel?" she asked once he was behind the wheel and had started the engine.

He turned and looked at her. "How about my mother's? You'll be safe there, and you won't be alone."

"Oh, Clay, I don't want to intrude on your mother's life."

"Ann, trust me on this. At least for the next day or two, it's the best place for you to be. She won't mind and I don't want you to be alone."

Nor did she want to be alone. It felt as if she'd been alone from the moment of birth and she ached with the need to be held, to be nurtured, to feel safe. She hugged Twilight against her breast, her fingers curling in the soft fur.

"You okay?"

She gave him a shaky smile. "Not really, but I will be."

His hand found hers on the seat between them and he squeezed it gently. She curled her fingers around his and closed her eyes. She knew why Twilight had come to Clay from beneath the bed. It was the same reason she was so drawn to him.

He was attractive physically, but that had little to do with the attraction. He had the spirit of a healer, the soul of the pure and good. Twilight had recognized it, and so did Ann.

Clay relinquished his hold on her hand to navigate the turn into the apartment complex where his mother lived. He pulled up against the curb, then got out and walked around to open the door for Ann.

The apartment door flew open as they approached. "Mom, I've got a favor to ask you," Clay began. "Ann needs a place to stay."

Rosemary opened the door and ushered them inside. "Well, of course she can stay here. What a fine kitty." She scratched Twilight behind his ear, then touched Ann's cheek gently. "You're welcome in my home as long as you need to stay."

Within minutes Rosemary had shown Ann to the spare bedroom. Ann remained in the room, unpacking a few things and giving Clay some time alone to explain the situation to his mother.

Twilight prowled the perimeters of the small room, then as if giving it his stamp of approval, he jumped up on the bed and curled into a ball.

"I see Twilight is settling in just fine," Clay said from the doorway. "Mom went next door to borrow some kitty litter from Mrs. Talbot. Mrs. Talbot has cats."

"I can't thank you or your mother enough. It's so kind of her to open her house for me."

Clay grinned. "Mom loves company. She should be thanking you." His smile faded. "As soon as Mom gets back I'm going to take off."

"You're going back to my house?"

He nodded. "You should cancel classes for a while," h
suggested.

"I can't do that," she protested. "I won't do that. My stu
dents depend on me, they've paid money for their courses
We're almost halfway through the semester. If I cancel classe
now they get stuck with a substitute who has no idea what I'v
been doing." More than that, Ann couldn't imagine sitting da
after day with nothing to do but think.

"At least cancel them for tomorrow," Clay urged. "We'
need you for more questioning and that will put us into th
weekend. We'll figure out where to go from there later."

"Okay." She sighed tremulously.

"Get some sleep, Ann. And if you think of anything, re
member anything at all that might be important, call me."

"I knew Gloria would have what we needed," Rosemar
said as she entered the room carrying a litter box. "I'll just pu
it here in your bathroom." She disappeared into the smal
adjoining bathroom, then returned a moment later. "Gloria als
gave me several cans of food, so this baby is all set." Sh
petted Twilight. "He looks like a noble warrior of life
wounded, but still with plenty of spirit."

Ann smiled. "Yes, that's what I've always thought."

Rosemary gave Twilight a final scratch, then moved to th
doorway. "What you need dear, is a good night's sleep. Clay
no more questions for tonight. Let her rest."

Clay nodded. "Good night Ann. I'll see you in the morn
ing."

Together mother and son left the room, closing the doo
behind them. For a moment Ann fought an impulse to run afte
them, not wanting to be left alone, afraid of where her though
would carry her.

She changed into her nightgown and got into bed. She didn
turn out the overhead light, didn't want to be alone in the dar
Closing her eyes, she thought once again of Tina.

The killer had sneaked up behind her, assuming Tina wa
Ann. "Who wants me dead?" she asked softly. What had sh
done to warrant such hatred?

If she had the answers at all, they were trapped in the swirling mists of her forgotten youth. Sooner or later she was going to have to plumb those dark depths of the past.

The thought terrified her.

By the time Clay got back to Ann's house, most of the other cops had left and Tina Mathews's body had been removed. He found Raymond at the kitchen table, taking notes and sipping coffee from a foam cup. He looked up as Clay sat down in the chair next to him, a frown furrowing his broad brow.

"I can tell you how he got in. I can tell you what the murder weapon was, but I can't tell you another damn thing. This guy is too good to be true. No fingerprints, no trace evidence, not a single clue that's been found so far."

"How did he get in?" Clay asked.

"Spare bedroom window. He cut out just enough screen and glass to be able to unlock it, open it and crawl in." He took a sip of his coffee, then continued. "I've got guys out canvassing the neighborhood, but so far nobody saw or heard anything."

"I feel like we're chasing a ghost," Clay said.

"It wasn't Casper who snuck in here and used a baseball bat on that poor woman. We've got a sick bastard out there, and I hope you don't intend to interfere with the investigation."

Clay looked at his friend sharply. "Since when do you worry about me interfering with an investigation?"

"Since you're sleeping with one of the material witnesses. You *are* sleeping with her, aren't you?"

Heat rushed over Clay's face. "She isn't a material witness, she's a victim." Clay intentionally didn't answer the question.

"Still, you were out of line pulling her out of here. I might have been able to break her."

"You were going to break her all right, and drive her right into shock where she couldn't be any help to anyone." Clay leaned back in his chair, thinking of what Raymond accused him of. Had he hurried Ann out of here because of his personal relationship with her? No. He would have reacted to any victim in the same way.

He leaned toward Raymond once again. "You were pushing too hard, buddy. You were treating her like a perpetrator, not a victim. She'd just found a dead body in her kitchen. You remember the way you felt when you saw your first dead body?"

Raymond sighed and raked a hand through his thinning hair. "You're right," he finally said grudgingly. "I was pushing too hard. But I can't help it. I've got the feeling she knows more than she's telling. I don't know, maybe she's protecting somebody."

"But who?"

"I don't know, an old boyfriend, a former student."

Raymond paused a moment to take another sip of his coffee. He put the cup back on the table and massaged his brow thoughtfully. "I just get the feeling the lady is hiding something. My instincts say she's got secrets that she's not telling."

Unease stirred inside Clay. He'd thought the same thing, had seen the whisper of secrets in the depths of her eyes. What were those secrets and did they hold the answers to what was happening now?

They were at Ann's house for several more hours, then finally left it with crime tape flapping in the early morning breeze.

Clay's eyes were gritty with lack of sleep as he drove home. Although he was exhausted, his mind still raced with questions. Who was this madman? What was his relationship to Ann?

Ann. Thoughts of her swirled in his head. The sweet taste of her lips, the warmth and beauty of her skin, the passion she'd exhibited when making love...all these things had indelibly marked his heart.

He'd spent the past week since making love to her attempting to gain some distance, keeping his contact with her brief and public. In four weeks he'd be gone and Ann would only be a pleasant memory. But before he left the department, before he even contemplated his own future, he needed to make certain Ann's future was guaranteed to be free of the monster who threatened her.

* * *

He'd killed the wrong woman and now Ann had moved out of her house. He parked down the street, close enough to see the yellow tape that crossed her front door. The early morning sun peeked over the treetops and sent out shafts of light that reflected off her windows.

He tightened his fingers around the steering wheel, thinking of that moment when he'd realized the woman in the kitchen wasn't Ann. Of course, by then it had been too late. He'd already plowed her in the back of the head.

It had been a stupid mistake on his part. An instance of blood lust overcoming rationality. He should have known Ann wouldn't be home in the middle of the day. He knew her schedule backward and forward.

He'd come to her house to leave a note, post a message, but instead he'd peeked in the window and saw the blond in the kitchen and all rational thought had fled beneath the fury of his need for final revenge.

Now Ann was gone.

He released his grip on the steering wheel and put the van into drive. It wouldn't do for him to be seen lingering in the area. Besides, he had work to do.

There was no doubt in his mind that he'd find her once again. Wherever she hid, whatever hole she'd crawled into, he'd find her. He knew the answer to her whereabouts rested with the cop. Clay Clinton.

He smiled. It was just a matter of time. He'd find her and when he did she would get no more second chances.

Chapter 12

"**I**'ve made us a nice cup of tea," Rosemary said as sh[e] came into the living room where Ann was curled up on th[e] sofa reading a magazine article.

"That sounds wonderful." Ann smiled affectionately at th[e] older woman and stood up to follow her into the kitchen. I[n] the last three days it had become a habit to share a cup of te[a] every afternoon before Rosemary started cooking dinner.

She slid into a chair at the table. "Clay told me you alway[s] gave him hot tea when he was sick and now he refuses to drin[k] it."

Rosemary laughed, her eyes twinkling merrily. "I only r[e-] member giving him hot tea once and if my memory serves m[e] right, it was heavily laced with honey and he loved it." Rose[-] mary shook her head ruefully. "I guess we all have a tendenc[y] to rewrite our childhoods in some way or another."

Ann didn't say anything. How she wished she'd had th[e] ability to rewrite hers. She'd opted for forgetting as much [of] it as possible instead.

"You like my son," Rosemary said.

"Yes, I do." Ann smiled. "You must be very proud of him. He's a good man."

"Ah, I'd like to wring his neck, knock some sense into him. This plan of his, this retirement dream, is crazy. Sheer nonsense. But, children rarely listen to their mothers." She eyed Ann slyly. "However, he might listen to you."

"Oh, no." Ann held up her hand in protest. "You aren't going to get me involved in this."

"But you're already involved, aren't you?" Rosemary's eyes held the wisdom of age, the cognizance of human emotion.

Ann shifted positions, uncomfortable beneath Rosemary's scrutiny. "I can't pretend that I don't care about Clay, but I also know he has to follow his heart, and his heart is set on leaving the police department to live a life that I can't live."

Rosemary squeezed a slice of lemon into her tea. "I'd hoped Clay would find a nice woman, settle down and have some children. That had been his dream until his father died, then everything changed for Clay." She frowned thoughtfully. "I'm not sure what happened then, but that's when he developed this harebrained retirement plan."

"But if it's what will make him happy…"

"What worries me is not so much that Clay wants to go to Hawaii and live a hand-to-mouth existence. I know my son. He'll tire of that soon enough and will find something else exciting and profitable to do with his time."

Rosemary paused to sip her tea. "What bothers me is his choice to remain unattached. I worry about him one day waking up old and lonely." Her eyes twinkled once again. "Oh, I know, you're thinking I'm old and alone, but I'm lucky. I have memories of a wonderful love to fill the lonely hours of my life. I want my son to experience that same kind of love." She frowned wryly. "Listen to me, I sound like a meddling old woman."

Ann reached over and touched her hand. "No, you sound like a loving, caring mother."

"What about your mother, Ann?"

"She's gone. She died when I was fifteen."

"Oh, honey, that's so sad. Who raised you?"

"I raised myself." Ann leaned back in her chair, remembering the day her mother died, the curious absence of grief that had haunted her ever since. "We had no family, no friends, nobody to even tell social services I existed."

"But how did you live?"

"I got lucky. I got a job at a family-owned pizza place. The owner, Mr. Carsetti, never asked me what my situation was or how old I was, and I never offered the information." She faltered, wondering if she was sharing too much, but Rosemary's eyes urged her on.

"Mr. Carsetti gave me a job and let me sleep in the back room. I went to school during the days and worked at night. I was lucky enough to get a scholarship to college. Finished my degree and here I am." Ann blushed, realizing she'd said far too much. But the brief time she'd spent with Rosemary had made her feel comfortable with the older woman.

"I don't think luck had anything to do with any of it," Rosemary said. "Strength and courage…that's what got you here." Rosemary stood and pulled Ann up from her chair. "I think you need a good hug," she said as she wrapped Ann in a loving embrace. Ann closed her eyes, breathing in the older woman's sweet lavender scent, enjoying the maternal feel of the arms that surrounded her. "Your mother would have been very proud of you," she said softly.

Tears burned at Ann's eyes, tears for the little girl she had been who'd never known the warmth of a maternal embrace, and tears because she knew Rosemary was wrong. Her mother wouldn't have been proud. Her mother wouldn't have cared.

"No matter what my knuckleheaded son does, when this mess of yours is over and he's gone to his paradise, you and I will remain friends, right?" She released Ann as the telephone rang. "Sit, drink your tea before it gets cold," she exclaimed as she hurried to pick up the phone.

Ann sank back down, her heart still warmed with the physical pleasure of Rosemary's hug. She stirred her tea and sipped it, half listening to Rosemary's end of the conversation.

"I'm sorry…I don't understand. Who told you this?" Rosemary's forehead wrinkled in consternation. "Well, there's been some sort of mistake. No, nobody here."

She hung up the phone and returned to her chair at the table. "That was odd."

"What?" Ann looked at her curiously.

"That was Barrows Funeral Home. Somebody called them and told them somebody here will be needing their assistance in the very near future, that someone in the household doesn't have long to live."

Ann's throat closed up as icy fingers walked up and down her spine. A roar resounded in her ears as her blood rushed both hot and cold within her. "It's him," she said. Her cup rattled against the saucer as she set it down. "He knows I'm here."

She stood, fear pressing against her chest, making it difficult to breathe, more difficult to think. She had to do something…go somewhere. "I…I've got to leave here." She started blindly for the door.

"Ann, wait." Rosemary approached her. "Honey, it's probably just a crazy mistake. They transposed the numbers or something." She followed Ann through the living room. "Come back and drink your tea."

"It's no mistake. He knows I'm here. He's toying with me." Ann went into the bedroom and pulled her suitcase out of the closet. Opening it in the center of the bed, she tried to keep her mind on the matters at hand, tried to shove away the fear that gnawed at her insides. If she allowed the fear to take hold, she'd be paralyzed, unable to make a single move. And she had to move…for her sake, but most importantly for Rosemary's sake.

"I'm calling Clay," Rosemary said and hurried out of Ann's room.

What kind of a monster was this man? Ann thought as she methodically folded her clothes into the suitcase. What kind of a mind did it require to think about having a funeral home call to taunt his next intended victim? Sick and evil.

She frowned, realizing her hands weren't working right, were shaking too hard to neatly fold her clothes. She laced her fingers together and closed her eyes, taking deep breaths to try to regain control.

Control. There had been a time she'd thought she had it. She'd overcome so many things to finally establish herself, her life, and now in the blink of an eye it had all been destroyed.

The home she'd worked so hard to build was no longer a safe haven. She wouldn't be able to live there anymore. Never again would she be able to walk into the kitchen and not see the horrifying vision of Tina's lifeless body.

She sank down on edge of the bed, hands still tightly linked together. She should have known. She should have known it was all too good to be true.

By all rights she should never have survived her childhood. It was as if fate had allowed her to endure solely for some perverse amusement. She'd survived, had begun to build a good life, and now it was all being stripped away piece by piece.

She'd cheated death years ago, and now it had come looking for her. She got up, a sense of urgency burning inside her. Finish packing and get out of here, a voice screamed inside her head.

"Ann."

She jumped and whirled around to see Clay standing in the doorway. "Don't sneak up on me like that," she snapped, then turned back to her task.

"What are you doing?"

"I'm packing."

"Why? Where do you intend to go?"

Ann smoothed a wrinkle from a blouse and added it to the pile of clothing in the suitcase. "I don't know where I'll go. I just know I can't stay here."

"Ann, stop for a minute. You're not thinking straight." He attempted to take her hands in his.

She pushed away from him. "You're right, I'm probably not thinking straight. All I know is that he knows I'm here, Clay. Somehow, someway he's found me."

"Ann, there's no reason to run."

"There's every reason to run," she said, her voice raised with an edge of hysteria. "I've already got one death on my conscience." She drew in a deep breath, then sank down on the edge of the bed and looked at Clay. "In the middle of last night, your mother crept into my room to put a blanket on me. She was afraid I'd be cold before morning."

She averted her gaze from him, unwilling to tell him how deeply his mother's simple action had touched her. Somebody who'd had that kind of caring all their life would never be able to understand the deep, aching hole the absence of such love created.

"Ann, my mother is a strong woman. She knows what's going on. Besides, there's no way I'd let anyone harm you or her."

"Like you didn't allow anyone to harm Tina?" She sighed and tucked a strand of hair behind her ear. "I'm sorry. That wasn't fair."

"No, it wasn't."

She stood once again and resumed her packing. "This man wants to destroy my life, take away everything I care about. He'd kill your mother and not blink an eye if he thought her death would hurt me. I can't take the chance, Clay. Not with your mother. She's been too kind to me. I couldn't live with myself if something happens to her."

This time it was Clay's turn to sit down on the edge of the bed. "I can't exactly get upset with you for wanting to protect my mother." She nodded and closed the suitcase. "Okay." He stood up and raked a hand through his hair. "I'll take you to my place."

She looked at him in surprise. "I thought I'd go to a hotel."

Clay shrugged. "If that's what you want. But this guy is good, Ann. He found you here and there's no reason to think he won't find you in some hotel. At least at my place he'll have to come through me.''

Ann hesitated. She didn't know what to do, what was best. "I don't know...I don't know what to do.''

"Ann, stay with me. It's the smartest thing to do.''

"Okay.'' The moment she agreed, Ann felt an overwhelming sense of peace coupled with a distressing sense of dread.

She knew she was falling in love with Clay and spending any more time with him would simply nurture the emotion already taking seed. He'd be gone in four weeks, out of the mainland, out of her life. Still, the thought of staying in a strange hotel room alone terrified her. She was grateful to be going home with him, but somehow, she had the feeling that in assuring her physical safety, she was about to sacrifice her heart.

Clay drove for an hour before finally pulling into his parking space at his apartment complex. He'd taken little-traveled streets, doubled back on his route and kept an eye on his rearview mirror to make certain they weren't followed.

Ann remained silent throughout the drive, Twilight in her lap. It wasn't until he shut off his car engine that she turned and looked at him, her eyes wide and luminous in the early evening light. "Do you think he'll find me here?''

Clay hesitated before answering, trying to gauge just how much she could handle. "Probably,'' he admitted. "Although it will take him a little time.''

"How do you think he knew I was at your mother's?''

"Who knows. Maybe he followed us the night I took you there, or perhaps he knows I'm in charge of your case and so decided to check the Clintons in the phone book. My mother is listed, but I'm not.''

"I hate this,'' she said suddenly, her voice filled with suppressed anger. "Running. Hiding. Looking over my shoulder. I hate feeling like a displaced person, without a home.'' Her eyes flashed with a bright spark of anger. "I hate what this monster has done to my life.'' The anger burned brightly for a moment, then faded, leaving the blue of her eyes dull and lifeless.

"Come on, let's get you inside. You'll feel better after tasting my hamburgers and home-style fries."

"You cook?"

"Yup. Hamburgers and home-style fries, that's pretty much the extent of my culinary expertise." He smiled, a gesture he hoped would reassure her, put the sparkle back in her eyes.

She smiled back, but it lacked heart. She looked beaten, hollowed out by the events of the last weeks. More than anything Clay wanted a moment alone with her monster, a moment to extract his own particular brand of vengeance.

"I'd better warn you," he said a moment later as he unlocked his front door. "This isn't exactly the Ritz."

"Yes, but the rent is just perfect." She touched his arm in appeal. "Please don't apologize for your home. I'm grateful you're opening the door to me."

Class. The woman definitely had class, Clay thought as he ushered her inside. Immediately he saw the place through her eyes. Functional furniture with no distinctive color or style. The kitchen area emitted no aura of warmth, nothing but stark serviceability. A temporary holding tank for a man without a life, Clay thought with sudden insight. Irritated by his thoughts, he swept a stack of newspapers off the sofa and gestured for her to have a seat.

"I'll just put your suitcase in the bedroom," he said, then disappeared into the adjoining small room. When he returned, Ann and Twilight had made themselves at home on the sofa.

"Clay, I can sleep here," Ann said. "I don't want to take your bed."

"I insist. Besides, most nights I fall asleep here on the sofa anyway." He clapped his hands together, summoning a burst of enthusiasm. "And now, to create my masterpiece meal."

Ann followed him to the kitchen area, separated from the living room by a bar with two stools. "What can I do to help?" she asked.

"There's a bottle of wine in the fridge. Pour us each a glass, then sit your bottom on one of those stools and watch a master chef at work.''

She smiled at him, apparently realizing he was working hard for just that effect. As she poured the wine, Clay got out the pound of hamburger and began to form patties.

''Good wine,'' she said as she took a sip and sat back down on the stool to watch him work.

''Yeah, I'm not much of a drinker, but I've always enjoyed a glass of wine to unwind after work.''

As Clay prepared their meal, their conversation remained light. They didn't talk about monsters, didn't speak about fear or the events that had brought her to his house.

Instead they talked about living in Kansas City, about the crazy midwestern weather, and how neither one of them had ever missed living in a bigger, more cosmopolitan city.

Their pleasant conversation continued as they ate. The hamburgers were juicy and full of flavor and the French fries were spicy with a blend of mysterious seasonings. The wine was sweet and chilled, and Ann knew she was drinking more than she should. But, each glass soothed frayed nerves and chased the edge of fear further away.

''You cooked, I'll wash,'' she said as they cleared the table.

''Okay,'' he agreed easily. ''I'll dry.''

Standing at the sink with Clay at her side as they washed and dried the dishes, Ann felt the magical pull of the moment. Anyone peeking in the window would assume they were husband and wife.

And if they were husband and wife, they'd finish doing the dishes, enjoy another couple of hours of talk, then go to bed together. They would make love, then fall asleep and perhaps dream of the children they would have, the future they would share.

Merely an illusion, she reminded herself. She and Clay were not husband and wife, would never share a future together. They wanted different things, needed different things.

''Why don't we take our wine and sit on my patio, watch

the sun go down?'' Clay suggested when they'd finished the dishes.

''That sounds nice.''

Evening shadows were just starting to fall as they sat down at the small table on Clay's patio. The western sky was ablaze with colors. Deep hues of pink and orange decorated the horizon, as if in gasping its final breath daylight had decided to leave with a spectacular final show.

''It's beautiful, isn't it?'' Clay said as if reading her thoughts.

''Gorgeous.'' She settled back in the chair, feeling loose and more relaxed than she had in days. ''I used to hate sunsets.''

''Why?'' He looked at her curiously.

She eyed the glorious sky. ''Sunsets mean the coming of night, and night always frightened me as a child.''

''I think most kids at one time or another are scared of the dark.''

She smiled. ''I suppose.'' She ran a finger around the rim of her glass, then took another drink. How could she tell him it wasn't the dark that frightened her, but the things that happened in the dark.

They both fell silent. As the quiet stretched between them it didn't grow awkward or uncomfortable, rather it became companionable, pleasant. The sun dipped down below the horizon and darkness descended quickly. Insects began their nightly chorus and in the distance a dog barked. Still they remained, drinking their wine and enjoying the quiet togetherness.

With the sun down, the temperature dropped into a comfortable zone as a light cool breeze appeared. As the breeze caressed Ann's skin, she found herself thinking of Clay's caresses. She wished they would go inside and make love once again. But she knew that particular wish was a foolish one.

''I'm going to have to move,'' she said, her thoughts skipping like a stone thrown across the surface of a pond. ''When this is all over I'll have to find another place to live. I don't think I'll ever be able to stay a night in the condo again.''

"Maybe you'll feel differently when this man is caught and put behind bars."

She looked at him, noting how his features had become obscured by the night shadows. "Your partner is still angry with me, isn't he?"

"Raymond thinks you know more than you're telling."

"And what do you think?"

"I think we should go inside now. It's getting late."

Yes, it was getting late and Ann had consumed far too much wine. She needed to go to bed, needed to stop thinking of being held in Clay's arms. "Yes, and I'm exhausted," she agreed.

"It will just take me a minute or two to get some blankets and a pillow from the bedroom, then it's all yours," he said once they were back inside.

"While you're doing that I'll just change into my nightclothes." She picked up her suitcase and went into the bathroom. It smelled of Clay. His aroma seemed to permeate the room, the scent of spicy cologne, of clean maleness.

Unpacking her nightgown and robe, she tried not to think about Clay. The single night they'd shared had been more than enough to convince her that he was a threat to her well-being, a hazard to the health of her heart.

Changed into her gown and robe, she left the bathroom, bumping into Clay as he came out of the bedroom. "Sorry." She blushed as they maneuvered around each other, her hands touching his chest, his brushing her thighs in the process.

After what seemed like an eternity, they managed to get past each other. "I put clean sheets on the bed. Let me know if you need anything," he said, his eyes simmering with an emotion that caused Ann's blood to heat.

I need you. I want you. The words teased on the tip of her tongue, but she bit down on them and swallowed. "Thank you, I'll be fine. Good night, Clay," she said, then turned and went into the bedroom.

Twilight was already there, curled up on the pillows as if he'd lived there all his life. In the past couple of days, between

Rosemary's loving care and the element of time, Twilight had come around, acting more like he had before the poisoning.

He meowed a complaint as she scooted him over to one side of the bed. "Come on, sweetie, you have to share," she said. Once beneath the sheets, she looked around the room curiously.

As with the living room, this room held little essence of the man who slept here. No personal photos, no special mementoes anywhere, just the bed, the dresser and the nightstand with a metal lamp. With a sigh, Ann reached over and turned off the lamp, plunging the room into darkness.

She closed her eyes, willing sleep to come. Instead she realized she'd been wrong. Clay's essence was everywhere in the room. His familiar scent lingered in the air, and she had the crazy feeling his dreams were trapped in the softness of the pillow.

"Get a grip," she whispered to herself, fighting a wave of yearning so great it nearly stole her breath away. She turned over on her side and hugged the spare pillow close to her chest, but still the ache resounded deep within her.

She replayed that moment in the hallway, when Clay's eyes had flared with desire. He wanted her. She wanted him. But it was crazy to continue, crazy to allow her heart to get anymore involved with him. Still, she couldn't simply shut off her desire for him like turning off the faucet on a sink. But, she could turn off his.

It was easy to do. She'd done it with Greg. All she had to do was tell Clay the sordid details of her past. He believed her past held the secret to the identity of her tormentor. She knew her past only held pain.

In sharing that pain, she had a feeling Clay would never again look at her with eyes filled with desire. And surely that would make her desire for him die.

Before she could change her mind, before giving herself a chance to lose her nerve, she flipped on the lamp and got out of bed. She pulled on her robe and left the room.

"Clay?" She peeked into the living room, where he lay on

the sofa, the lamp next to him on and the television barely
audible.

"Yeah." He sat up, his chest bare, a sheet covering the
lower half of his body. He punched the Mute button on the
remote.

She nearly faltered. His chest looked so broad, so strong and
her fingers remembered exactly how it felt, so warm and sexy.
She drew in a deep breath and crossed the room to sit on the
overstuffed chair next to the sofa. "I want to talk to you."

"Okay." He started to rise, the sheet gripped around his
waist.

"No, please. Stay where you are," she protested. "Just relax."

"Ann, what's going on? What do you want to talk about?"

She curled up in the chair and wrapped her arms around
herself. "Raymond thinks I'm hiding something in my past.
He's right, although it's not the identity of the man who's after
me." She frowned, knowing she wouldn't be able to tell him
her secrets with the light shining on her face. "Could you shut
off the lamp and the television?"

Two clicks and the room fell into darkness. Ann cleared her
throat, wondering where to begin. "My mother died in my
arms when I was fifteen. Acute alcoholism. That was the end
of the nightmare I called my childhood."

"Ann, you don't have to do this if you don't want to."

"Yes, I do. I want you to understand that I'm not intentionally hiding any important clues, not withholding information
that might help you find this man." More than this, she knew
it was the easiest way to erect a barrier, keep her safe from
falling any more deeply in love with Clay.

She pulled her legs up beneath her and collected her
thoughts. "My mother loved three things—singing, drinking
and men. She insisted she was going to be the next Dolly Par-
ton."

"Was she any good?" Clay asked softly.

"She sang like an angel when she wasn't drinking. Unfortunately, those times were rare." For a moment Ann tilted her

head, her memory bringing the sound of her mother's voice back like a distant sweet echo. The memory faded, usurped by unpleasant reverberations from the past, her mother screaming in rage, crying in torrents, laughing hysterically.

She shook her head slightly to rid it of those particular details. "We lived in a variety of horrid motels and in the back rooms of bars. When I went to sleep at night, I never knew where I'd be or what I'd find the next morning." She rubbed her shoulders, seeking warmth from the cold chill of her memories.

"I believed if I was good enough, smart enough, Mom would eventually stop drinking and be a real mother to me. It never happened." She paused a moment, taking a step deeper into the mists of the past, knowing what she'd told him so far was only the beginning.

"Clay, I can't tell you for sure if there's somebody in my past who might want to seek revenge on me. I spent a long time trying to forget those years and I finally managed to suppress them into a place where they aren't easily retrieved anymore. There were men in my mother's life, usually mean drunks."

Alone in a dark room, the scent of stale liquor and mustiness permeating throughout. She curled into the corner of the bed and watched as the door slowly creaked open. "Mommy?" Her voice echoed off the dirty walls. It wasn't her mother. The shadow that moved toward her was too tall, too broad to be her mother.

She squeezed her eyes tightly closed to dispel this particular disturbing memory. She didn't remember what happened after the door closed behind him, knew it was one of the memories she'd shoved into the darkest recesses of her mind. She drew in a deep breath and released it on a mournful sigh. "There are things in my past that I don't want to ever remember, but I can't imagine there being a man I somehow wronged. I was powerless, the adults in my life had all the power."

"And abused it." The lamp clicked on.

Ann shielded her eyes from the glare with the back of her

hand. "Don't..." She protested the light, preferring the anonymity of darkness.

"Why?" Clay left the sofa and knelt at the edge of her chair. "What are you afraid I'll see?"

She shrugged, wrung out by her foray into the past, too exhausted to hide the resulting emotions that still flooded her.

"Ann, let me tell you what I see." He cupped her face in his hands, his eyes compelling her to look at him. "I see a strong, beautiful woman who survived horrors and thrived in spite of her childhood."

His thumbs caressed her cheeks. "I see a courageous woman who was once a victim, a survivor who had become a vital, passionate, caring woman."

Tears blurred her vision of him, cathartic tears of release. She'd told him more, far more than she'd told Greg, but Clay hadn't turned away. His face came closer to hers and his lips touched hers in a kiss of such sweetness, such gentleness, her heart convulsed in her chest.

Ann wrapped her arms around him, realizing her plan to emotionally push him away had backfired. She'd survived a hellish childhood filled with emotional and physical abuse. She hoped she was strong enough to survive the futility of loving Clay.

Chapter 13

Dawn chased the night shadows out of the bedroom, washing the room in the pale golden light of a new day. Clay watched daybreak claim the room. His arm was sound asleep, trapped beneath Ann as she slept, but he was reluctant to move.

They'd not made love the night before, but rather had talked as he'd held her in his arms. She'd given him more pieces to her past, snippets of information that horrified him and filled him with compassion. He was humbled by her strength, her will to survive and the way she'd managed to put the past behind and move on with her life.

He turned his head and looked at her. In sleep her features were soft, almost angelic as the morning light bathed her face. His heart convulsed as he thought of the child she had been, the experiences she'd suffered with her mother.

He now understood her need to lock her bedroom door each night before going to sleep. He now understood her lack of intimate friends, the need to keep herself protected from any more hurt. She had suffered the ultimate betrayal in not being able to trust her mother to keep her safe.

For Clay, it was impossible to imagine a childhood where he would not have been able to depend on his mother. Rosemary had meant stability, unconditional love, and from the moment of birth he'd trusted her to nurture him.

In his job, Clay saw the results of poor parenting and dysfunctional childhoods every day. By all percentages, Ann should have become an alcoholic, a drug user, a criminal. He admired the fact that she'd been smart enough to use education to climb out of the muck of her past.

More than anything, Clay wanted to give her back her safety, return to her the life she'd worked so hard to achieve. He needed to find the man who was after her, and he needed to do it in the next four weeks. When he left for Hawaii, he wanted to know Ann was all right.

And he couldn't do it lingering in bed. He suddenly felt the pressure of time running out. His time on the job was winding down. He'd disposed of all his cases except this one. Twenty-seven days to find a madman.

He gently withdrew his arm from beneath Ann's neck, stifling a groan as the needles and pins sensation indicated the return of blood flow.

Her eyelids fluttered, then opened as he sat up on the edge of the bed. "Sorry," he apologized. "I didn't mean to wake you."

"That's okay." She stretched like a languid cat and shoved a cloud of hair away from her face. "What time is it?"

"Early. Only six-thirty. Go back to sleep."

"No, I've got to get up and get ready for work."

Clay frowned. "Ann, can't you take a leave of absence or something until this is all under control?"

"No." She sat up and grabbed for her nightgown strap as it slid off her creamy shoulder. Her gaze held no indecision, no wavering of emotion. "He's taken away too much from me already. I won't let him take away my work. It's all I have left." She held up a hand to still Clay's protest. "I'm surrounded by people at the college. You've told me again and again this man is smart. Surely he's smart enough to know if he tries anything there he'll be seen.''

Her strap slipped again, giving him a tantalizing view of the curve of her breast. He averted his gaze, trying to keep his mind on her safety, not on her sweet, unconscious sexiness.

"Clay, I'll be far safer at work than I would be here alone all day."

He raked a hand through his hair, realizing she was probably right. "Okay, but only if you let me take you and pick you up."

"I can't let you do that," she protested. "You have a job to do."

"And you're my job." He stood. "Give me ten minutes to shower and shave, then the bathroom is all yours."

A job, he reminded himself a few moments later as he stood beneath the shower spray. She's just a job. Protect and serve, then get on with the rest of your life.

He was almost grateful they hadn't made love again, didn't want to feel any more drawn to her than he already did. He sure as hell didn't want to fall into the love trap, with all the trimmings of a thirty-year mortgage, bottles and diapers, and the sacrifice of adventure and fun.

No, he absolutely refused to love Ann. He could and did admire her, respect her and desire her, but that didn't mean he was in love with her.

He closed his eyes, imagining himself on a warm beach sipping a rum-flavored drink. He waited for the resulting contentment the vision always brought.

When it didn't immediately come, he grunted in irritation and turned off the shower. No wonder the vision didn't bring any kind of excitement or serenity. How could it when he had Ann's life dangling in front of him.

Until she was safe and the murderer was behind bars, Clay couldn't take pleasure in thoughts of his retirement plans. Usually Mondays were his days off, but he didn't intend to take another day off until he solved this case.

He dried, then dressed quickly and left the bathroom. As he

stepped into the hallway the scent of freshly brewed coffee greeted him. He followed it into the kitchen where Ann stood against the counter, sipping a cup.

The early morning light crept into the window, lovingly caressing sparkling strands into her pale hair and radiating on her smooth skin.

She saw him and smiled. "I hope you don't mind. I found the coffee in the cabinet and helped myself."

"Mind? I'm grateful." He poured himself a cup and sat down on one of the bar stools. "What time is your first class?"

"Eight o'clock."

"What about the rest of the day's schedule? What's it like?"

"I've got classes until noon, then a two-hour break. My last class of the day is over at five."

Clay sipped his coffee thoughtfully, then looked at her once again. "What do you normally do during your break time?"

She shrugged. "It depends. Usually I spend the time in my classroom grading papers."

"Until we find this creep, do me a favor and take your breaks in the student union where you're surrounded by people."

There weren't many women who wore morning well, but Ann was definitely one of the lucky ones. Her skin glowed and her eyes shone as a result of her sleep. Her hair, rather than being messy, curled around her shoulders in charming disarray.

The silk robe did little to hide her feminine curves and instead emphasized her slender waist and the thrust of her breasts.

"You'd better get dressed or we'll be late," he said more sharply than he intended, irritated by the swift boost of desire that rocketed through him.

She nodded, placed her cup in the sink, then disappeared down the hallway. He breathed a relieved sigh. More than anything, he wanted to make love to her again. More than anything, he didn't want to make love to her again.

He sighed and picked up his coffee cup. Twenty-seven days. He had twenty-seven days to find a killer…and hang on to his heart.

* * *

"Hey, Clay. Got somebody here I want you to meet." Lieutenant Sanders gestured for Clay to enter his office. As he walked in, a tall, thin officer stood.

"This is Officer Bob Linfield," the lieutenant explained. Clay and Bob shook hands. "He's the man going to take over for you when you retire. From now until you leave, I'd like him to tag around with you and Raymond, kind of get a feel for things here at our station."

"Sure, we'll be glad to work with him."

"If there are no other problems, then get the hell out of here and get to work." The lieutenant dismissed them both with a curt nod of his head.

"Retirement, huh?" Bob said as they left the office. "Lucky you."

"Yeah. You'll learn quickly that this is a small department, requiring the officers to wear a number of hats. Before I leave for retirement, I've got a case I'd really like to solve." Clay looked at the man walking next to him. "I hope your fresh eye can give us some insight."

"What kind of a case is it?" Bob asked. They'd reached Clay's desk. Clay hesitated a moment, then gestured Bob into his chair behind the desk. It was a conscious relinquishment of his space, and he felt a tiny stab in his heart as Bob sank down in the chair where Clay had sat for the past twenty years.

Clay pulled up a folding chair and sat down at the edge of the desk. "The case began with a woman receiving threatening notes and calls. She's a teacher, so initially we assumed it was some sort of student prank. Things escalated when somebody tried to run her down in a shopping mall parking lot and poisoned her cat. Last week it became murder. The perp killed the victim's housekeeper. The housekeeper and the potential victim were approximately the same height and hair color."

Bob frowned. "It's really wild, but this sounds like a case I was working on about three months ago. Threatening notes and nasty phone calls were a prelude to murder. As far as I know, that case is still open."

"We checked the computer for similar cases, why didn't the one you're talking about pop up?"

Bob shrugged and smiled ruefully. "You should know the lag time between working a case and getting it fed into the central computer. I don't know about you guys, but we ran six months behind in getting things into the computer."

Clay nodded, well aware of the inefficiency involved in computerizing crimes and information. "All I know is we need to get a break before Ann Carson winds up dead."

Bob stared at him. "Ann Carson?"

"She's the victim, the one the killer was after."

"Oh, man. This is wild. This is really wild." Bob rubbed a hand across his chin and leaned back in the chair. "The victim in the case three months ago? Her name was Anntoinette Carson…all her friends called her Ann."

The information sent a wave of adrenaline shooting through Clay. "Ann Carson. It's a fairly common name, right?"

"Right."

"What do you suppose the odds of coincidence are that in a three-month period in a city the size of Kansas City, two Ann Carsons would be targeted for murder and the cases wouldn't be related?"

"Oh, about a million to one."

Clay nodded. "That's kind of what I thought. Who do I need to talk to in order to get the records of this Anntoinette Carson case?"

"Roger Buress was the officer in charge. I can contact him and get copies of everything we had," Bob offered. "Although there isn't much. We didn't have any leads, got no breaks at all with the case."

Clay gestured to the phone. "Why don't you get on the horn right now and get us whatever they have?" A burst of optimism surged through him. Maybe they'd get lucky. Maybe this was the break he'd been hoping for.

"Clay, got something for you."

Clay turned to see Raymond. He introduced Bob, then looked at Raymond expectantly. "What's up?"

"A little birdie whispered in my ear and told me Greg Thorton was charged with battery on his girlfriend before Ann."

"You're kidding?" Clay grabbed Raymond's arm and moved him away from Bob, not wanting to disturb Bob's phone conversation. "What happened?"

"Case was dismissed."

"Who was the birdie?"

"Somebody in the prosecutor's office."

"Did you get a name of this previous girlfriend?" Clay asked.

Raymond grinned. "Name and address. Thought you might want to check it out."

"I'd love to check it out," Clay agreed, although he still wasn't sure whether his dislike of the slick lawyer had a basis in his cop instincts or in his male instincts. He disliked the man for making a stink with the captain, but he disliked the man more for emotionally hurting Ann.

"Clay." Bob called to him, his hand held over the mouthpiece of the phone. "They can either fax us what we want, or we can go down to the station and pick it up."

"We'll pick it up," Clay said. As Bob continued his phone conversation, Clay turned back to Raymond and quickly explained what Bob had told him about the previous case.

"Wow. I can't wait to get my hands on the reports and compare things with Ann's case." Raymond grinned. "I've got a feeling we just got closer to this creep."

Clay nodded. Yes, they were one step closer to finding the perpetrator, a step closer to guaranteeing Ann a safe life, and closer to the time when Clay walked away from her. He steadfastly ignored the small pang of his heart at the thought of never seeing her again, never holding her in his arms again.

Surely it wasn't love he felt, nor was it regret for what his future held. It hadn't been a heart pang at all, he decided. It had been a heart jump. Excitement, that's what it had been. The excitement of closing in on his quarry. It had absolutely nothing to do with loving Ann.

* * *

"You're my job." Clay's words rang in Ann's head all day, reminding her over and over again that loving him would only bring a new heartbreak. But it was too late for caution.

He'd listened to her tell her childhood tales without recriminations, without judgment. Nor had he offered her useless pity. He'd validated her experiences, held her close as she'd recounted each and every one, then had spoken about strength and growth. And in those night hours in his arms, Ann had completely, irrevocably given him her heart.

She'd long ago given up dreams of happiness, had always suspected that happiness would remain elusive in her life no matter how hard she sought it.

Fate teased her, giving her brief moments of joy, days of contentment that eventually were always shattered.

She knew better than to dream of a life with Clay. In the last couple of weeks she'd learned not to look for happiness, not to anticipate a happily-ever-after, but rather simply to exist, to survive. Day by day.

A buzzer sounded, indicating the end of class. "See you on Wednesday. Don't forget your papers are due then," she reminded the students as they left the classroom.

When the last student had drifted out Ann looked at her wristwatch. She had two hours before her next class, and she'd promised Clay she'd spend those hours in the student union, where she was surrounded by people.

Gathering up her papers and purse, she tried not to think about Clay, about the fact that he'd be off the force in a month. What if the case wasn't solved before he left? Raymond Misker would probably take over as lead investigator for the case, and he lacked Clay's compassion, suspected Ann knew more than she was telling.

She entered the student union and spied an empty table near the vending machines. Buying an apple, a package of cheese crackers and a soda, she looked around the crowded room. Several people waved to her and she waved back. She loved being a teacher, knew she was a good one and was respected and liked by most of the students she taught.

As always, when she had a quiet moment to herself, she thought of the man who was after her, the man who burned with the need to get revenge. What had she done? What possible motive could this crazed man have for wanting to kill her?

Was the motive trapped in those memories she could no longer retrieve? Was the identity of the man logged in the darkness of her past? God knows, she'd tried to sift through the nightmares, filter through the memories seeking some kind of an answer.

She unwrapped her crackers and started to take a bite of one when her eyes locked with Barry Namath's. He sat facing her across the room. Although he was some distance away, she could feel the intensity of his gaze. Angry, burning with emotion, it caused a shiver to race up her spine.

The cracker stuck in her dry throat and she picked up her soda to wash it down. Was he the one? Had he poisoned Twilight? Killed Tina? The police had said he had a previous record. Apparently violence was no stranger to him. But why target her? Always the questions came back to why?

"Ms. Carson?"

She gulped and jumped at the deep voice right next to her. "Dean." She forced a smile as he pulled his wheelchair up to her table.

"I'm really glad to see you here today," he said as he placed his books on the table. "I'd heard you've been having some problems and was afraid you might take some time off."

"No, no time off." She smiled at him warmly. "I'm afraid the students won't get rid of me so easily."

"I'm glad. This place wouldn't be the same without you around."

"I don't plan on going anywhere," she said firmly.

"I went by your house yesterday. I was going to leave you another story, but there was crime tape across the door and I heard on the news about the woman who was killed. You must be terrified."

She drew a deep breath, uncomfortable with the path of the

conversation. "I'm handling it. It's been rough, but I'm getting by." She cleared a lump from her throat. "Do you have you new story with you now?"

He nodded and pulled several sheets of paper from his note book and handed them to her. He smiled apologetically. "It' a murder mystery. Maybe you want to wait to read it. Yo know, until things are back to normal in your life."

She was beginning to wonder if things would ever be norma in her lifetime. "Thanks, Dean. I'll keep that in mind."

"Ann?" The secretary to the president of the college ap proached. "Dr. Bainbridge would like to see you in his offic right away."

Ann looked at her in surprise. "Oh, okay. I'll be righ there." As the secretary walked off, Ann quickly gathered he things. "If you'll excuse me, Dean."

As she hurried out of the student union, Barry's gaze fol lowed her. Walking toward the administration buildings, sh dismissed Barry from her thoughts, far more concerned abou the summons to the President's office.

"You can go right in," the secretary said. "He's waiting fo you."

Ann entered the plush office and was instantly greeted b Dr. Bainbridge. "Sit down, Ann. I'm sorry to take up some o your break time."

"No problem." She sat down and looked at him curiously She could count on one hand the number of times she' spoken with Dr. Bainbridge in the time she'd been teaching a the college.

"Ann, I received a disturbing letter today in the mail." frown etched deep across his forehead, marring his dignifie attractiveness. "I got a similar one yesterday and dismissed i but with the arrival of this one today, I decided perhaps should speak to you." He reached to hand her the letter.

Ann read the contents, horror sweeping through her. Sh fought back a wave of frustrated tears and looked back at D Bainbridge. "This is a vicious lie." Ann's face burned wit the fires of humiliation and anger as she tossed the letter bac on the top of his desk. "I would never do something like this. Never."

Dr. Bainbridge smiled sympathetically. "Ann, I never give any merit to a letter that's sent anonymously. You're an excellent, committed teacher and I know you'd never jeopardize your position here by indulging in an intimate relationship with a student." His smile faded and his frown once again caused his forehead crease to reappear.

He leaned back in his chair and Ann steeled herself as she saw regret darkening his eyes. "Ann, I've heard about the things going on in your life right now. Your housekeeper's death. I think it would be best for the college if you'd take some time off." He held up a hand to still her protest. "Ann, you're a good teacher, one of our finest. But this letter, coupled with the personal problems you've been going through, makes me think perhaps a little time off would be good for you."

Ann knew better than to argue. She could tell by the expression on his face his mind was made up. "Can I finish out this week? That will take us to midsemester."

He nodded. "That will be fine. I'll call in a substitute to begin next week."

She stood up, fighting an overwhelming sense of hopelessness. There was no doubt in her mind who'd sent the anonymous letter.

"Ann, this is temporary," Dr. Bainbridge said as she started for the door. "Your teaching position will be here when things are settled."

She nodded and left.

She didn't want to go back to the student union, would have preferred the quiet of her classroom to nurse the wounds from this latest blow. But, she'd promised Clay she'd spend her free time in the student union where she'd be surrounded by people.

As she walked back toward the student union, she bit the inside of her mouth in an effort to stop the threat of tears. Everything. She was losing everything.

Anger stirred inside her, an anger bred from helplessness. Who was this man who was stealing her peace, her triumphs, her life piece by piece? He'd tainted every element of her existence. He might as well kill her…he'd already stolen the spirit of her life.

There was a single small comfort in the knowledge that there was nothing more he could do to her, nothing more he could take away from her. Except for her very life, she had nothing left that she cared about.

Clay. She froze as his vision filled her head. If the killer was systematically taking from her everything she held dear… perhaps she wasn't the next intended victim. Perhaps the next victim would be Clay.

Chapter 14

Clay entered the student union eager to find Ann and tell her what they'd discovered that day. He looked around the busy area and finally spied her. She sat alone at a table near the vending machine, her attention focused on a stack of papers in front of her.

For a moment he merely stood inside the door and gazed at her, noting the way her hair shone in the sunlight streaming though the windows, the way her lips moved as she read from the papers before her.

He strode over to her, feeling the gazes of students watching him as he progressed toward her. He should have changed out of his uniform.

"Hi," he greeted her, eager to share the information they'd gleaned today with her. "Ready to go?"

She nodded, her gaze cool, impersonal. She stood up and gathered her papers in her arm. "Officer Clinton, if you intend to escort me to and from work, the least you could do is be on time." Her voice was loud, carrying throughout the room.

Clay felt like a little boy reprimanded by the teacher in front of an entire class of students. "Bad day?" He smiled, bu couldn't retain the gesture beneath the coldness of her eyes "Ann, what's wrong?" He reached out to take her arm, bu she jerked away from him.

"Just take me home, Officer." Without waiting, she took of for the door.

Clay hurried after her, wondering what in the hell was going on. "Ann…wait up," he exclaimed as she continued to walk briskly to his car. Before he could reach her, she slid into the passenger seat and slammed the door.

"I want you to take me to a motel," she said when he go in and started the engine.

He turned and stared at her. "You want to tell me what's going on or are we going to sit here and play guessing games?"

"There's nothing going on. I've just decided it was a bad idea to stay with you." She didn't look at him but rather ap peared to be fascinated by the sight of his dashboard.

"And why is it such a bad idea?"

"It just is. I don't need a reason for the way I feel." She crossed her arms and averted her gaze out the passenger win dow. "Please, just take me to a motel."

Clay put the car in drive and took off, irritated by her mood by his own ignorance as to what had caused it. He'd grown accustomed to her ready smile, the spark in her eyes whenever he smiled at her. The lack of her warm response caused a pang of something alien to his heart, and that irritated him.

He tightened his grip on the steering wheel, averting his self irritation outward to her. She wanted to go to a motel? Tough She wasn't going anywhere except his place until he got some answers.

"This isn't the way to any motel," she finally said, her words clipped and cool.

"We're going to my place and we're going to talk."

"You want to talk?" For the first time since leaving the college, she looked at him, her eyes blazing with anger. "Find this madman and put him behind bars, then we'll talk."

Clay swerved into his parking space at the apartment, then

cut the engine and glared back at her. "That's what this is all about? We aren't moving fast enough for you, so you're pissed? Lady, we're busting our butts on this case. We all want this guy behind bars and we're doing the best we can. If that's not good enough for you, tough."

They both exited the car, tension thick in the air between them. It had been a long day and Clay wasn't sure whether his irritation with Ann was solely due to her mood, or because of his frustration with the case.

"It's just as well we came here," she said as they went into the small apartment. "I can get my things together then you can drive me to a motel or I'll call a taxi. Either way, I'm not staying here another night."

"Ann." He grabbed her hands and led her to the sofa. "Sit down." Her hands were icy cold in his. "Tell me what happened today that has you so upset. Please…you owe me that much."

She tried to pull her hands away, but he held on tight. She finally stopped struggling and sagged with defeat. When she looked at him her eyes were hollow, devoid of hope.

"Dr. Bainbridge, the president of the college received a letter about me today. The letter accused me of having an affair with Simon Casmell. Simon is only eighteen years old, for God's sake." She closed her eyes and drew in a deep, unsteady breath. "It was vile, the letter was filled with horrible accusations."

"Surely your boss didn't believe them."

Ann shook her head. "No, he didn't, especially since the letter was sent anonymously. But he did tell me he thought it would be better if I took some time off."

For the first time since they'd sat down, life flashed in her eyes and her fingers squeezed into Clay's hands. "This man…this monster is taking away everything that's dear to me. He's systematically destroying everything I care about." She jerked her hands out of Clay's and stood. "He's killed a friend, taken my home, tried to kill my cat, stolen my job…there's nothing left except..." She bit down on her lower lip and in her eyes for just a moment, Clay saw the answer to everything.

"Except me." He stood up and approached her, for a moment his throat too full of emotion to speak.

She turned away from him, her posture rigid. "I just think it would be best if I go to a motel."

"Ann." He placed his hands on her shoulders and turned her around to face him. Her gaze went from one side of him to the other, never directly connecting with his. "You're afraid for me." He felt a curious wonder, a surge of warmth as welcome as a blanket on a wintry night, an awe the likes of which he'd never felt before.

"Yes." The word shot out of her as if unbidden, unwanted. "Yes, I'm frightened for you." She sagged against him, her arms reaching up to wind around his neck. "I'm terrified that by being here with you I'm putting a target on your forehead. I'm terrified that he'll take some sick pleasure in killing you next."

"Shhh." Clay pulled her tight against him, so close he could feel the pounding of her heart against his chest. "And so you are willing to stay alone in a motel room to distract this nut from me. And the scene in the student union..." He chuckled. "You missed your calling, you should be teaching drama."

"It's not funny," she said indignantly.

"No, it's not," he agreed, reaching up to tangle his hands in her sweet-smelling hair. He pulled her head away from his chest, wanting to look at her face, see into her eyes. "Ann, I'm a cop. I'm trained to keep myself alive."

"But how can you protect yourself against an unknown attacker? How can you stay safe when you don't know where or from whom the danger might come?"

Clay placed the palms of his hands on either side of her face. He gazed into her eyes and saw the shadows of fear...fear not for herself but for him. He'd never experienced this kind of unselfish caring before and again his heart filled with a wonder that swept all other thoughts from his mind.

Without thought, functioning on sheer emotion alone, he

lowered his lips to hers. What began as a simple need quickly flamed out of control.

Her mouth was hot. Greedy. And in the space of a heartbeat Clay's desire soared to unstoppable proportions. He thrust his tongue into her mouth, a sweet invasion she welcomed and returned.

Her arms wound around his neck, her fingers tangling in his hair as she pressed herself against the length of him. Their hips moved in ageless rhythm, the intimate friction shortening their breaths and increasing their frenzy.

Clay didn't want to think about whether making love to Ann again was a mistake or not, he only wanted to drown in the sweet sensation of kissing her, touching her…loving her.

As their kiss broke apart, Ann removed her hands from around his neck and began unbuttoning his shirt. She didn't speak, but her eyes burned with the flames of desire, a language Clay didn't need verbalized to understand. His breath caught in his throat as she removed his shirt and her fingers danced at his belt buckle. Within seconds he stood before her, naked and so aroused he thought he might lose his mind.

He sat on the sofa as she backed away from him and slowly, sensually removed her clothes. Clay had never before understood the pleasure some men had from watching women undress, of men turned on by strippers. As he watched Ann reveal herself in slow, languid movements, he suddenly understood. He burned with the desire to kiss and caress each inch of skin she exposed, ached with the need to meld his flesh with hers.

When her clothes were finally removed, he reached out and took her hand and pulled her down on top of him on the sofa. Again their mouths found each other.

Hungrily his hands caressed the silkiness of her breasts, the pebbled hardness of her nipples. She moaned her pleasure, the low, throaty sound increasing Clay's delight. He wanted her moaning, gasping, weak for him…as he was for her.

Her body was warm, the heat centered where their hips joined and moved erotically together. She moaned again and raised up to take him into her. As he felt her velvet moistness surround him, he looked into her eyes, wanting the eye contact to deepen their intimacy.

Her blue eyes shimmered with tears of emotion and in the naked love emanating from her, Clay realized he was not going to be able to walk away from the case or her unscathed. Somehow, some way, he'd lost all his objectivity. He'd fallen in love with Ann.

He closed his eyes, breaking the eye contact, not wanting to see into her soul, not wanting to fall in any deeper. Instead he focused solely on the physical sensations sweeping through him.

"So, what you're telling me is that it's possible somebody is trying to kill me because they don't like my name?" Ann looked at Clay incredulously.

They were in bed, a platter of crackers, cheese and fruit between them. They had made love on the sofa, then showered together. While Ann got dressed and dried her hair, Clay had fixed the plate of food for them to share while he filled her in on what he'd learned that day.

"That's about the size of it." Clay popped a grape into his mouth and chewed thoughtfully.

"But that's crazy." Ann smiled ruefully at her own words. "Why should anything surprise me at this point in time?"

"From the police reports we read today, Anntoinette Carson was being stalked, receiving frightening notes and messages. Tomorrow we're going to try to get a look at the notes and see if they match up with the ones you received."

"You're sure they will match."

He nodded. "It's just too damned coincidental that two different perpetrators would be involved."

"So, what do I do? Change my name?"

Clay smiled. "Unfortunately, I don't think that will work. It's more than your name…it's what the name Ann Carson means to the perp. If we could figure that out, we could probably figure out his identity."

Ann reached for a cracker, her heart aching for the woman

named Anntoinette Carson, a woman who hadn't survived. Months from now would another woman be thinking about the second Ann Carson? How sad it was that she hadn't survived? She placed the cracker back on the plate, as her appetite fled beneath the morbid thoughts.

"You okay?" Clay asked.

She nodded. But she wasn't okay. She had a crazy person after her, a man who wanted to kill her. She'd lost her home and her job and each day she spent with Clay she knew brought her closer to the heartbreak of her life.

"I've got Raymond checking with the computer, seeing if we can find anything that might have to do with the name Ann Carson. I don't know that it will do any good, but it's the only lead we have to follow up on at the moment."

Ann sighed in frustration and pulled her legs up to her chest. "I keep going back, wondering if somehow the answer is in my past. There are holes in my memory, dark patches of time without memories." She reached up and rubbed her temples, the beginning of a headache pounding to life. "If the answer to this mystery is locked in my lost memories, then Anntoinette Carson's death is directly on my head."

"Don't you believe it," Clay replied, his jaw tight. "There's only one person responsible for Anntoinette Carson's death, and that's the person who stabbed her. You are no more responsible than I am."

"Logically I know you're right, but emotionally I feel responsible."

Clay sat up, displacing Twilight who'd been curled at his feet. "Like you felt responsible for your mother's drinking? Like you felt responsible for the abuse you suffered?"

"No." Ann raised her chin. "No, I know I wasn't responsible for those things. I was a victim of my mother's life and choices. I won't accept the responsibility for the things that happened because of it."

"Good." Clay nodded, satisfaction lighting his eyes.

"But if the identity of this crazy man is trapped in my memories, then maybe I should see somebody about being regressed or hypnotized to remember the lost time.''

Clay didn't answer for a long moment.

She looked at him, wondering if he thought it a good idea or not. ''Clay?''

When he looked at her, his eyes were filled with an emotion she couldn't quite understand. ''Retrieving those memories might be the most painful thing you'd ever do. You forgot those things for a reason.''

''Yes, but if it would help find this madman... I survived the reality of my life, surely I can survive the memory of my life.''

He averted his gaze from her and instead focused on some indefinable point on the ceiling. ''Sometimes your strength absolutely blows me away,'' he finally said softly.

''I'm no stronger than anyone else,'' she replied. ''I just know if you think it might help, I'll go through whatever process is necessary to get all my memories back.''

''Let's not make a decision about that right now. Give us a couple of days to check out what we have, see what we can come up with before you do anything rash.'' He got out of bed, surprising her with his sudden movement. ''I've got some reports I need to go over and you'd better get some sleep.''

He pulled on a pair of jeans and picked up the platter of goodies. He started for the door, then hesitated and turned to her. ''You know, I was just thinking. You mentioned that you are going to need a place to stay. I'll be leaving this apartment in less than three weeks, but the rent is paid up through the end of the month. There's no reason why you couldn't stay here until you decide what you want to do about your condo.''

''Thanks. I appreciate the offer. I'll think about it.''

He nodded and left the room, pulling the door closed behind him. A hollow ache gnawed in Ann's chest. She had a feeling he'd intentionally distanced himself from her, not only by leaving the bed, but by reminding her he would be leaving in a short time.

She knew he cared for her, felt it when he looked at her

when he touched her. Were his feelings for her strong enough to make him forget the dreams he'd worked toward for the past twenty years? And did she really want him to sacrifice his dreams for her?

No. She wished his dreams included her, wished his desires for a future were the same as hers. But, she didn't want him to relinquish his goals and stay with her, then grow bitter for having made such a choice.

He'd leave and she'd survive. Surviving is what she did best. She plumped her pillow and reached over to turn off the bedside lamp at the same time that Twilight curled up against her warmth.

She turned off the light, plunging the room into darkness, then pulled the cat into her arms. "You and me, Twilight. We'll be fine." Tears burned hot at her eyes and she knew this time her tears were not for the child she'd once been, but for the woman she'd become and the heartache of loving Clay.

"Dammit." Clay slapped the reports down on the top of his desk and shoved his chair back. Raking a hand through his hair, he glared first at Bob, then at Raymond. "I was sort of hoping we'd find a connection between Greg Thorton and this Anntoinette Carson, but there's nothing to tie him to her."

"Would have been nice to tie things up that neatly," Bob agreed as he grabbed the last slice of pizza from the take-out box. "But we know Thorton is clean. He's got an airtight alibi for Anntoinette Carson's murder. He was giving a speech at a dinner in front of a hundred other people at the time she was killed."

"And after talking to his ex-girlfriend, I'm not so sure there's anything to the charges of abuse. I spoke to the prosecutor in charge of the case and the way she remembers it, the girlfriend was mad because Thorton had broken up with her. She trumped up the charges of abuse to get even with him." Raymond scratched his belly thoughtfully. "I'm still working the computer and looking at back records to see if the name Ann Carson pops up anywhere."

"Yeah, and I'm running down the list of her students, checking backgrounds and looking for red flags," Bob added.

Clay nodded. "Anything that might tie one of the students to both Anntoinette Carson and Ann." He sighed in frustration. "Okay, lunch break is over, let's get back to work."

As his two partners walked away, Clay stared down at the paperwork in front of him. He wasn't sure whether it was the pizza or the lack of leads that had given him a case of heartburn.

The captain had taken him and his partners off street patrol, wanting them to focus on closing up the Carson case before Clay left the department.

Twenty days. Twenty days were all he had left before he had to walk away from the case. Dammit, why couldn't they get a break?

It had been days since the latest contact from the man they hunted. Not a word, a note, nothing since he'd called Clay's mother's house. The silence worried Clay. Had the perpetrator discovered Ann was now staying at his apartment? And if he knew…what plans had he made for her?

The silence was as loud as a ticking time bomb, and Clay couldn't anticipate when the explosion might come or what form it would take.

He reached into his top drawer and pulled out a package of antacid tablets. As he chewed one, he contemplated the possibility of not solving the case before he left the department. He could always put off his retirement for a week or two, however long was needed to break the case. His flight plans could be changed with a simple phone call to the airline.

The alternative was to walk away from the case…walk away from Ann knowing she was still in danger. His heart convulsed and he wasn't sure whether it was because of the thought of leaving while Ann was still at risk, or simply the thought of leaving Ann altogether.

There was no way to negate the positive presence she'd had on his life. The apartment that had always been merely a place to hang his hat and sleep, now breathed with a new life. Pieces of Ann were everywhere, from the bottles of perfume on the dresser in the bedroom, to the robe hanging on the hook behind the bathroom door.

Even the kitchen, which had always been so impersonal, so sterile, now seemed imbibed with the spirit of Ann. On the ride home from the college the night before she'd insisted he stop so she could buy a bouquet of flowers from a vendor on the corner. The bouquet had greeted him first thing this morning, an explosion of yellow blossoms in a vase in the center of the kitchen table. Yellow. Her favorite color. The color of hope.

"I'll have all the flowers I want when I get to Hawaii," he muttered irritably.

"Pardon me?" The officer at the desk next to Clay's looked at him.

"I said I'm not changing my retirement plans for anybody."

"Sure, Clay, that's fine with me." The young man looked at him as if he'd lost his mind.

Clay felt the heat of a blush sweep over his cheeks. He looked back down at the papers, shoving aside any thoughts he might have entertained about postponing his retirement. This was a good police department, and the officers working on Ann's behalf were fine men. They'd make certain she was safe. She didn't need him...and he sure as hell didn't need her messing up his plans.

One thing was certain. He wasn't about to make love with Ann again. She was a temptress, stealing pieces of his dreams each time he made love to her. He had to keep some emotional detachment until he gained some physical distance.

By the time he picked her up from school that evening, he felt he'd once again gained the objectivity he felt so necessary in dealing with her. "What do you want to do about supper?" he asked as they drove toward his apartment. "I'm sure you're fairly sick of my hamburgers by now."

She smiled at him. "Maybe just a wee bit. Why don't you stop by a grocery store and let me buy dinner."

"You can pick whatever we cook, but I'll buy."

She reached over and placed her hand on his arm.

"Please, Clay. Let me do this. It's such a small thing for me to do to repay your kindness."

Clay hesitated a moment, then nodded. He knew for her it was a matter of pride.

It was nearly seven o'clock by the time they got back to Clay's apartment, two bags of groceries in hand. "Why don't we eat on the patio?" Ann suggested. "The weather is so nice and I bought stuff for a kind of picnic."

"Okay. I'll wash down the outside table and set it."

As Clay disappeared out the back door, Ann busied herself unloading the food they'd bought. Walking in the grocery store side by side, as he pushed the cart and she placed the items in it, Ann had seen a whisper of what might have been. If Clay loved her. If Clay stayed.

But he'd never spoken of love, and he'd reminded her daily that he would be leaving in a matter of days. She shoved these thoughts from her mind. She didn't want to think about the future. Tomorrow was her last day at the college and soon Clay would be leaving to follow his dreams.

At the moment, the future held little interest to her. She preferred focusing on the here and now. Tonight she didn't want to think about tomorrow. She didn't want to remember the circumstances that had brought Clay into her life. She just wanted to enjoy a wonderful meal with a handsome man and the beauty of a warm summer night.

By the time they sat down to eat, darkness had fallen. Clay turned on his porch light, illuminating his patio in a pale golden glow.

"What a feast," he said as they sat down at the table. He eyed the platter of fried chicken, the bowls of potato salad and cole slaw. Sliced cucumbers, chunks of cheddar cheese and hot rolls added to the meal. "There's enough food here to feed an army."

Ann smiled. "We'll just eat leftovers for the next couple of days." Again she felt a whisper of what might have been. They sounded like husband and wife, talking about leftovers. But Clay didn't want a wife. He didn't want any encumbrances.

"Mrs. Woninski came in again today," Clay said as they began to eat.

Ann frowned at him in confusion. "Mrs. Woninski?"

"Remember I told you about her…the old woman who keeps filing missing person reports on her dead husband."

"Oh, yes. How sad."

He paused a moment to help himself to some more potato salad, then continued. "Today I decided it was time somebody helped her out. I called social services, then I called my mother."

"Your mother?"

Clay grinned. "I think what Mrs. Woninski needs more than anything is a friend. Mom called her and invited her to join their bingo group. Mom said Mrs. Woninski was delighted and I have a feeling the police will be seeing less and less of Mrs. Woninski."

Ann thought of Clay's mother, her warmth and loving. Yes, the lonely old woman would thrive beneath Rosemary's friendship. "Loneliness is a terrible thing."

"I suppose." He pushed away from the table. "How about some coffee?"

"No, thanks, none for me." She looked at her watch. "If I have caffeine this late at night, I'll never get to sleep." By the time they got the table cleared and the kitchen cleaned up, it was nearly eleven o'clock. "There's about two glasses of wine left in this bottle," Clay said, holding out the wine they'd drank several evenings before. "How about a nightcap?"

"That sounds good." Ann curled up on the sofa and watched as Clay poured the wine and joined her. "To the good guys…may they always catch the bad guys," he toasted.

"Here, here." She clinked her glass against his, then took a sip.

The phone rang.

Ann looked at Clay sharply. It was eleven o'clock. Who would be calling at this time of night? The wine in her mouth suddenly tasted with the bitterness of vinegar. She swallowed. "It's him," she said softly.

Clay's jaw tightened as he set down his glass and jerked up the phone. "Clinton," he barked. Ann held her breath. He visibly relaxed. "It's Raymond," he told her.

Ann sagged against the sofa, her heart resuming a steady beat. Okay, so it wasn't him. This time. But if he didn't know already, sooner or later he'd discover that she was here.

The pleasantness of the evening shattered beneath the cold harshness of reality. She could pretend she was safe here, could even pretend she and Clay were building something lasting, but the reality was that neither was true.

She refocused on Clay as he hung up the receiver. "I've got to go to the station," he said.

"Now?"

He nodded. "Raymond thinks he's got something. He wouldn't go into it over the phone. I'll be back as soon as I can." He stood and disappeared into the bedroom. He returned a moment later, holding a small gun in his hand. "This is a snub-nosed .38. I want you to keep it."

"No…I don't know anything about guns." Ann eyed the weapon with apprehension.

"You don't need to know anything but how to remove the safety and how to pull the trigger." He sat back down next to her. "I can't leave you here alone without some protection." He held the gun out to her. "It's loaded and ready to fire. All you have to do is remove the safety here."

Ann took the gun from him. "It makes me angry that I even have to think about handling a gun."

"Yeah, well, better angry than dead." He stood and grabbed his car keys. "I don't know how long I'll be. Raymond could have something…he could have nothing."

Ann got up and followed him to the door. "You'll call me?"

"Of course." He hesitated at the door, his gaze lingering on her. "You know the routine, don't open the door for anyone. If you hear anything or see anything that doesn't seem right, call 911. Keep that gun next to you until I get back home."

"Don't worry. I'll be fine."

He touched her cheek in his sweet, familiar fashion, then turned and was gone.

Ann closed the door and carefully locked it. Her gaze landed on the gun lying on the coffee table. She didn't know whether its presence made her feel safer or not. Would she be able to use it on somebody? She didn't know.

She sat on the sofa, hoping, praying Clay wouldn't be gone long and that while he was gone no monsters would come.

Chapter 15

The ringing phone awakened Ann. She opened her eyes, sur
prised to find herself on the sofa in Clay's living room. The
she remembered. Clay was at the station. She'd fallen aslee
while awaiting his return.

The phone rang again and she checked her watch. A littl
after six. Almost time for her to get up anyway, she thoug
as she answered the phone.

"Ann, it's me."

She shoved her hair away from her face and smiled at th
sound of Clay's voice. "Good morning."

"Michael Johnson."

She frowned into the receiver. "Pardon me?"

"Michael Johnson...does that name mean anything to you?"

"No, not off the top of my head. Should it?"

"Twenty-one years ago Michael Johnson was tried and con
victed of murder. The sole witness against him was a six-year
old girl named Ann Carson." Clay's voice rang with excite
ment. "Was it you, Ann?"

Ann frowned, playing and replaying the name in her min

searching back over her distant childhood for memories of a trial. "I...I don't know, Clay," she finally admitted.

"That's the time where I don't have many memories at all."

"Ever been to Englewood Park?"

"Sure," she answered, thinking of the northland community park. "I occasionally go there to feed the ducks."

"I mean as a kid. Were you ever there with your mother?"

Again Ann frowned. "I don't know, Clay. Probably. Whenever the weather was nice and we had no money, we sometimes slept in parks. Why?"

"Ann Carson and her mother were at the park late one night. Ann saw a man putting something into a garbage Dumpster. The man was Michael Johnson and he was throwing his girlfriend's body into the trash." Ann gasped. "Does that jog loose anything...anything at all?"

"No," she answered softly, horror sweeping through her. "But that's the kind of heinous thing a child would want to forget, isn't it."

"Yeah, I guess it is." He hesitated a moment. "In any case, it doesn't matter whether it was you or not. Apparently Michael Johnson thinks it's you."

"So you're sure this Michael Johnson is the man after me?"

"Nothing is sure, but it all makes sense. Michael was released from prison six months ago, just in time to stalk and kill Anntoinette Carson. The notes you received said revenge was sweet when it was long in coming. I'd say twenty years in prison might have produced a burning need for revenge."

"But I don't know a Michael Johnson."

"Unfortunately, our information is still sketchy at best. We're trying to locate Samantha Whitling. She was the assistant prosecuting attorney who handled the case. She retired several years ago. We're hoping once we find her, she can fill in some blanks."

"And in the meantime?"

"In the meantime, we know for sure that Michael Johnson is at least forty years old, so anyone younger is no longer suspect." He hesitated a moment. "Ann, I really hate to leave

here to get you to work this morning. Why don't you ski
today."

"Clay, I don't want to do that. Today's my last day an
there are several students I specifically need to talk to befor
the substitute takes over their classes." She frowned. "Look
I can call a taxi to take me to work and bring me back her
when I'm through for the day." She felt his disapproval em
anating over the line. "Clay, please. It's just one more day. I'
be fine."

"Take the gun with you."

"But, I'm sure I'll—"

"Dammit, Ann, take it with you," he interrupted. "Carry
in your purse or whatever. Just don't leave without it. An
forget about the taxi. I'll send a car to pick you up."

Ann hated the idea of a policeman taking her to work, b
she knew better than to press the issue. "All right," she agree

"I'll have a patrol car there by seven-thirty. You can ca
the station when you're ready to come home and we'll ser
somebody back to pick you up…and Ann…be careful."

"I will." The conversation ended with Ann promising
call Clay on her lunch break. She hung up the phone and leane
back against the sofa cushions.

Michael Johnson. If Clay was right, it was the name of Ann
monster, the man who'd systematically tried to destroy her lif
He was the man who'd killed Tina, tried to kill both Twilig
and herself. Definitely a monster.

Had she been the little girl who'd testified against him
Wouldn't she remember something as unusual, as important
a murder trial? Maybe…maybe not. She'd repressed and fo
gotten so many things in that particular period of her life. Pe
haps the trauma of testifying had helped to create the blac
holes in her memory.

She stood and went into the kitchen to make coffee, awa
of the silence of the apartment around her. Funny, she'd grov
accustomed to spending the early morning hours with Cla
While he showered, she made the coffee, then they'd share
few minutes drinking the fresh brew and talking. She misse

him being here now. It was amazing how quickly he'd become a habit in her life.

"A habit that will be broken," she murmured, a catch in her heart at the thought. She should have known better than to become intimately involved with him. He'd made it clear from the beginning that his priorities and desires for life were different from hers.

However, fate had conspired to throw them together and the chemistry between them had been undeniable. Not only had she been drawn to him physically, but emotionally as well. He'd become the left foot to her right, the heart of her soul. And when he left, he'd take with him pieces of her she would never, ever be able to get back. Shoving aside these thoughts, she headed for the shower.

As she dressed, she thought of Clay's offer for her to stay here in his place after he left. She'd probably take him up on it.

He'd told her the night before that her condo had been released. She intended to hire a cleaning crew, then put it on the market. She'd never stay there another night. As soon as Michael Johnson was no longer a threat, she'd begin house hunting.

At precisely seven-thirty a patrol car pulled up outside Clay's apartment. Ann eyed the gun on the coffee table. She didn't want to carry it, didn't even want to touch it. But, she'd promised Clay. She checked to make certain the safety was still on, then slid the weapon into her purse.

As she walked out to the patrol car, the purse, hanging on a strap over her shoulder, bumped against her stomach. She imagined she could feel the cold steel of the gun through the leather. She wondered if she walked too fast, if the gun would somehow go off, shooting her in the stomach and accomplishing Michael Johnson's goal for him.

The patrolman who drove her to the college was young, and kept up a stream of nervous, inane chatter. Ann suspected he was a rookie and considered transporting her an important job.

"Clay said for me to remind you to call the station when

you're ready to leave," he said as he pulled up at the campu main entrance. "He said for you to be sure to wait for an office to take you home."

"I will, and thank you for the ride," she said as she got o of the car.

As Ann walked toward the English building, a bitterswe pang went through her. Today would be her last day here unt Michael Johnson was caught and put behind bars. Hopefull now that the police had his name, he would be caught soc and she could get her life back.

The morning passed quickly. Keeping in mind the info mation Clay had given her on the phone, Ann found herse studying all the male students who looked to be around the aʝ of forty. There weren't many, but each one suddenly seeme suspect in her mind.

Although she'd had her last creative writing class the nig before, she immediately saw Barry Namath sitting with a grou of other students in the student union when she took her lund break.

Barry was approximately the right age. But, the police ha checked into his background the day he'd been at her hous Surely had he been in prison the last twenty years, that fa would have shown up in the police files. Barry couldn't ！ Michael Johnson. Barry was just a man with a bad attitud But what about the others? Two of the men seated with Bar were also approximately the right age to be Michael Johnso She frowned, realizing she was obsessing.

Before sitting down for lunch, she went to the pay pho and called Clay. "It's me," she said when he got on the lir

"Everything all right there?" he asked.

"Fine. Anything new with you?" She held her breath, ho ing, praying he'd tell her they'd found Michael Johnson ar he was now behind bars.

"We located Samantha Whitling. She now lives in St. Lou Unfortunately at the moment she's out shopping and there's ￭ way for her husband to contact her. We're expecting her return our call any time. Hopefully she can give us something that will help us identify Michael Johnson.''

"So, we don't know any more now than we did this morning.''

"Ann, with every minute that passes we get closer. We're going to get him. Hopefully by the time you go to sleep tonight, you'll no longer have to worry about Michael Johnson.''

"I hope you're right.''

As Clay hung up, he wondered if he'd been too optimistic with her. So far the day had worked on Murphy's Law... everything that could go wrong was going wrong. It had taken them all morning to locate Samantha Whitling, only to discover her out shopping. The computer had gone down for two hours, leaving them helpless to continue background checks. Even the prison that had released Michael six months before couldn't find the photo they'd taken on the day he'd arrived to begin serving his term. One frustration after another.

Adrenaline had been pumping through Clay since the moment Raymond had called him back to the station in the middle of the night. But with the passing of each hour and the lack of any more progress, the adrenaline had begun to fade little by little, leaving behind a weary frustration.

He looked up as Bob approached. "I've hit a dead end,'' Bob said as he sank down in the chair next to Clay. "I've checked every male over forty years old on Ann Carson's student list and nothing comes up as suspect.''

"Why doesn't that surprise me?'' Clay said dryly. "Nothing about this case has come easily.''

Bob frowned thoughtfully. "Are we sure this Michael Johnson is a student?''

"We aren't sure of anything.'' Clay leaned back in his chair and drew a deep breath. "But I can't believe Michael isn't somebody directly in Ann's life. He's displayed too intimate a knowledge of her daily routine, her work schedule, all the little nuances of her life not to be somebody she sees regularly.''

"What about the security guards at the college, the maintenance people...other teachers?''

Clay nodded. "Check them out. Any male approximately forty years old."

"Got it."

As Bob left, Clay once again felt the overwhelming burn of frustration. Who in the hell was Michael Johnson? What name was he using? What mask did he wear now? As always, Clay had the feeling of time running out. Not only because his retirement approached, but because he somehow felt as if he'd tuned into Michael Johnson's rage...felt it simmering to mammoth proportions. An imminent explosion. It was coming, and if they didn't figure out who Michael Johnson was, Clay was afraid that the eventual explosion would destroy Ann.

Ann stood on the curb at the campus main entrance, waiting for the patrol car to return to take her back to the apartment.

It had been a long, difficult day. She hated relinquishing her classes to a substitute, hated the feeling that she was somehow letting down her students. Her life was no longer in her control, and she hated that more than anything.

Sighing, she looked at her watch, wondering what was taking her ride so long. She was anxious to get home, kick off her high heels and share the bittersweetness of her day with Clay.

Summer heat had returned and Ann found herself thinking longingly of the pool at Clay's apartment complex. Although she hadn't used the pool since moving in with Clay, she'd often heard the splashes and laughter coming from the area as she and Clay walked from their car to the apartment.

She wondered if tonight she could talk Clay into a quick dip. Her face warmed as she imagined Clay in a pair of swimming trunks, his broad chest and muscular legs bare.

"Hi, Ms. Carson."

She turned and saw Dean Moore, his wheelchair squeaking softly as he approached. "Hi, Dean. Going home?"

"Yeah, it's been a long day. How about you?"

She noted how the sun gave his gray hair a slight silver cast. She would miss Dean and the stories he always wanted her to critique. "I'm just waiting for my ride."

"You need a ride? I'll be glad to take you wherever you're going," he offered.

"Thank you, Dean. But my ride should be here anytime."

He smiled at her shyly. "I know it's a lot to ask, but would you look at a few more of my stories? I have them in the back of my van, along with a self-addressed, stamped envelope so you can mail them back to me."

"Sure, I'd love to look at them."

"You sure you don't mind?"

Ann smiled, thinking of how little this man seemed to have in his life, how important his writing appeared to be to him. "I don't mind at all."

"Great...I'll just go get it and bring it back to you."

As he started across the parking lot, Ann called after him. "Wait. I'll go with you and save you the trip back."

"Thanks, I appreciate it." He flashed her a bright smile.

Together they moved across the asphalt that still retained the heat from the day. Ann noticed beads of sweat across Dean's forehead and above his lips. "Warm, isn't it?" she said.

"Yeah, days like this I wish I could wear shorts, but my legs are...well...they don't look so hot in shorts."

Ann wanted to ask him if he'd been the victim of an accident or an illness. What had put him in the chair? But she didn't know the political correctness of asking such questions and so didn't.

"Here we are," he said as they reached the van. He unlocked the back door and struggled to open it.

"Let me," Ann said, stepping forward to help. "If you'll just tell me where the papers are, I'll get them."

"Great. They should be just inside on the carpeting."

Ann leaned forward into the interior of the van, not seeing any paperwork on the stained carpeting. "I don't see them."

"Maybe while I was driving they shifted and moved up front more."

She leaned farther, still unable to see any papers. "Dean, I don't think they're here...." She gasped as something slammed into the back of her head, knocking her feet out from beneath her and sprawling her on the carpet inside the van. Before she could catch her breath, before she could even begin to assimilate what was happening, she was hit on the head again. For a moment stars danced, then faded into the darkness of the deepest night and she knew no more.

It was after five when Samantha Whitling finally called Clay. Unfortunately, she had little to add to their investigation. "Michael Johnson and Ann Carson have haunted me for years," she said in the same strong, vibrating voice that had served her so well as a prosecutor. "Never have I seen the battle between good and evil so well-defined. The innocence of a child against the raging madness of a sociopath. Why your interest in this ancient case now?"

"I have a dead woman and a threatened woman, both named Ann Carson, both blonde and in their late twenties and Michael Johnson was released from prison six months ago," Clay explained.

"Hmm, then I'd say it's definitely Michael. The day he was taken to prison he swore to get Ann Carson."

"Anything you can do to help us locate where Michael is now or what alias he might be using?"

A long pause filled the line. "Hmm, I can't think of anything. His mother lived there in town, have you contacted her?"

"His mother? There was nothing in the files about her."

"I remember her as a pathetic thing. Old, thin, with life's weariness on her face."

"You remember her name?"

"No, I'm sorry." Genuine regret resounded in her voice. "She only came to the trial one day for a little while. I never even personally met her."

When Clay hung up, he felt no closer to solving the puzzle than he'd been a week before. He pulled out the list of potential suspects and stared at it for the hundredth time.

There were now twelve names on the list...students, other teachers and maintenance workers at the college who were approximately the right age to be Michael Johnson. Twelve names. As he read them over, one by one, something niggled at the back of his brain. Something he'd forgotten, or dismissed, something important.

"Clay."

He looked up at Bob. "What's up?"

"They all check out." He gestured to the list in front of Clay. "None of them have prison records, none of the names appear to be aliases."

"Dig deeper." Clay swept a hand through his hair. "Michael Johnson was in prison for twenty years. In that time he probably made contact with men who are experts at creating new identities. Whole lives and pasts can be manufactured."

"Okay, I'll dig deeper." Bob stood.

Clay frowned, something still whispering in the back of his head. He stared at the list on his computer screen, the same list Bob was using to check backgrounds. "Bob, would you tell Raymond I want to talk to him?"

"Sure."

While Clay waited for Raymond, he once again looked at the list of potential suspects, trying to listen to what his instincts seemed to be trying to tell him.

"What's up?" Raymond eased down in the chair across from Clay's.

"You made up this list of suspects, right?"

"Right. Why, what's wrong with it?"

"Nothing wrong." Clay hesitated, staring at the names one last time. "Why isn't Dean Moore on this list? He's about the right age."

"I'd think the reason he's not on there would be pretty obvious. The man is in a wheelchair."

"Do we know why he's in the chair? What's wrong with him?"

"No," Raymond stretched the word into two syllables. "I see the wheels spinning, Clay. What are you thinking?"

Clay leaned back in his chair and rubbed the center of his forehead thoughtfully. "I don't know…maybe I'm grasping at straws, but something's been bothering me since we went to talk to Dean Moore.''

''At this point straws are all we have to grasp. What's bothering you?''

Thinking back over that day when he and Raymond had gone to speak to Dean, Clay tried to figure out exactly what had been niggling at the base of his brain. ''The house where Dean lives…it's an older house. The doorways were narrow…too narrow for a wheelchair to go through. Why would a man in a wheelchair choose to live in a home that wasn't equipped to handle his handicap?'' Clay rocked forward, something else now in focus. ''And why would a man relegated to spending the rest of his life in a wheelchair rent the chair?''

Raymond's eyes narrowed. ''What are you talking about?''

''The chair. On the side of Moore's wheelchair was a little tag that read B and B Rentals.'' Clay slapped his hands down on his desk. ''That's what's been bothering me. Why in the hell wouldn't Moore own his wheelchair?''

''I think you're on to something, partner.'' Raymond's eyes gleamed with renewed fire. ''I'll do a background on him right now.''

Clay nodded. ''And I'll call B and B Rentals and see what they can tell me.''

Twenty minutes later Clay, Raymond and Bob met in the quiet of an interrogation room. ''He doesn't check,'' Raymond said the minute they were all seated at the table. He enrolled in the creative writing class, but because it's a community education course, he didn't have to show any sort of identification or credentials. He isn't registered in any other classes.'' Raymond looked at Clay. ''What'd you find out from the rental place?''

''Dean Moore rented a wheelchair from B and B Rentals three months ago. The clerk remembered him because it was the first time they'd rented a wheelchair. Dean walked in and carried the chair out. He told the clerk his mother was infirm and coming to visit.''

Raymond frowned. "But Dean Moore looks too old to be Michael Johnson."

"Twenty years in prison can make a man look older than his years," Clay said dryly. "I want him brought in for questioning."

"Unless you're ready to book him, I say we'd better go slow. So far all we know for sure is he's probably using a wheelchair under false pretenses...hardly a crime."

Clay glared at Bob, emotion fighting reason. "Dammit, if what we think is right, this man is responsible for two deaths that we know about." Reason won. He drew a steadying breath. "But you're right. We can't blow this. The man is smart and if we spook him he's liable to disappear where we'll never find him. We need more. We need to tie Dean Moore directly to Michael Johnson." He looked at Raymond. "Check out Dean's address. Samantha Whitling said Michael Johnson's mother lived in the area. See who owns the place where Dean lives."

"And I'll see if I can draw a link between Dean and Anntoinette Carson," Bob said.

Clay nodded tersely. They all turned as the door to the interrogation room opened and a young, fresh-faced officer stepped in. "Clay? She wasn't there."

Clay stared at the young man, for a moment unable to make the transition from one subject to another. As his brain assimilated who the officer was talking about, a chill swept over him.

"I waited around for her, even went into several of the buildings and asked about her, but she was nowhere to be found." The officer's voice shook, his face a sickly pale as he waited for Clay's reaction.

"Did anyone see her?"

"One of the students said he saw her standing in front of the administrative building, but he went on to class and doesn't know what happened to her."

Clay swept past the officer and raced to the nearest phone. He picked up the receiver and quickly punched in the seven numbers to ring his apartment. "Be there," he breathed. Maybe she took a taxi, or caught a ride from a girlfriend. But neither scenario felt right. The phone rang once…twice…three times. With each ring a cold knot of terror hardened in Clay's chest. Four rings. Five rings. Six rings. He felt beads of perspiration appear on his forehead.

He hung up the receiver and turned to look at Bob and Raymond. "She's not there." His voice was a mere whisper. "Where is she? Where's Ann?" he asked.

Nobody answered aloud, but the answer was in the dread that radiated in the air between them. He had her. Michael Johnson had Ann.

Chapter 16

Ann came to slowly, fighting her way up from a black void. She knew she was lying on a bed, but how had she gotten here. And where was here?

She sat up and opened her eyes. Immediately a stab of pain pierced the back of her skull. She moaned and squeezed her eyes closed, willing away a wave of nausea. Tentatively, she reached her hand up to the back of her head and felt a bump the size of an avocado.

She winced, her fingers exploring to find further damage. Other than the goose egg, she seemed to be all right…except for the fact that she had no idea where she was.

Attempting to separate clear thoughts from the haze of pain, she tried to think. She'd been at the college…she'd been standing at the curb waiting for a ride. She could remember the heat from the pavement radiating upward, the desire to get home and share her day with Clay. Her eyes flew open as she remembered walking to Dean Moore's van. Dean. Had Dean done this?

She sat up straighter on the bed, looking around in an at-

tempt to sort out where she was. It was dark, the only ligh
seeping in around the edges of heavy curtains that hung at a
single window. The room was small, with only a bed and a
dresser.

Where was she? The place smelled like a million place
she'd been in her past. The musty scent of other people, o
lives passing through, lives without hope.

She wanted to get up and get out, but fear kept her immobile
If it had been Dean who'd knocked her out and brought he
here, where was he now? Why was she here? Her thought
were confused, jumbled, but more than anything a deep, abid
ing fear kept her planted on the bed, afraid to move.

She realized she was crying, tasted the bitter salt of her tear
on her lips. Her tears were the flavor of fear, a fear bred from
knowledge. Dean Moore was Michael Johnson. The knowledg
swam through her, filling her with a terror she'd never expe
rienced before. Dean Moore was Michael Johnson and he in
tended to kill her.

Hope washed away from her through the tears. And with th
absence of hope came a wave of resignation. There was a cer
tain amount of peace in the resignation, the knowledge tha
soon she'd be dead.

It seemed this had been fate's intention for her since the tim
of her birth. What her mother and that life-style long ago ha
not managed to accomplish, Michael Johnson would finish.

Where was he now? Light seeped in from beneath a close
door. Was he in the next room, waiting for her to regain con
sciousness?

Where was Clay? Why wasn't he here to save her? Fres
tears fell as she thought of Clay. Never again would she fee
the strength of his arms surrounding her. Never again woul
she gaze into his eyes and see the special warmth he held in
side. Although he'd never told her he loved her, she knew h
would grieve for her. Small comfort.

She froze as she heard footsteps. Her crying stopped
usurped by sheer terror as she stared at the door. With the smel

of the room, the surrounding darkness, and the deep, abiding fear, she was plunged backward in time.

Once again she was a child, waiting for her mommy to come home, needing her mommy to protect her. She watched the door. Waiting. Waiting. Her breath caught in her throat as the footsteps drew closer. "Mommy?"

Please, please, please...let it be my mommy. I'm scared. Please Mommy, come and hold me tight.

As the door creaked open, Ann cowered in the corner of the bed. It wasn't her mommy. The dark shape that entered the room was too big, too bulky to be her mommy. A sob caught in her throat as she realized she was alone with a monster.

"I don't want to go up there with guns blazing," Clay said to Raymond and Bob. They were a block away from Dean Moore's house and being followed by two more patrol cars. "If Ann is inside, I don't want to spook him into doing something foolish. You've got the warrant, right?" he asked Raymond.

Raymond nodded. "Right here." He patted his breast pocket.

They'd managed to get a search warrant in record time once they'd established that the house where Dean Moore lived had been owned by Margaret Johnson, mother of Michael. The upkeep of the house was still being paid by Margaret Johnson's estate. The link had been established and they now knew Dean Moore was Michael Johnson.

Clay watched in his rearview mirror as one of the patrol cars left the parade and turned the corner. That particular car would go down the alley between the houses to the back of the Johnson residence. Clay pulled over to the curb to await the radio acknowledgement that they were in place.

Tension swelled inside Clay. Let her be there. Let her be all right. Dear God, don't let us be too late. He refused to admit that it very well might be too late, that Ann might already be another of Michael Johnson's victims. He couldn't let that thought take root, fill him with despair. He had to hang on to hope.

He thought of the bouquet of flowers in the center of his kitchen table. Yellow blooms as big as his fists. Yellow. The color of hope.

His radio crackled. "Unit three is in position."

"Ten-four. Don't move until you hear my command. You copy unit two…unit three?" As they acknowledged him, Clay pulled away from the curb and headed the rest of the way toward the Johnson place.

"I think it would be best if I just go to the front door and tell him I have a few more questions about Barry Namath," Clay said. "Play it cool and hope he doesn't get suspicious. Maybe I can get inside and perhaps get an idea of where he has Ann."

"Maybe he doesn't have her," Bob said with a surge of optimism. "I mean, it's only been a little over an hour since the officer missed her at the college. Maybe she decided to go shopping, or visit friends."

"No way," Clay replied tersely. "If she'd gone anywhere other than my apartment, she would have called me. She, more than anyone, knows the stakes in this game, knows that a single careless mistake might cost her her life."

"If Michael Johnson has her, then the odds are she made a careless mistake," Raymond said.

Clay shot him a sharp look. "No, she didn't make a careless mistake, we did. Dean Moore should have been on that list." Raymond flushed. "I'm not blaming you, Raymond," Clay continued. "We all missed him. I'd looked at that list a thousand times and didn't see the omission."

He pulled into the driveway, his heart thudding an anxious rhythm. "Okay, everyone stay cool," he said both into the radio and to his partners. "The last thing we want is to tip this guy before we find out Ann's welfare."

As Clay walked to the front door, he tried not to think about Tina's body…how in those first moments of seeing her he'd thought she was Ann. What he wanted to do was crash through the door with guns blazing and not give Michael Johnson a chance to defend himself.

He drew a deep breath, steadying himself, gaining control of his rage, trying to ignore the terror that filled him as he thought of Ann.

He knocked on the door, trying to school his features into a semblance of relaxed irritation. There was no telltale movement behind the curtains, no whisper of sound beyond the front door.

Clay's stomach knotted, his heart once again pounding anxiously. He knocked again, this time a loud, rapid tattoo. No answer. He leaned his head against the wood, trying to still his heartbeats, his breathing, so he could hear any noise, any sign of life behind the door.

He froze. Was that a sound? A creaking of a floorboard beneath a foot? Why didn't somebody answer the door? What was happening inside? Where in the hell was Ann?

"Move in," he yelled into his radio. He tried the doorknob and found it locked. Stiffening his shoulder, he rammed it into the door, the blow jarring his teeth.

Bob and Raymond came running and together the three of them managed to break in the door. They entered, guns drawn. At the same time they heard the officers entering at the back of the house. "Check the bedrooms," Clay said to Bob.

"I'll take the kitchen," Raymond said.

Clay nodded and moved to the door he assumed led to the basement. A cold calm descended on him as he opened the door and stared down the dark flight of stairs.

He could smell evil. It permeated the walls, saturated the very air. Perspiration beads appeared on his forehead as he clicked on the light and started down the stairs, not knowing what he might find when he reached the bottom.

As his foot hit the last step, he looked around, dread roiling in his stomach. His breath whooshed out of him in relief. A basement. Nothing more. A bare lightbulb dangled from the center of the room, shining faintly on boxes, an old Christmas tree, a rocking chair with a broken rocker. No bodies, no tools of evil, no Ann. Just the remnants of a life. Clay checked the

writing on the boxes, unsurprised to read Margaret Johnson'
name.

He took the stairs two at a time back up to the main floo
of the house, wondering what the others had found. He foun
them in the living room.

"House is secured, there's nobody here," Raymond sai
"No sign of Michael or Ann."

"But there is something you need to see," Bob said.

Again dread balled up in Clay's chest as he followed Bo
down the hallway and into a small bedroom. A single bed wa
shoved against one wall and a computer desk took up the spac
of another wall. Clay immediately spied what Bob had wante
him to see.

The wall behind the computer desk held a bulletin board an
tacked there were photos. About a dozen were of a woma
Clay didn't know. They showed her getting out of her ca
walking down a busy street, going into a health spa. Snapsho
of pieces of her life. "That's Anntoinette Carson," Bob sai
The last picture of her had a large red X drawn across her fac

The other dozen or so photos were pictures of Ann. The
showed her getting out of her car in front of her condo, ste
ping off the curb at the entrance of the college, exiting a gr
cery store and standing in her doorway with Clay.

"Son of a bitch," Clay said beneath his breath as he realize
how closely Michael had been watching her…watching the

His heart convulsed painfully in his chest as he saw the la
picture on the board. Ann's face…with a bold red X draw
through it.

"Put out an APB on Michael Johnson," he said, his voic
hollow as he continued to stare at the picture of Ann. "I wa
every cop on every corner looking for him. We're going
turn this city upside down. And we're going to pray that it
not too late."

Without waiting for any reply, too sick to say another wor
Clay headed back up the hall, then out the front door. For
moment he drew in deep breaths of the hot summer air, tryin
to erase the stench of evil that had filled the house.

What now? He looked up and down the street, wondering where in the hell Michael Johnson would be. Where would he take Ann? He knew in order to find the madman, he was going to have to think like a madman.

The park. Englewood Park. Had he taken Ann there? Back to the scene…back to where she'd watched him dump a body?

He turned to see Raymond hurrying toward him. "Bob is going back to the station with one of the other cars to man the phones and put out the APB."

Clay nodded and together he and his partner got into the car. "Where are we headed?" Raymond asked as Clay peeled away from the curb and hit the siren.

"Englewood Park. It's a long shot, but that's all I can think of."

Raymond smiled with a touch of admiration. "I wouldn't have thought of it." He hesitated a moment. "Clay…no matter what happens, no matter what the outcome of this, you've done your best. You're one hell of a cop."

Clay looked at his partner in surprise. He and Raymond had often been at odds over the years, yet always there had been an unspoken respect and admiration for each other.

Raymond smiled ruefully. "I figured I should say that once before you leave the department."

"Thanks." Clay frowned and clenched the steering wheel tightly. "I just hope we're good enough cops to get to Michael Johnson before anything happens to Ann."

It took them only minutes to get to the park. The playground equipment was decorated with children in brightly colored summer wear. An older couple sat on the bank by the lake, tossing bread to ducks that quacked their pleasure.

Such an idyllic scene, yet Clay's gut twisted as he scanned the small park, looking for something, anything that might point to Michael Johnson and Ann being in the area.

Nothing. They knew he drove a navy van, but there were no vans in the parking area, no vans anywhere around. "Maybe we should check out the rest rooms?" Raymond suggested.

Clay nodded, although his instincts told him Michael Johnson wasn't here and hadn't been here. He pulled up in front of the rest room structure and together he and Raymond checked the facilities. Nothing.

"Dammit." Clay banged his palm on the steering wheel. He'd been so sure. It had felt right, that Michael would take Ann back to the scene of his crime, back to the place where she had watched him dispose of a body.

With every minute that ticked by, the odds of them finding Ann alive diminished. For all he knew, she might already be dead.

Surely not, he thought. Surely if she were already dead he'd feel a void deep in his heart, at the core of his soul. As dear as she'd become to him, he felt certain that he would instinctively know if she'd drawn her last breath.

Where are they? Where would Michael have taken her? Hold on, Ann. Be strong. Don't give up. He concentrated on the words, hoping somehow she'd hear them wherever she was. She'd survived so much already. Was she strong enough, smart enough to survive Michael Johnson?

His heart jumped as a new thought blossomed. Of course Michael wouldn't bring her back to his home. And he wouldn't have taken her to the park, either. The park wasn't the scene of the initial crime, it had only been the final dumping ground.

"Raymond, call the station and see if you can find out where Michael Johnson killed his girlfriend years ago. If I remember right it was somewhere on the west side of town. Get the name and location."

Raymond picked up the radio as Clay pulled over and parked at the curb. As Raymond waited for the information, Clay impatiently clicked his fingers against the steering wheel.

He had to be right. Time had become the enemy. Every minute wasted was a gamble with Ann's life. And as he thought of those yellow flowers in the center of his kitchen table, he wanted to weep.

"The Night Sky Motel," Raymond said. "It's on Kimble Street."

Clay nodded and hit the siren as he pulled back on the road

"Pray I'm right," he said as he maneuvered the patrol car through the late evening traffic.

"I am," Raymond answered softly. "And I'm praying we're in time."

The light in the room flicked on and Ann stared into the face of her monster. Dean. Dean standing upright, without a wheelchair, a pleasant smile curving his lips. "Hello, Ann."

For a moment, past mingled with present, creating confusion in Ann's mind. The confusion cleared and she realized she wasn't six years old, and her mother was never going to come to save her.

The man standing before her wasn't one of the monsters from her past, but he was a monster nevertheless.

"Dean?" With the light on she realized she was in a motel room. She didn't move from her position on the bed, afraid that any sudden movement would set off the insanity that gleamed from Dean's eyes. No...Michael's eyes. But she felt that salvation rested in playing dumb...buying time. "Dean, why am I here? What happened?"

His smile grew, like the Cheshire cat from *Alice in Wonderland.* "I hit you over the head and brought you here. God, you made it so easy for me, walking with me to the van, bending over to get those papers."

"But why?" Her pulse raced, pounding loudly in her temples.

"Ann, you know why. And we don't have to play games here. You know my name is Michael Johnson. I told you years ago that we'd see each other again. Surely you haven't forgotten." He leaned against the door, a smile of amusement still playing at the corners of his mouth.

"Michael, you have the wrong person," Ann said, dropping any pretense. "I'm not the person you're after."

"Shut up." The smile died and anger snapped in his eyes. "I know it's you. You can't lie to me. I know you're that girl. I knew it the minute I saw you." He pulled himself away from the door and started to pace. "You think I don't remember?

You think your image didn't play in my mind every minute of every day that I was in that stinkin' hole of a prison? I remember the dress you were wearing the day you testified against me, I remember the pink bows that sat on top of your pigtails. I remember everything like it was yesterday.''

Ann said nothing, afraid the mere sound of her voice would set him off on a rampage of death. And yet his words confirmed what she hadn't been sure of; she now knew with a certainty she was not the Ann Carson he sought. But she also knew it didn't matter anymore.

He stopped pacing and sank down on the edge of the bed, the smile once again lifting his mouth. ''I could have killed you in the van while you were unconscious. One draw of my knife across your throat and it would have all been over. Revenge sated. But it seemed right that I bring you here. Sort of poetic justice.''

''Where's here?'' Ann whispered.

''This is the motel where I killed my girlfriend twenty-one years ago. Don't you remember? It was her body you saw me dumping at the park. She was going to leave me, had decided she didn't love me anymore. I slit her throat right there on the bed.''

Despair swept through Ann like the bleak winds of winter. It blew any lingering hope away, leaving behind only a deep, abiding weariness. She felt as if she'd been fighting the war of survival all of her life, and at the moment, she had no strength left to fight.

Michael stood up and began to pace once again, telling her the details of the night he'd killed his girlfriend, as if wanting to inspire terror. What he didn't know, couldn't know was that she was beyond terror. She was beyond caring. She closed her eyes, simply wanting it over and done.

With her eyes shut, a mental image formed in her head. Clay. His warm brown eyes radiated admiration, respect and love. ''Your strength awes me,'' wasn't that what he'd told her? The night she'd bared the secrets of her haunting past, he'd held her, told her she was a survivor.

Yes, a survivor, and now this monster wanted to take her life, steal the breath from her body. Her heart banged against her ribs as anger surged within her. How dare he?

She'd been a victim as a child, helpless to cope with the dysfunctional adults surrounding her. She was no longer a child, and she would never be a victim again. She wasn't about to give up without a fight. She wasn't dead yet.

As if to prove that fact to herself, she raised a hand and placed it against her chest. Her heart beat fast, but strong. As she dropped her hand, it encountered the strap of her purse.

"Look at me," Michael demanded. Her eyes flew open. He smiled in satisfaction. "I want to see the terror in your eyes."

The gun. If he would just look away…give her half a minute, she would be able to get it out of her purse.

"The game is over, Ann." He pulled a knife from his pocket. "Finally…finally I'll have my revenge."

Chapter 17

Clay heard the gunshot as he pulled up in front of the Night Sky Motel. The explosion rent the relative silence of the night and blasted fear through Clay's veins.

"It came from over there," Raymond said as he pointed to the motel units just ahead.

As they started to leave the patrol car, one of the unit doors opened and Ann staggered out. Blood covered her. She took several steps, then sank to her knees.

"Ann!" Clay ran toward her, his heart thudding painfully. All that blood. "Call for an ambulance," he yelled back at Raymond, then crouched down next to her.

"It's too late for an ambulance," she said softly.

A cold chill of horror ripped through him. "Don't give up, Ann." He wanted to hold her, but didn't know where she was hurt, was afraid of inflicting more damage. He kept one eye on the door to the motel unit, knowing Michael Johnson was still inside.

She raised her pale face to him. "He was going to cut my throat. He didn't give me a choice. I had to shoot him."

"You shot him?" Some of Clay's fear ebbed away. "You aren't hurt?"

She shook her head and looked down at the blood that saturated her clothing. "It's his blood. I'm all right." She smiled faintly.

In that moment, Clay recognized the depth of his love for this woman. But he knew now was not the time to explore his sudden insight.

"Ambulance is on the way," Raymond said as he joined Clay and Ann. "Johnson still inside?"

Clay nodded. "Ann says she shot him."

Raymond drew his gun. "We'd better check it out."

Clay stood up and pulled his gun. "Ann, go get in my patrol car. We'll be out as soon as we check out the situation."

They waited until she'd gotten into the back of the patrol car, then together Clay and Raymond advanced on the room.

The first area they entered was a small sitting room. A sofa, television and an old kitchen table with two chairs was the only furniture. A doorway straight ahead led to the bedroom.

They listened for a moment, trying to hear any sound that would indicate life. Nothing. The scent of fear lingered, along with the coppery smell of spilled blood mingled with the burnt odor of spent gunpowder.

Clay and Raymond exchanged glances, and Clay knew his partner wondered the same thing he did...was Johnson dead? Or was he lying in the bedroom waiting for them to come through the door?

As if thinking with one brain, they positioned themselves on either side of the doorway that led to the bedroom. With the synchronization of longtime partners, together they swept into the room in shooter stance.

Empty. The curtains billowed and blood dripped down the wall below the opened window, pointing to Michael Johnson's means of escape.

Clay cursed. Holstering his gun, he went to the window and looked out. A dense wall of woods stood just beyond the motel building, creating hiding places for evil.

''We'd better call for more men.'' Raymond slapped Clay on the back. ''We'll find him. He's obviously hurt. He won't get far. At least Ann is all right.''

Ann. Her name screamed in Clay's head. He raced out of the motel room just in time to see his patrol car pulling out of the parking lot.

It's over. It's finally over. Ann lay in the back seat of the car. She didn't move or open her eyes when she heard the door open and the engine start. Exhaustion kept her immobile and the back of her head ached with nauseating intensity. But beneath the overwhelming tiredness and the pain in her head, relief flooded through her. No more fear, no more danger. It was over.

''Is he dead?'' she finally asked. No answer. She realized the patrol car was going fast. As it squealed around a corner, alarms went off in her brain. ''Clay?''

She sat up and looked at the driver, shock riveting through her as she saw Michael at the wheel.

''Hello, Ann.'' His gaze met hers in the rearview mirror, his radiating a madness mixed with rage and pain.

''No.'' A sob welled up in her chest, pressing tight against her ribs and for a moment she couldn't catch her breath.

It couldn't be him. She'd shot him. His blood still covered the front of her dress. This must be a dream. A nightmare produced by the blow to her head. But it wasn't a nightmare, it was far too real to be merely a dream.

She could smell him, the scent of blood and sweat. The sound of his harsh breathing filled the car. His gaze met hers once again. ''Unfortunately for you, I'm not dead.''

As if with a life of their own, her gaze still focused on him, her hands scrambled to find the door handle. She realized her only hope was to get out of the car, throw herself to the curb before he could carry her someplace where nobody would ever find her when he finished killing her.

Where was the damned door handle? She finally looked at the door. The sob that pressed against her ribs released itself as she discovered there were no door handles in the back seat. Trapped. She was trapped in the car with evil.

The gun. She grabbed her purse, but the gun was no longer there. She'd dropped it on the bed after she'd shot him.

Helpless. She was once again helpless, one more time a victim. And the greatest irony of all was that she was an innocent victim. She knew with a certainty she was not the woman Michael sought. She'd never seen him in the park, had never testified against him at a trial. It was the ultimate betrayal by fate that she would die at the hands of a man who believed she'd done something she hadn't.

She would never again feel a man's arms holding her with love, never experience the joy of giving birth. Never again would she see the beauty of a sunrise, or smell the sweetness of the earth after a gentle rain. She would never see Clay again.

"No." The denial fell as a whisper from her lips. "No." This time she said it more firmly, feeling it in her heart. She wasn't going to let Michael just drive her away, take her to her own grave. If she was going to die, she'd do it with dignity, fighting for her life.

Escape wasn't possible, and she had no weapon. All she had was the purse over her shoulder. She fingered the leather strap and looked at Michael. He was concentrating on driving as fast as possible down the suburban streets. She knew instinctively he was heading for the interstate, where he could elevate his speed.

Once we get on the freeway, it will be too late, she thought as she drew the purse strap over her head. On the interstate he'd be going too fast, the odds were too great.

Do it now, a voice screamed in her head. It's your only hope…your only chance. Ignoring the sharp pain that felt as if it were trying to split the back of her skull, she focused only on the back of Michael's head.

Without giving herself a chance to consider the possible outcome, in one fluid motion she slid the purse strap around his neck and pulled tight.

"You stupid bitch." His words were garbled, ending in a

guttural cough as she tightened her grip. She hung her weight on the strap, praying the leather held, sobbing as his choked rage filled the car. His hands left the steering wheel and scratched and clawed at the strap that cut off his airway.

In horror, she saw the traffic light ahead of them change to red, saw the semi truck pulling out in front of them. She recognized Michael no longer had control of the car. With a scream, she dropped behind to the floor. She had a split second to pray before the impact. Then nothing.

Clay rearranged the yellow roses a final time in the vase on the table, then stepped back and eyed them critically.

Perfect.

He checked his watch. Almost time to get Ann from the hospital. He'd get her settled in here, stop by and say his goodbyes to his mother, then catch his seven o'clock flight to Hawaii.

"Hello? Anyone home?" Raymond's voice called from the front door.

"In the kitchen," Clay yelled back. "You just caught me, I was just about to leave to get Ann," he said as Raymond entered the room.

"Yeah, I heard she was being released today." Raymond sank into a chair at the table and scratched his belly thoughtfully. "I gotta say, she's one hell of a woman. Not many would have had the presence of mind or the guts to do what she did."

For a moment Clay was thrust backward in time, back to the moment when he and Raymond had approached the smoldering wreckage of his patrol car. Michael Johnson had died on impact. In an ironic twist of fate, Ann's life had probably been spared by Michael. The crash had thrown her up and over the front seat, but she'd been saved, cushioned by Michael's body. She'd sustained cuts and lacerations, a broken rib, and a severe concussion that had kept her hospitalized for the past nineteen days.

As they'd waited for the ambulance, Clay had held her hand

and she'd flashed him a triumphant smile. "He was a stubborn cuss, but we finally got him, didn't we?"

He shoved the image out of his mind, not wanting to dwell on the love he'd felt for her at that moment. Love he was consciously turning his back on now. "I've got to get going," he said to Raymond as he checked his watch once again. "I want to make sure Ann is settled in here before I catch my plane."

Raymond stood up. "You know, I thought when push came to shove, you'd stay. But, you're really going, aren't you?"

Clay nodded. "I've spent the last ten years working toward this. What good are dreams if you don't actively pursue them?"

"Guess you're right, although by the time I get home from work, play with the kids and bond with Ginger, I'm usually too contented to dream." Raymond walked to the front door, Clay behind him. "In any case, I'm going to miss you, partner." They shook hands and Clay once again shoved away an edge of regret.

When Raymond had left, Clay got into his car and headed for the hospital. As he drove he realized he'd not only miss Raymond, he'd miss all the other fellow officers in the department. He'd miss the bad coffee, the terrible jokes, the sense of camaraderie. Finally, he'd miss the thrill of the hunt, the positive feeling he got when he was instrumental in taking a criminal off the streets.

He focused on the imaginary vision of a sandy white beach, blue waves crashing to the shore, the hot sun tempered by balmy breezes. By this time tomorrow he'd be stretched out on the beach. "It's what I want," he murmured as he parked in front of the hospital.

As he walked in to get Ann, he steeled himself against any weakness he might feel while looking at her. He prepared himself and summoned the strength necessary to tell her goodbye.

She was waiting for him, looking pale and weak, yet oddly radiant. With a minimum of fuss and a multitude of paperwork, her release was secured and within an hour they were in the car heading back to Clay's apartment.

"How are you feeling?" Clay asked once they were settled in the car.

"Surprisingly well." She flashed him a beautiful smile that caused muscles to clench like a fist in his chest. In the past five days as he had visited her in the hospital, they hadn't spoken of Michael Johnson, or the accident that had killed him.

She leaned her head against the seat and smiled again, the tranquil gesture of a woman at peace. "It's strange, but I've never felt so cleansed, so emptied of pain. It's as if in saving myself from Michael, I saved a piece of the little girl I used to be."

She looked at him, her eyes as blue as the brilliant summer sky overhead. "I wasn't the Ann Carson he was after."

"I know. Samantha Whitling called the station yesterday. She remembered that Ann's mother had mentioned relocating to Chicago after the trial. Ann lives there now with her husband and two children."

"I'm glad she's safe and I hope she's happy."

He cast her a sideways glance. "How did you realize you weren't the right one? Did you remember something?"

She nodded. "Michael told me he'd never forget the ribbons I wore in my pigtails the day of the trial. That's when I knew it wasn't me. My mom kept my hair short, too short to pull into pigtails. He was so sure I was the one he was after."

"What are your plans now?" Clay asked.

"I intend to take a few more days off to recuperate, then go back to work. I called Dr. Bainbridge yesterday and told him I'd like to be back at work the first of next week. I also put my condo on the market. The real estate agent thinks it will sell fast so I need to decide where I want to live."

"You know you can stay at my place for as long as you want. The rent is paid through the end of the month and my landlord says if you want to stay longer he'll make the necessary arrangements."

"What time is your flight?" she asked.

"Seven o'clock, but I've got to stop by my mother's before going on to the airport. I figured I'd get you settled in, then take off."

Silence fell between them, a silence that weighed heavy with unspoken words. Clay mentally grappled, trying to find words to fill the void. He could no longer deny that he loved Ann, but he refused to speak of it, refused to acknowledge it, afraid that somehow he would end up sacrificing all he'd worked for, the fulfillment of his dreams.

The silence stretched until they got to Clay's apartment, broken only when Ann was greeted by Twilight. "Hi baby," she said as she scooped up the cat and held him close to her chest. "Oh, I've missed you." She hugged Twilight, but her gaze sought Clay's. "And I'm going to miss you," she said softly.

Again the fist balled up in Clay's chest. "Ann, come with me." The words exploded out of him.

She closed her eyes and expelled a whispered sigh. He held his breath, wanting her to say yes. Her eyes opened and she placed Twilight back on the floor. When she straightened and looked at him once again, what he saw in her eyes stole his breath away. Love...pure and sweet flowed from her gaze.

"I can't, Clay. I can't go with you." She looked away from him and Clay felt as if the sun had suddenly been stolen from the sky. She sank onto the sofa, her gaze still not meeting his. "I love you, Clay. More than anyone I've ever loved in my life. When I was in that motel room with Michael, I lost hope, I was ready to give in to death, but it was a vision of your face that gave me back the will to survive." She paused a moment and cleared her throat. "But I can't forget who I am and what my needs are to go with you in the pursuit of your dreams. Your dreams don't coincide with mine."

Finally she looked at him once again, and this time in her eyes he saw her love, but he also recognized resigned sadness. She stood up and approached him. Gently, she placed her palm against the heat of his cheek. "I would never ask you to sacrifice your dreams for me, but I can't chase them with you. I *need* the stability and routine you're leaving behind."

He nodded and stepped away from her touch, afraid that i he felt it another minute he'd do something crazy, somethin; stupid. "Well, guess it's time for me to head out. The refrig erator is stocked and there's a good supply of cat food o hand." He didn't look at her, couldn't look at her. Instead h stared at his suitcase by the door. "You'll be all right?"

"I'll be fine. I'm a survivor, remember?"

He looked at her then, saw the shimmering strength that botl drew him and gave him the ability to walk away. "Goodbye Ann." He picked up his suitcase and walked out the door with out looking back.

He hadn't realized leaving would be so hard. He hadn't re alized regret tasted so bitter. But better taste it now than fiv or ten years down the road, he thought as he drove toward hi mother's apartment.

"This is what I want," he said aloud. This was what he' worked so hard to achieve for the past ten years. He had healthy nest egg and he intended to enjoy retirement while h still had youth and energy on his side.

By the time he got to his mother's, he'd managed to pu thoughts of Ann in the back of his mind and he felt firm an resolved about his following through on his goal.

"So, you're really going," his mother greeted him at he door.

"Mom, please don't start. I just stopped by to tell you good bye." He sat down in the chair that had belonged to his fathe

Rosemary sat on the sofa opposite him. In her eyes, he sav no judgment, but rather confusion. "I just don't understand son. I don't understand this need you seem to have in you."

"It's not a need. It's a want." Clay struggled to put it al into words for his mother. "When Dad was so sick all he talke about was the deep-sea fishing trip he'd wanted to take. He' wanted to be captain of a ship, spend his days on the ocea reeling in big fish. But, he had you and me...responsibilitie that made his dream impossible.

"Sea sickness, that's what made his dream impossible," Rosemary interrupted. Her eyes went hazy and a soft smil urved her lips. "Your dad and I went deep-sea fishing on our oneymoon. We spent four miserable hours on a boat in the niddle of the ocean. Within fifteen minutes of leaving the dock, our father was green and throwing up." She laughed and hook her head ruefully. "It was a joke between us. He was oing to be a sea captain, and I was going to be a famous ancer. We both knew I don't have a lick of rhythm, just like e knew he'd never willingly spend another hour on a ship."

Clay stared at his mother in surprise. "Why didn't you ever ll me that before?"

She shrugged, a tinge of pink staining her cheeks. "I never ought about it. It was just one of those silly things between married couple."

"Yeah, well I still think Dad sacrificed a lot of his dreams ecause he had to work every day and support us."

Rosemary looked at him sadly. "Oh honey, your father ought loving and supporting us was the single most important ing he would ever do. For him, it was an honor, not a duty." he got up and went to the bookshelves. She pulled out a photo lbum and held it out to him. "Here…take it with you. Thumb rough it and tell me that's a man who wasn't happy, who lt like he'd lost out. Taking care of us was his dream."

Clay took the album and stood. "I'll call you, Mom," he aid as he walked to the door. "We'll talk at least once a eek."

She nodded and followed him, her eyes misty with unshed ars. "What about Ann?" she asked as they reached the door. She loves you, you know."

Again an arrow of regret pierced through him. He shoved it ack. "Ann will be fine. She doesn't need me."

"That's probably true, but sometimes that's the best love of l, when you don't need somebody, but rather want and choose have them in your life." Rosemary leaned forward and issed him on the cheek. "You know my only concern is your appiness. And if it takes this move to Hawaii to make you appy, then you have my blessing."

"Thanks, Mom." He kissed her, gave her a hug, then turned

and walked back to his car, the photo album tucked benea
his arm.

As he headed for the airport, he concentrated on pulling for
the vision of sandy beaches, balmy breezes, no work, no co
mitments. Instead, his mind filled with Ann's image.

Funny, he'd never realized before how her eyes were t
color of the Hawaiian skies, how the flavor of her lips wou
rival any sweet drink he might ever taste. She smelled as e
otic, as fragrant as any flower blossoming anywhere in t
world.

He tightened his grip on the steering wheel. Stop it, he d
manded himself. She'd be fine without him. Eventually she
find a nice man who shared her dreams and she'd live a hap
life.

He breathed a sigh of relief as the airport came into vie
And in a mere matter of hours, he'd be living his dreams.

If memories could be packed into a suitcase and carri
away, Ann would have begged Clay to take hers with hi
Perhaps then his absence wouldn't hurt so much.

He'd left behind a vase full of yellow roses, memories
love and her. When he'd gone, she sank down on the sofa wi
Twilight in her arms. Tears burned at her eyes and her he
was as heavy as stone.

The most difficult thing she'd ever done was tell him s
wouldn't go with him. Although he hadn't told her he lov
her, hadn't said the actual words, at least he'd ask her to
with him and share his dreams. And she'd told him no.

She stood, fighting back tears, and went into the kitch
where the roses filled the air with their pungent scent. S
placed a finger on one of the fragile velvety petals, wishi
things could be different, that she could be different. But s
couldn't. She'd lived a childhood of uncertainty and now s
needed stability. She'd survived Michael Johnson but knew th
if she chased after Clay and tried to live the life-style
wanted, they'd eventually grow to hate each other. She'd rath

ave memories of his love, than try to be something she could
ever be.

She knew it was a smart decision, but smart hurt. In those
ours of being with Michael, she'd realized how isolated she'd
een in living her life, how afraid she'd been of giving up her
eart to anyone. Clay had burrowed beneath her fear, sneaked
eyond her boundaries; she loved him as she'd never loved
nother. She loved him enough to stay and let him go.

Although it was still early evening, she decided to take a
ap. The nurse had given her a final dose of pain medication
hat morning and she was tired, drained both from the physical
ffort of leaving the hospital and the emotional disturbance of
aying goodbye to Clay.

She closed and locked the bedroom door, then changed into
er nightgown and crawled into bed. Dusk's golden light
lowed into the room and played on the wooden door. How
nany nights had she locked her bedroom door before sleeping?
A lifetime's worth. As she stared at the door, she realized the
ubtle whisper of fear that had always been with her was no
onger there.

She got out of bed and opened the door, a curious peace
weeping through her as she got back beneath the covers. Her
ast no longer mattered. Those long-ago days and nights of
hildhood, those memories she'd buried no longer tormented
er.

Instead, torment came in her aloneness. She imagined she
ould still feel Clay's body warmth in the folds of the sheets.
he closed her eyes and hoped she'd dream sweet dreams,
reams of Clay telling her he loved her, dreams in which he
ecided to stay.

Twilight joined her on the bed, curling up in the crook of
er legs. "You and me, Twilight," she murmured tiredly.
"We'll be all right. We always are." She closed her eyes
gainst the tears that began to fall.

"Ann."

The voice came from somewhere in her dreams. Clay's

sweet, deep voice. She smiled, wanting the voice to keep tall
ing.

"Ann. Sweetheart, wake up."

A gentle touch on her cheek pulled her out of her drean
and into wakefulness. She opened her eyes to see Clay sittin
on the edge of the bed. For a moment dreams battled wit
reality. Confusion swept through her as she sat up and shrugge
off the last of her sleep.

"Clay...what are you doing here? Did you forget som
thing? You're going to miss your plane."

"There will be other planes." He reached out and pushe
her hair away from her face. "You were sleeping with th
bedroom door open."

"Yes. I don't need it locked anymore. My monsters are a
gone."

"I'm glad." He turned on the bedside lamp, illuminating th
room in a soft glow. "I have something I want you to loc
at." He handed her a photo album. She looked at him cur
ously, wondering why he was here and not on the plane, wh
could have possibly made him change his plans. "Look at
Ann. Tell me what you see."

She opened the first page and gazed at the pictures insid
The first photo was of a young couple holding a newborn bab
"That's your mother, isn't it?" She recognized a muc
younger Rosemary, her face glowing with love.

"Yeah, my mom and dad and me."

Ann studied the baby in their arms and smiled. "You we
bald as a cue ball."

He winced. "Please, no comments from the peanut galle
on the cuteness of the kid." He gestured for her to keep turnir
the pages. "Go on. Look at all of it."

Still confused, unsure what he wanted from her, Ann looke
at each and every picture contained in the album. Clay as
little boy playing catch with his father in the yard. Clay ar
his dad sporting fishing rods at the edge of a lake. Clay's da
and mom sitting at a picnic table, their faces lit with lov

Clay's growing older chronicled through pictures taken year by year.

She reached the last page then looked at him once again, searching his features, trying to discern what he wanted from her. "I'm not sure I understand, Clay."

"Just tell me your overall impression of the people in the pictures."

"A happy family. Love. Commitment."

"But not sacrifice, or unhappiness," he prompted. He swept a hand through his hair and took the album from her. "I've spent the last ten years of my life believing that somehow my dad sacrificed all his dreams for my mom and me. That he'd put aside his desire for adventure in order to work a nine-to-five job, get a mortgage, provide the necessities of life for his family." He flipped the pages of the album once again. "But as I look at him in these pictures, I don't see a bitter man, I see a man whose face radiates the kind of contentment I want. I see a man whose dreams all came true."

A lump filled Ann's throat as she saw the stark emotion on Clay's face. Grief for the father he'd lost darkened his eyes as he stared down at the album. He cleared his throat and placed the picture collection aside.

When he looked at her once again, her heart thudded sharply. Gone was any residue of grief, and instead a new emotion shone from the depths of his brown eyes.

"I almost got on that plane," he said softly. "But I don't want Hawaii alone. Hell, I don't want Hawaii at all anymore. Somehow over the past weeks, my dreams have changed. I didn't realize it until I was sitting in the airport, waiting to board. I realized I didn't want to be there, I wanted to be here with you. I want you, Ann. I love you."

Ann's heart felt as if it would pound right out of her chest. For a moment she held herself rigid, afraid to believe this wasn't another cruel trick of fate, afraid that she would reach for him and discover this was all an incredible dream. Beautiful, but only a dream.

"Ann, before I left here this afternoon, you said you loved

me more than anything else. Did you mean that?'' He reached out and touched her cheek in the achingly familiar way that arrowed straight through to her heart.

She knew by his touch it wasn't a dream, and fate wasn't laughing. Fate was smiling at her through the warmth and love in Clay's eyes. ''Oh, Clay, I love you so much it almost scares me.''

She flew into his arms, tears blurring her vision as he held her close. She felt his heart beating against her own, the individual rhythms inseparable from each other. His lips sought hers, evoking fires of pleasure and the deeper, more lasting emotion of a forever kind of love.

''Marry me, Ann,'' he said as he broke the kiss. He captured her face between his palms, his eyes gazing into hers. ''Marry me and give me what my father had, what Raymond has, those things that are more important to me than any exotic beach.''

''You mean things like a thirty-year mortgage and bottles and diapers?'' she said half-jokingly.

''Exactly,'' he replied, his gaze making a connection deep inside her, right into her soul. ''And things like love and family. And forever. Will you marry me, Ann?''

''Yes, oh, yes.''

Again they kissed, sealing a promise, a vow of the heart. As the kiss ended, he took her hand and pulled her up from the bed. ''Why don't you get dressed and we'll go tell Mom that her harebrained son finally came to his senses.''

Ann's nightgown strap slipped from her shoulder and she smiled shyly. ''Are you sure you want to tell your mom right now?''

His eyes flamed as he gazed at her bare shoulder, the gentle curve of her breast. He grinned. ''Being married to you is going to be the most exciting adventure of my life.'' As he joined her on the bed, Ann saw her future in his eyes, a future filled with the greatest adventure of all…love.

* * * * *

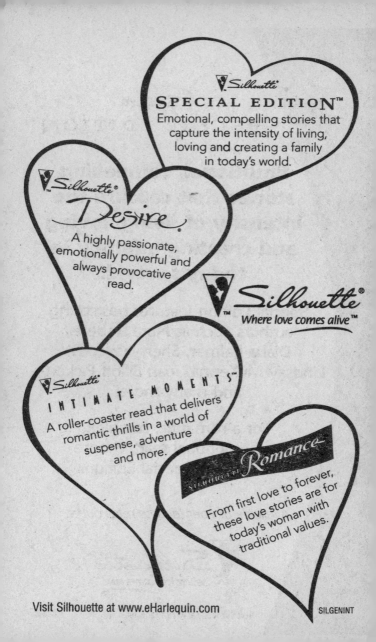

▼ *Silhouette*®

SPECIAL EDITION™

Emotional, compelling stories that
capture the intensity of living,
loving and creating a family
in today's world.

▼ *Silhouette*®

Desire.

A highly passionate,
emotionally powerful and
always provocative
read.

▼ *Silhouette*®

Where love comes alive™

▼ *Silhouette*

INTIMATE MOMENTS™

A roller-coaster read that delivers
romantic thrills in a world of
suspense, adventure
and more.

Silhouette Romance

From first love to forever,
these love stories are for
today's woman with
traditional values.

Visit Silhouette at www.eHarlequin.com

SILGENINT